Cold Spring in Russia

Olga Chernov Andreyev

Foreword by ARTHUR MILLER
Translated by Michael Carlisle

ardis / ann arbor

Olga Chernov Andreyev
Cold Spring in Russia
Translation by Michael Carlisle,
Foreword by Arthur Miller,
Copyright © 1978 by Ardis.
ISBN 0-88233-303-8 (cloth)
ISBN 0-88233-306-2 (paperback)

Published by Ardis, 2901 Heatherway,
Ann Arbor, Michigan 48104

TABLE OF CONTENTS

Part V: Wanderings through Russia

Part VI: The Dacha in the Woods

Part VII: The Lubyanka

Part VIII: The Cheka Ambush

Part IX: Off to Bashkiria

Part X: The Second Arrest

Part XI: The Hotel National

Part XII: Life with Peshkova

Part XIII: The Homes in Serebryany Bor

Part XIV: Last Days in Russia

Illustrations

Frontispiece: Olga Chernov. Paris, 1916.

Photographs following page 99:

> 99a (top): Villa Ariana. Alassio, 1914.
> 99a (bottom): Left to right: Natasha, Nyanya, Olga, Vadya. Vyborg, 1908.
> 99b: Victor Chernov. Spezia, Italy, 1911.
> 99 c & 99d: Members of the SR Party. Left to right: Victor Chernov, Vasily Sukhomlin, Olga Chernov, Dasha. Alassio, Italy, 1915.
> 99e: Victor Chernov and Adya. Paris, 1924.
> 99f: Victor Chernov with André Reznikov (son of Natasha) and Olga Andreyev Carlisle (daughter of Olga). Paris, 1936.

FOREWORD

It is always the winners who write the history, and so it has to be. That the Bolshevik Revolution should have come down to us in fundamentally Bolshevik—(or anti-Bolshevik) renderings is merely to say that Christianity described by Christians may leave something to be desired from the Moslem or Jewish viewpoint. For some reason which I can only guess, however, I had not been aware until reading the present book of how profoundly I had been brainwashed by the victors, and by their enemies, and if it was to a lesser degree by the latter, the fact nevertheless is that Olga Chernov Andreyev's autobiography manages to implicitly frame the usual dogmatisms by conveying the experience of revolution in a uniquely informed yet emotionally vulnerable way, so that the dilemma of such an explosion—its promise and its dreadful toll, its nobility and vileness, come together in an undifferentiated flood of impressions which finally have the feel of life.

And the all but forgotten nub of it all is that the by far single most numerous political party in Russia was the Socialist Revolutionaries, a more or less Socialist-Liberal type of movement by Western standards, and that the armed takeover of power by Lenin's Bolsheviks was primarily a matter of seizing the reins not any longer from the Tsarist forces but from those who expected to govern in parliamentary democratic style. Inevitably the brother-socialists would be hunted down in the years that followed, or driven out altogether. But that the fact of their very existence should so totally cease to have mattered—that the majority party of the time, bumbling and outmaneuvered and bludgeoned finally as it was, should have been simply erased from almost all educated consciousness, is another example of the age-old human capacity for intellectual surrender to overwhelming and victorious force. That the Bolshevik side won, and won everything, ultimately served to cover the majority party with contempt and in the long run a nearly total obscurity.

But it would be wrong to characterize her book as a partisan one when each individual who crosses her path is so freshly seen and justly dealt with. It is a book, a kind of account, which only a woman could have written. She stands at that juncture where the wand of great events makes contact with human flesh, burning and stinging and leaving its scars. It is always the women who are left to carry on what life is left to live in such cataclysms and for this reason they see human presumptions with the eye of the gene, the smaller particles of living substance, the little specks where God lives and tests lies and truth.

In the present instance, however, that view is remarkably novelistic; the tidal surges, the troughs of retrospection, the looming of important personages and their disappearances—doubtless her life was like this in those terrible years, but that she should have been able to give such form to her account is a literary accomplishment rather than merely a feat of memory after a lapse of nearly half a century. So that finally a transcendant quality is clearly reached where the political bitterness of defeat and the lost chance no longer control emotions; instead, a tragic quietness, a sorrow beyond sadness, a kind of amplitude which may even embrace the enemy holds all in place. It seems to me a book which will enter the record and remain for a very long time.

Arthur Miller

COLD SPRING IN RUSSIA

INTRODUCTION

Olga Chernov Andreyev's memoirs, describing the years 1917-1921 in Russia, give a first hand account of the Russian Revolution and of the Civil War as they were experienced by a family of Socialists. The adopted daughter of a well-known political figure, Victor Chernov, Olga Chernov Andreyev was a witness and sometimes a participant in the events she describes.

Victor Chernov, a leader and a theoretician of the Socialist Revolutionary Party since the early nineteen hundreds, was elected to the chairmanship of the Constituent Assembly, the only parliamentary body ever assembled in Russia through a democratic process. This Assembly, which convened in January, 1918, held one dramatic session before it was disbanded by the Bolsheviks. It was during this single session that Victor Chernov made his famous opening speech, the last free political utterance to be heard in Russia to this day. He did this under the menace of Red sailors' bayonets and machine guns; the Bolsheviks were moving in against all those committed to democracy.

Little is said today about the Socialist Revolutionaries who emerged ideologically from the nineteenth-century populist revolutionary party of Russia, the "Will of the People." They had been "Europeanized" at the turn of the century through the efforts of moderates like Victor Chernov. They were the non-Marxist Socialists, drawing their support from the peasants of rural Russia, who constituted a sizeable majority at the time. Meanwhile, the Socialist Democrats, Mensheviks and Bolsheviks relied on factory workers for support. In the opinion of these Marxists, the workers were the only class which mattered to the future of Russia.

Victor Chernov always opposed Lenin's ideas and fought against them. An economist specializing in agrarian problems, he was the author of a land reform bill based on the creation of free cooperatives which would have been presented to the Russian public for consideration early in 1918.

References to the Socialist Revolutionaries, or SRs, as they were often called, are almost never found in Communist books and periodicals. Before the Revolution, the SRs were equally unpopular with the Tsarist authorities and the right wing parties of that period, notably the Monarchists, who rejected any notion of Socialism for Russia. The SRs, whenever they are mentioned at all in the Soviet press today, are treated with contempt. Few are aware that in 1917 they embodied the hopes of the overwhelming majority of Russians. But precisely because of their respect for the democratic principles, the SRs proved unable to retain power in the face of armed assaults by the Bolsheviks. Theirs is a tragic story, one not without a lesson for us today.

Olga Chernov Andreyev grew up in a family which had to emigrate under the Tsarist regime because of its stand against autocracy. She describes her childhood in Paris and on the Italian Riviera, where she encountered a great many revolutionaries like Vera Figner and Natasha Klimova, legendary figures in their time in Russia In her parents' house as a small child, she saw the famous Azef, one of history's most spectacular double-agents. There were also encounters with men like Maxim Gorky, who subsequently was to play an important role in the cultural history of the USSR.

This memoir relates the story of a family caught in the midst of great historical events. It is the story of how people act and become shaped by profound events.

M.V.C.

PART I

Moscow 1919-1920

We were slowly dying in a hungry and frigid Moscow. During the winter of 1919-1920, there were huge snowfalls and, because the streets were not cleared, snowdrifts grew throughout the city. Piles of ashes and garbage strewn in the backyards were periodically covered with new-fallen snow, and looked white and festive. Then came frosts and Moscow glittered with crystals and sparkling stalactites. Moscow was beautiful and solemn.

The tramways did not run, except for the A and B lines, but they were so overcrowded that it was best not to try to get on. Daredevils rode on their footboards in clusters, hanging precariously from the handrails as the trams gained speed. Soon all transportation within the city stopped completely.

Bundled from the cold in whatever they could find, people walked on foot, careful not to slip. They carried shopping bags over their shoulders, which were known to Moscow inhabitants as "Appendix Dorsalis." The more fortunate pulled along small sleds loaded with food-stuffs they had somehow procured, and with pails of water for household use. In most houses water pipes had frozen and burst.

The average citizen was terrified. Rumors were spreading about a group of night robbers. They were known as the "jumpers," and were said to have spring-like attachments on their feet which enabled them to jump high and far, and thus escape the militia. Certain frightened Muscovites maintained that the "jumpers" possessed phosphorescent green eyes. Others claimed that they simply held electric flashlights with which they blinded the Muscovites who ventured out late at night. From time to time—and this was quite real—passersby were forced to undress on deserted side streets. Their furs and warm overcoats were carried off. Other thieves, called "raiders," broke into apartments under the pretext of conducting a search, and then cleaned the premises of all valuables.

At night, the streets of Moscow were quite empty. Occasionally, trucks filled with Red Army soldiers in pointed, cloth-covered helmets, holding their rifles high, bayonets sticking out at an angle, broke the silence of the night. Other trucks carried men in black leather coats. The rare passersby backed away fearfully. The Cheka was off on its next mission; another search, another act of repression, was underway.

We led an underground cavelike existence. My stepfather, Victor Mikhailovich Chernov, the leader of the Socialist Revolutionary Party and the elected chairman of the disbanded Constitutional Assembly, was wanted by the Bolsheviks. Our entire family lived in hiding. We saw few people—most of our friends and acquaintances were afraid to meet with us. Their fear was not without foundation; we could be searched and arrested at any moment.

My sister Natasha and I are twins. We had just turned sixteen, having graduated from the gymnasium the previous spring, but neither of us had any prospect of going on with our education. At that time, the background of anyone applying to the University was carefully investigated. Getting a job was equally impossible for us because of our lack of identity papers.

Five of us—Mother, Victor, Natasha, Adya, my nine-year old sister, and I—all lived in a single, large room. In addition, we shared this space with a sixth person, a friend of Mother's, Ida Samoylovna Sermus, whom Mother had befriended in 1917. Our room, into which we had moved that Fall, was located in a small, one-storied house near the Yauza Gates, a section east of Moscow situated near the confluence of the Moscow River with its tributary, the Yauza. After the nationalization of housing in Moscow, a certain Sinitsin, a past member of the Socialist Revolutionary Party, was put in charge of this particular house. He had given us one room on the recommendation of SR

Party Comrades. In any case, he was obliged to share his lodgings; the new housing laws prohibited his occupying an entire house alone with his wife. In addition to ourselves, another couple lived in a room at the opposite end of the house. Their name, oddly enough, was also Chernov. Both of them worked, and they were rarely at home; we hardly ever saw them.

Originally a merchant's residence, our house was solidly built in the old Moscow style. It had thick walls, large tile stoves and sturdy double windows. The layout of the rooms was intricate. Our windows opened onto the street, but the Sinitsins alone were allowed to go out through the front entrance—we used the back door. A winding corridor connected our room to the front door, which was upholstered in oilcloth in the traditional Russian fashion. This door was bolted from the inside; it had no doorbell, and visitors often had to knock for quite a while before being let in.

Sinitsin was a practical man. After the Bolshevik takeover, he had obtained a good position in the Food Distribution Offices. In addition to this he owned a fortune: huge stacks of birch logs neatly piled up in the back yard of the house. Youngish, heavy set and broad shouldered, Sinitsin appeared rather coarse and unsociable. His pregnant wife was meek and subservient and she remained noncommittal in her relations with us.

Three beds and a small couch fit into our room. Natasha and I took turns sleeping on makeshift bedding on the floor. A writing table stood near the window; there was another larger dining table in the center of the room. We cooked on a small, square stove, the kind that was then called a "burzhuyka," a "bourgeoise." It worked excellently with small logs, wood chips, or even sawdust. After our wood had run out, we started to burn newspapers, paper and old magazines in it in order to prepare our spartan meals.

We never entered the Sinitsins' kitchen, nor their bathroom. Our water came from a faucet in the hall, and to wash ourselves, we made use of a large enamel basin in which we also washed our clothes. Washing clothes was a difficult task, made harder by the lack of soap.

Although Sinitsin avoided us from the start, we were directly and permanently linked with him through a wall-high, built-in, Dutch stove which was located along the wall separating our quarters from his. The moderate, but steady heat which came into our room from the back of the huge, white-tiled stove helped us survive that winter.

Sinitsin resented the fact that "his" heat was warming our room at no cost to us—an extreme instance of life's unfairness. He discussed this with Mother, noting that, in all justice, we should heat the stove with our own logs at least twice a week. Mother, who was always exceedingly considerate in her dealings with strangers, had to explain to him that we simply could not do this. We had no logs, they were impossible to buy, and even if we had found some on sale, we could not have paid for them. As it was, we barely managed to get enough small logs and wood chips with which to cook our meals in the "burzhuyka."

When he had let us stay in this house, Sinitsin had probably expected that Victor, because of his position in the Party, would receive financial assistance, either from the Moscow SR organization, or from the provincial Party branch. But this had not been the case and he was infuriated. He became extremely hostile towards our family. He could not change the laws of physics which were sending out "his" warmth into our room, but the free heat which we were getting became an obsession with him. Whenever he passed one of us in the hall, he brought up the argument again, and was rude and disgusting.

In periods of stress such as war, occupation or terror, people tend to reveal their true nature. They may be classified into two distinct groups between which there is little middle ground. Either they blossom forth and reach a certain level of spirituality, or else their bad instincts triumph. During that period we came upon people, relatively well off materially, who, when they heard the doorbell or a knock at the door, quickly hid their provisions and brushed the crumbs off the table. Others, half-starved themselves, put out whatever they had to feed friends who happened to come in. Sinitsin, who would have been an "ordinary" person under "ordinary" conditions, became something of a scoundrel under the pressure of these years. His wife, who may well have been a kindly woman, feared him and was silent while he persecuted us.

-2-

Our life was difficult from the financial point of view. Little money remained from the advance Victor had received for the memoirs he had started to write. At first this advance had seemed substantial, but with every day the price of food grew and money lost its value. We lived under assumed names, and only three out of the six of us had been able to register with the authorities. Rations exchanged for our three "third category" cards for the unemployed were insignificant, despite the patriotic message they bore—the center of the cards printed on rough, gray paper was stamped with a poem by an unknown author:

Two worlds are clashing,
The old world and the new one.
A stormy sea rocks the ship,
But over our proletarian sufferings,
Concrete, steel and granite are ringing out.
Within a few, intrepid years,
On a pedestal of concrete,
We'll build a proletarian world of steel.

It often took an entire day of searching and standing in line to obtain our food allotments. All stores were closed except for the state ones, where from time to time food was sold to those who had coupons. Workers received rations of groats, vegetable oil, sugar and kerosene, but no one in our family worked and our rations were minimal. "He who doesn't work, doesn't eat" was the motto of those years.

Private trading was forbidden, but both on the legal and the illegal markets a lively exchange of goods took place. There, one could purchase foodstuffs, second-hand clothes, kitchen utensils, and every kind of luxury item. Despite the ban on bringing produce into the city, peasants sold bread, grain, milk and meat from the countryside. They traded these for things they needed—salt, kerosene, clothing, household articles, chinaware, and nails. "Baggers" or "speculators" performed the transaction. They carried large bags of foodstuffs into the city, taking home manufactured goods in their place, thus saving the population of the cities from total starvation.

The Soviet government was waging a ruthless campaign against these "baggers" and "speculators." Whenever caught, they were summarily shot. The lack of provisions, the devastation and the hunger throughout Russia were blamed on these enterprising, small-time merchants. This was of course an absurd notion. In reality, the Bolshevik government, coming to power, had alienated the peasantry. In accordance with the teachings of Marx, the platform of the Socialist Democratic Party appealed to the urban proletariat only. It disregarded the fact that Russia was a patriarchal, agricultural country.

When War Communism was proclaimed, a program of requisitioning was introduced. The government forcibly collected an entire crop and left the peasants only a minute share of it, based on the size of the particular family involved. As a result, the peasants were doomed to starvation. Moreover, they lacked the grain needed for planting future crops. They began to hide their grain. To counter this, harsh measures were taken: punitive detachments were sent into the countryside. They searched for and confiscated the hidden grain, executing guilty peasants on the spot. Finally, in the spring of 1921, a more rational system of taxation, the "Prodnalog" was instituted, whereby peasants gave over to the state only a part of their production.

The open markets of Moscow, those of Sukharevka, Smolensky and Trubnaya squares were typical of those times. Some traders stood in line next to each other, offering their goods for inspection, while others sold their wares as they walked around. They all shouted and praised the qualities of their merchandise. The crowd was so thick that a customer could barely get through the crush of people. The old country women, dressed in their reddish sheepskin coats with black furred seams, wearing gray knitted kerchiefs low over their eyes, were settled next to their cans and pails of frozen milk. In their hands, they held bags of groats and flour, and cottage cheese wrapped in frozen rags. Men stood behind open bags of dark, frozen potatoes, beets and cabbages. The city tradeswomen came to the markets with wooden boatshaped containers hanging from their shoulders on leather straps or on cloth braids.

"Here, who'll buy these? Hot *pirozhkis*! Hot meat-cakes! Who'll have these? Step right up!"

"Cookies, freshly baked rye cookies!"

Mirrors, paintings, bronze statuettes, and porcelain trinkets were offered for sale by ladies old and young. The women were from the "old world" and looked cold and sad; until recently, these objects had adorned their apartments. During that period, one could buy old miniatures, portraits, jewelry and rare books for very little. In the fall, Mother had bought us necklaces at one of the open markets. Natasha chose one made of rock crystal, while I picked out a heavy, dark red coral one. We still have them—these necklaces were among the very few things that we were able to bring out of Russia.

Young boys darted about the market, livening it with their shouts, and adding to the bustle:

"Cigarettes! Matches."

"And here's some toffee, fresh toffee!"

"Matches, Swedish matches! Soviet matches stink first and burn later! Get your Swedish matches instead!"

A young child's voice rang out:

"Cigarettes! Ira, Yava, run, run, run! They're rounding us up!"

From time to time, seizures were made at the markets, as the government attempted to catch the "speculators." At the first sign of alarm, panic broke out among the peddlers. They wrapped up their goods in haste, grabbing their sacks and packages. Dragging their wares as best they could, they took shelter in the neighboring side streets and alleys. The market place was clear of people within minutes. Loud whistles were heard as the Chekists were cordoning the market place off. A few peddlers were usually caught and arrested. Their customers' identity papers were also checked.

With every day food was becoming scarcer. Muscovites stood in endless lines for the little that was available: beets, small frozen heads of cabbage, carrots, and terrible looking black potatoes. People were bitter; they watched the line carefully to make sure that no one would cut ahead of his place, but certain customers managed to butt in anyway, pushing their way forward.

I remember overhearing an exchange as I stood in a long line, hoping to buy some vegetables. Next to me, a middle-aged woman, tired and out of breath, spoke in a conciliatory, cultivated voice:

"No meat? Oh, well.... A spoonful of carrots makes a drop of blood, as Leo Tolstoy has said."

The person behind us replied tersely, "That is not the only stupid thing your Leo Tolstoy has said!"

Back home, cooking the vegetables posed serious problems. We cut the beets in fine slivers and we were happy whenever we could bring them to boil in our small saucepan. We ate the carrots raw, having warmed them in the "burzhuyka" oven. We rarely had bread or groats. Occasionally we bought frozen milk, which thawed out in our room. I loved to suck on the frozen bits of milk. It seemed to me that there was nothing tastier in the whole world.

Once, in the course of that winter, we were able to

procure a bag of onions. Since we had nothing else in the house, we ate them alone for several days on end. We baked them in the oven, and they were delicious, soft and sweet. Their aroma filled the room. Another time, friends from the provinces sent us a piece of lard, an extraordinary treat. We had no bread, no flour, no groats, no vegetables at that particular time, and we ate the lard alone. Soon it was gone, which was too bad—we could have stretched it out for a long time had we had something else to go with it.

Since we had come to Russia, almost all our belongings and books were lost in the course of our constant displacements. Our clothes were wearing out. Some of our things were stolen, others had been sold. By the end of 1919, we had almost nothing left that we could have sold or bartered. But we did have an important asset—a samovar, loaned to us by good friends: the kind who were happy to share. We had no coffee or tea, but we brewed dried apple skins or thinly chopped carrots, the two best replacements for tea. We had tried and rejected the various substitutes on sale at the time in the open markets. Among these, I remember a completely fraudulent packaged product, made of something resembling chicory. The package, made out of gray paper, was decorated with raspberries. The label read: "Sweet Tea—to be used with sugar or jam."

Our stove and our samovar were our prize possessions. Our "burzhuyka," also procured through friends, was a great deal better than the usual, small model which heated the majority of the apartments in Moscow. Not unlike a Franklin stove, it stood on solid, cast-iron legs and had two burners. In these times of misery, Muscovites listened avidly to rumors suggesting that somebody, somewhere, had obtained a marvelous object which no one else had. Thus, Victor had heard from friends that a certain type of "burzhuyka," by the trade name of "Bromley," used very little firewood and gave off maximum heat. It was said to be a wonder, the best stove available.

"If only we could get ourselves a 'Bromley,' " Victor sighed every morning as he lit our stove.

At the time of our departure from the Sinitsins, after Victor had to go into hiding once more, Natasha and I decided to shine our stove before returning it to its owners. We scraped and scoured it and, next to the pipe, we found the factory trademark stamped into the cast iron. "Bromley Co." We had had a real "Bromley" all along!

-3-

Books were our salvation. At night, after the hunt for food had ended and the dinner dishes were cleared, we drank our carrot tea and read. That winter, Natasha and I read Dostoyevsky for the first time. Books, like food, were hard to come by, and I will forever be grateful to the people who lent us volumes from their libraries during that period.

In Moscow that winter, the electricity often went out. Whenever this happened, providing we had some kerosene left, we lit the lamp above the round dinner table. Mother, who had always loved reading aloud, read to us while we listened and drew or mended our clothes. Victor, who was hard at work on his memoirs, would then join us and take turns with Mother, reading Shakespeare, Gogol or Leskov. Nekrasov was his favorite poet and Victor, who had a marvelous memory, often recited from his works. He liked Nekrasov's "Frost, the Red-nosed," and "Who is it that lives well in Russia" best.

The year 1919 was coming to an end. In some other world people my age were studying at the university, joining the Communist Youth Organization which was already known as the Komsomol, and dancing the fashionable dances of the period:

"The students dance the Hungarian waltz
nineteen-nineteen is on its way..."

These young people were proclaiming a "new truth" which was entering Russian life as a legend—a legend which has been maintained in Russia for nearly sixty years. But we saw the world from a point of view different from theirs. We were living in total isolation.

A very few friends continued to see us. Among them was the family of a well-known attorney, Logorov, who had given us shelter when we were homeless. On two occasions when we had stayed with them, Mother had become violently ill and Logorova nursed her with devotion. The Logorovs had registered Natasha and myself at their home, enabling us to receive our food rations.

With their three children the Logorovs lived in a marvelous, well-furnished apartment. Before the Revolution, they had been wealthy. But that winter their house, built in the "modern style" of the early part of this century with steam heating, thin walls, an elevator, and a large stairwell, became terrifying. Every heating and plumbing pipe burst, and water flooded the entire building. It turned into an enormous icebox. There were no flues anywhere in their apartment and, like most Muscovites, the Logorovs could heat only one of their many rooms. They too had a "burzhuyka," its pipe coming out of a window.

I do not know what happened to the kindly Logorovs after the Civil War. Shortly before our departure from Russia I heard a rumor to the effect that Logorov had been denounced and arrested because of his friendship with Victor Chernov. It is easy to imagine what happened afterwards to these warm and generous people.

Our family was also close to the two brothers, Alexander Rabinovich and Yevgeny Rabinovich, who were Mensheviks. They were bachelors and worked in a publishing house. Their life was comparatively comfortable: they lived in a large apartment and would spoil us with rare sweets and books.

Among the people who did drop in on us occasionally, there were certain members of the Central Committee of the SRs, notably Mother's close friend Evgenia Ratner. She perished with many other SRs in the aftermath of the 1922 trials.

The wife of another Central Committee member, Timofeev, would also come by to see us. Her husband had been arrested that winter. One night, he had asked a passerby on the street for a light. The man who gave him a light turned out to be a Chekist who recognized the SR in the flickering light of his match and arrested him on the spot.

Our best and most trusted friend was Yulia Zubelevich, whose Party nickname was "Dasha from Kronstadt"— Dasha Kronstadtskaya. Of Polish origins, this then-famous revolutionary was a Russian intellectual of the old school. She had joined the Party at an early age and had worked in the revolutionary underground in Russia, spreading Socialist propaganda among the sailors at the Kronstadt Naval Base. She had been one of those who had prepared the uprising of 1905. As part of the conspiracy, she had worked under the name of Dasha as a servant in an officer's family. Hence her nickname.

Dasha had not been able to pursue her calling: the medical profession. She had had to leave the University in her third year because of her revolutionary activities. She was an unusually gifted person, one of those who seeks truth throughout their entire life. Dasha possessed a mystical belief in the goodness of the Russian people. Had she belonged to an earlier generation of revolutionaries, she would have been one of those who "went to the people." Sensitive and conscientious, she was often displeased with herself. Whenever she argued with anyone, she always tried to perceive the other person's point of view.

Tall and slender, with an elongated face and sunken cheeks, she had the appearance of an early Christian mystic. Her light green eyes were full of kindness and sorrow. She dressed simply, almost poorly, giving her better clothes to younger women, whom she thought needed to look their best. At the same time, she was marvelously neat, her clothes properly mended and freshly ironed. Dasha was a great mender of clothes, and she taught Natasha and myself the art of mending. She told us that even in her adolescence she always took up mending whenever she had to make an important decision—it helped her relax.

She liked art and played the piano. She was attracted to Mother because, in contrast to many Socialists of that generation who leaned towards asceticism, Mother took an open, enthusiastic interest in the emerging arts of that decade and did not object to the paths modern art was taking. The Symbolists were recognized in our household, along with the so-called "Decadent" poets. Most of my parents' friends had not gotten beyond Nadson, applying Tolstoyan principles to the fine arts, while we read Blok, Remizov, Prishvin and Akhmatova.

When the Revolution of 1917 broke out, Dasha was staying with us in Italy. Together we had returned to Russia. After the defeat of the Socialist Party in 1918, she did not side with its left wing which collaborated with the Bolsheviks. She tried to get away from politics, taking up teaching. In the winter of 1919, she traveled through provincial Russia with a research commission investigating orphanages throughout Russia. There were several million orphans in Russia at that time, the result of World War I and especially of the Civil War.

During the winter of 1919, Dasha would occasionally come and spend the night with us. As she put it, "she'd stop in to warm herself by our fire" between her travels. How happy we were to see her! We rushed to greet her and helped her with her frozen clothes, which she called "her skins," and which covered her adequately from the cold. We unwound her long muffler, rubbed her hands and sat her down in a warm corner at the back of Sinitsin's stove. We tried to comfort her, for after weeks of vain efforts expended in the fight against misappropriations and irresponsibility in the various state orphanages which she had visited, Dasha was tired, disappointed and hungry. We helped her relax: "Somehow, you iron out my nerves," she would say. And, resting up and gaining strength during these respites, she would once again embark on overcrowded, unheated, exhausting train rides.

-4-

Days were growing shorter and winter was moving in, icy and merciless. One day with a shudder, I realized that we had not yet reached mid-winter. For all of us, in our small room in Moscow, life seemed without hope.

In our family, I had grown up within the ideal of the Russian Revolution. The lives of those around us had been dedicated to it. The Revolution was considered both desirable and inevitable—and not necessarily easy. But the course it had taken was not the one which the adults had predicted when they used to say in my childhood: "During and after the Revolution, a far-reaching political struggle will be inevitable. The ruling classes will not easily give up their privileges. As enormous new perspectives will be opening up before Russia, the country will need all of its forces for the creative task ahead. We will all have to work hard and be selfless." Yet, how could this "creative task" be pursued within our illegal existence dominated by cold and hunger?

Once, towards evening, I was coming home to our house near Yauza gates, walking alone along empty side streets. I was bringing home a small package of millet which I had obtained somewhere. On a street corner, I saw an elderly woman bundled in a gray woolen shawl. She was carrying two buckets of water which were so very full that with each step water splashed out, turning to ice instantaneously. The old woman could not manage both buckets at the same time—they were too heavy for her. A few steps at a time, she carried one bucket, then the other. Clearly she did not want to let either of her two buckets out of her sight. I came up to the old woman and offered to help her. She looked at me sideways. She agreed reluctantly. Perhaps she feared that I would go off with one of her water buckets? Silently, side by side, we walked to the iced stoop of her wooden, one-storied house. Careful not to slip, I carried one and then the other bucket up the stairs. I said goodbye to the old woman. Distractedly she thanked me.

As I was coming up to our house I kept thinking that this somber old woman had to be a fairy out of a tale by Perrault. She would thank me for my good deed by bringing about some change within our life, some marvelous surprise. After banging at our door for a long time, I was let into our room. No happy transformation had occurred there. Our stove burned feebly, the small saucepan of lukewarm water atop it ready to receive the millet I had brought home. Natasha was adding small woodchips to the fire. Mother was straightening up the room while Victor was sitting at the desk, writing. Next to him Adya was drawing a picture.

I rubbed my numb face with a towel and settled by the stove to warm my hands.

This second winter in Russia, after our years in France and Italy was particularly hard on all of us. It seemed almost impossible to believe that little more than two years had elapsed since we had lived on the shore of the Mediterranean, and mimosa and orange trees had blossomed in our garden. Everything that was happening around us had to be a nightmare from which we would wake up simply with strong will power. Yet it was all quite real. It was not a bad dream which was paralyzing us, try as I might to make it one, reliving over and over again the memories of my childhood.

PART II

Childhood—The Years of Exile

I have retained glimpses of my childhood from a very early age. I see myself lying on a big white bed, tightly swaddled. Now I am in the arms of my wet-nurse, after a bath, wrapped up in a blanket, my head bundled in a white knit shawl. I recall Yalta, when I was only two years old, the wide, sunlit terrace which served as my father's studio, with its smell of warm wood and oil paints. Or even earlier, in Odessa, I can remember the clatter of hooves in the street below, and the nurse's shriek: "The Cossacks! The Cossacks!" She was carrying me away from the window, far from the chaotic noise and the shouting of a pogrom.

In 1906 my mother was married, for the second time, to Victor Chernov. I vaguely remember Victor in the Finnish village of Papula, but it is in Vyborg that I can first clearly picture him. Our nurse referred to him as "your new papa," but Mother preferred us to call him Viktya.

Mother had been extremely young when she was married for the first time to my father, the artist Mitrofan Fedorov, a student of Repin, the well-known Russian realistic painter. Fedorov, a graduate of the Petersburg Academy of Fine Arts, was known as a distinguished teacher of painting. He was an interesting, talented man, yet no one in Mother's family had approved of the marriage. There was a great disparity of age, upbringing and character between my mother and my father, who was said to have a strong, domineering personality. My parents separated stormily, when our older brother, Vadya, was three and Natasha and I but a year old. During this crisis our nurse, Nyanya, proved to be an extraordinarily reliable friend to our mother. But the trauma of my parents' separation left me with a sense of anguish, of impending disaster. A feeling of tragedy imprinted itself on my conscience forever. In Mother too, there remained an irrational dread. After her break with Fedorov she tried to forget everything about her first marriage. Unable to come to terms emotionally with what had happened, she wanted to strike it altogether out of her memory—and that of her children. With her own particular brand of optimism, Mother thought that this might be possible. No one ever mentioned Fedorov in our home and we, the children, took the family name of Chernov, who adopted the three of us legally. Victor had suffered at the hands of an unfeeling stepmother when he was young, and he wanted the family to feel as one, without the notion of stepson or stepdaughter interfering with the closeness of the family circle.

However, the three of us remembered our father well, and this made us feel uneasy, almost guilty at times. We were not supposed to say a word about him and we never did, even among ourselves. Only much later, as adults, Natasha and I exchanged letters with our father, but the Second World War interrupted our correspondence forever. Our father, a professor of Fine Arts at the Leningrad Academy, died in the Blockade in 1943.

In the summer of 1970, a retrospective exhibition of his paintings and drawings was held in the Ukrainian city of Kharkov, where he had taught for a long time. Alas, Natasha and I were not able to attend it.

-6-

My whole childhood was marked by the personality of Praskovya Nikifrovna Nikifrova, our nurse. She was an exceptional woman, selfless and warm-hearted. She had never known her own parents, having been taken as a young child from a foster home in Petersburg. In those years, the government offered small rewards to peasant families who selected children from orphanages and brought them up in their own homes.

Praskovya was my nurse's first name—her patronymic

and family names were those of her godfather. Her nickname was Pasha. She had grown up in an extremely poor but kindly family in the village of Velygory in the Novgorod region. Nyanya, as we called her, was deeply attached to her foster parents, who loved her no less than their own children. Her adoptive sisters regarded her as dearer than blood kin. But because of their poverty Nyanya needed to leave her family to become a domestic. A very young girl, she went to work in Petersburg as a servant. On the eve of her departure, her adoptive father pressed two precepts upon her: not to marry and not to wear the fashionable sleeveless undershirts with a plunging neckline worn in the city. He was a man of severe principles. Our nurse never married, but she found herself wearing the sleeveless shirts during her long years abroad.

She had come to us when she was about thirty-five, in answer to an advertisement. Our older brother Vadya was two at the time; Natasha and I had not yet been born. As far as I remember, Nyanya never mentioned her age, and when she was still young, counted herself among the "old folks." She was a small woman with an elongated face, regular features and smooth chestnut-brown hair, parted in the middle. Her face was quite delicate and gave no clue about her ancestry. She dressed with extreme neatness, always in dark clothes covered with a billowing white apron, immaculately clean and freshly pressed. She loved children passionately and she took upon herself all the duties connected with our well-being, in addition to the household chores, thus freeing our mother from these responsibilities. At the time Mother was still a very young woman.

Unlike certain other nannies I have known, Nyanya was always fair. She never discriminated against other children for the benefit of her own charges. A stranger to sentimentality, our nurse was exacting and worried about us fitfully, as if foreseeing what lay ahead for us. She instructed us at an early age in housework. Not only did we take care of our own rooms as our mother expected us to do, but Nyanya taught us to launder our clothes, to do the ironing and wash the dishes. She scolded us whenever we were messy; she herself maintained the strictest standards of cleanliness wherever she went.

She loved nature, both the north country of her native village, and the southern beauty of the Mediterranean shore where we had lived amid palms and roses in the Italian town of Alassio. She had that special gift which Dostoyevsky calls "the ability to be touched." She held dear all the things of Creation—animals, flowers, every plant, bud and blade of grass. She would get upset whenever we cut flowers for bouquets. "What a shame to destroy such beauty!" she would say.

Nyanya spoke in the natural voice of the Novgorod province, an exquisite and inexhaustibly rich language. Her speech was punctuated with proverbs, always fresh and unexpected. Where did she learn them? How could she remember them? She never repeated any of her sayings—always coming up with another with a slightly different meaning. Ridiculing our foibles, she gave us nicknames: "Lady Lisanska," "The doll from Borovichy," "The old man Shlinskoy." Much later, studying a map of the Novgorod region, I found the town of Borovichy and the rivers Shlina and Shlinka.

Nyanya had a rare sense of humor and was forever the instigator of pranks and tricks. She loved practical jokes and she always succeeded in duping adults and children alike on April Fool's Day. Her joy was completely good-natured.

As children we used to enjoy flipping through our nurse's photograph album, a small, thick affair made of green plush with metallic fastenings. In it were pictures of her family sitting on chairs, the women with restrained faces staring out from under severe black kerchiefs, the men in embroidered peasant blouses under their jackets. Another photo was of a young woman with gigantic shoulders and an attractive face swimming in fat with three huge folds of flesh hanging over a lace collar which was pinned with a brooch. This was the wife of the deacon for whom Nyanya had worked for several years in Petersburg. Nyanya sometimes told us about her: "The mistress of the house would come home after an evening out, sit down on my bed, and say, 'Pasha, I am hungry!' She would cut a loaf of French bread open, spread it with butter, add four cold cutlets, and gobble it down. Thus, eating, eating, she wore out two of my piqué bedspreads. The deacon would say to her, 'Maska, you can't be eating again?' He himself was thin and ate little, although he drank a lot!"

During her stay with the deacon Pasha lost her faith in the church. She no longer went to religious services. She had seen how, during Lent, the clergy gathered at the deacon's home, one pulling out a bottle of vodka from under his cassock, another a sausage. This had troubled her and caused her to rethink her convictions. But being by nature a religious person, our nurse remained a believer and lived her life as a true Christian.

When she came to Mother, Nyanya met the revolutionaries who frequented our house—Vera Figner and the members of the SR Central Committee, Gershuny and Gotz. She was impressed by their dedication and asceticism, and she came to believe in their struggle, accepting it as well. She revered them. Their pictures were included in her precious album. Thus from my childhood I remember Tolya Rogozinikova, a young SR terrorist who had been executed, a fresh-looking girl with an enormous braid of hair, dressed in the checked dress and white collar of a schoolgirl; and the young face of Nastya Mamaeva, another SR who had been condemned to death; Michael Gotz, ill with crippling rheumatism caused by beatings suffered at the hands of the prison police, was wrapped up in a plaid blanket. One of the founders of the SR Party, Gershuny, looked out from his photograph with bright, dark eyes. I was a little afraid of the picture of Vera Figner, who looked young and beautiful but very stern, as in real life.

All the Socialist Revolutionaries, friends of our

parents, loved Nyanya and trusted her. Sometimes they asked her to hide compromising papers such as the minutes of a meeting or some illegal pamphlet. Nyanya would slip these behind her icon case.

-7-

In 1906 we lived in Finland in the small town of Papula; by 1907 we had moved to Vyborg, into a large apartment which became the center for the SR's party in Finland. One of the rooms at the far end of the apartment, away from the children's quarters, was set aside for Vera Figner, a member of the "Will of the People," the populist party out of which the SR Party developed. She was then slowly recovering from a twenty-year term in the infamous Schlusselburg Fortress. Vera Figner avoided us. Children's voices, their laughter and weeping disturbed her. We saw her only once in a while in the hallway, and the severity of her appearance awed us. Because she suffered from acute insomnia, she took long walks before bedtime. Mother always accompanied her on these.

Victor was a member of the Central Committee of the SRs, and the other Central Committee members, as well as comrades from Russia and abroad would come to stay with our family—sometimes for weeks at a time. Mother, young, outgoing and generous, considered this natural. Once there was a misunderstanding; a member of the SR Party who had arrived on business thought that he had come to the Party's collective apartment, and became rather demanding. When he understood his mistake, he was embarrassed and apologized to Mother. The same thing happened once again in Italy, while we lived in Alassio. Mother's sense of hospitality was boundless.

Natasha and I were four years old when we settled in Vyborg; our brother, Vadya, was six. I remember Vyborg vividly—clean streets and stores, walks around town and

[30]

across the bay, frozen in the wintertime.

Our nurse's room connected with ours. I can still remember her treasure—a small, white plaster house with
windows of different colored glass, standing on a full chest
of drawers. When a candle was lit inside, the windows glowed
red, green and blue in magic patterns. An icon light cast a
bluish light on Nyanya's icons. One was of the Savior,
others showed the "Virgin who touches hardened souls"
and the "Virgin with three hands." It hung in the holy corner of the room, on the right-hand side as one came in.

In Vyborg I had a bad case of scarlet fever; luckily
Vadya and Natasha were not infected. The doctor forbade
Mother, who was pregnant with Adya, to enter my room.
Nyanya looked after me day and night. I remember vaguely seeing her white figure through my delirium. She was
dressed in the kind of enormous undershirt that her father
would have approved, with long sleeves and a drawstring
neckline, a long, white petticoat gathered at the waist, over
it. I remember her black stockings, and her long dark hair
in a braid. She gave me water to drink and touched my
forehead and applied wet compresses to it. When I recovered, it was discovered that I had been left with a slight
heart ailment. This was to have a profound effect on my
childhood and adolescence. I was regarded as having "delicate health"; strenuous physical activity was forbidden to
me.

In 1905, Victor became the ideological leader of the
Party. He was the author of the SR political program
adopted at that time. Among the Central Committee members who frequented our house in Vyborg was Evno Azef,
known as "Ivan Nikolaevich." No one knew of this yet,
but he was an *agent provocateur,* a revolutionary who also
served in the Okhranka, the Tsarist Secret Police. I remember seeing Azef in 1908 when we lived in Mendon, a suburb
of Paris. These were the days just preceding his exposure.
He came to congratulate Mother on the birth of Ariadne,
on December 25. He brought her an enormous bouquet of
red roses. On that very day Victor had gone to Paris to

confer with Burtsev, the SR journalist, who had just obtained proof of Azef's treachery from the former head of the Okhranka, Lopukhin.

The encounter between Burtsev and Lopukhin took place in the train between Paris and Berlin. In the course of a long conversation Lopukhin had not denied Azef's connection with the Okhranka. Having become one of the leaders of the Combat Section (the terrorist organization within the Party), Azef had organized a whole series of terrorist acts which had earned him the confidence of the SR Party. In particular, he was responsible for the killing of the Grand Duke Serge, and that of the Minister of the Interior, Pleve. Because of Azef, a great number of SRs throughout Russia were arrested.

Following his own inclination Azef revealed to the Secret Police terrorist actions planned by the revolutionaries. He gave the names of his comrades, who were then seized and often condemned to death. The real reasons Azef became a traitor remain mysterious, although many historians have attempted to interpret them.

Victor, who knew him well, thought that cupidity—Azef's services were lavishly paid for by the Tsarist authorities—was not the principal motive behind his actions. Intoxication with his own dark power, a taste for risk, a difficult childhood in a poor Jewish family, all can be considered as partial explanations, although Azef remains an enigma to this day.

Thus for many years Azef had led a double life. He was an excellent family man, but this did not prevent him from maintaining a mistress in Berlin, an entertainer in a *café chantant.* To pay for this, he used both his earnings as an agent of the Okhranka, and the SR Party funds.

Azef had an unpleasant appearance. He was a big man with hardly any neck at all and a broad, fleshy face; his skin gleamed and he had a heavy gaze. In spite of this repulsive exterior, his comrades trusted him. And how could they not trust him, when he was head of the Party's Combat Section, and took part in the preparation of many successful acts of terrorism?

Mother used to tell us that from the first moment she had met Azef he had terrified her, but stubbornly Victor, who was quite a bit older than she, would repeat to her the revolutionaries' consensus about Azef: "Behind Azef's coarse and forbidding appearance is hidden the noble, self-sacrificing soul of a true revolutionary. Just look at his sad, pensive eyes." At night, Azef was known to toss and turn and moan in his sleep, as the comrades who shared his room well knew. "It is his hypsersensitive conscience," they said. "He is tortured by the thought of slain comrades, of Jews killed in pogroms. The victims of terrorist assassinations burden his soul. This is why he cannot sleep." In reality, during that period it was the Tsarist government which was intentionally staging the pogroms in question.

In our family, we often recalled Nyanya's first encounter with Azef. When he rang the doorbell, our nurse had opened the door a crack and then quickly dashed upstairs. Azef had asked for Olga Eliseyevna in a self-assured voice. Nyanya had become terrified and ran up to Mother's room: "Olga Eliseyevna, some sort of spy is asking for you."

"What do you mean, a spy?"

"He must be from the police—he looks like a spy."

Mother went into the hall, and recognizing Ivan Nikolaevich, burst out laughing. She showed Azef into the dining room, where other guests had already sat down to tea. Mother told everyone about the amusing mistake made by Nyanya. Everyone chuckled. Azef laughed longer and louder than anyone. He was seized with a paroxysm of laughter; he could not stop laughing. His heavy face rocked; he was choking.

Mother often recounted this story—of Nyanya's intuition and the diabolical laughter of the *provocateur*. She also told of another episode concerning Azef. In Vyborg the entire household had rallied around Vera Figner, who had lived through her long prison sentence with remarkable courage and honor. She was then recuperating at our house —the eldest person there. Not only the children, but also the adults were slightly intimidated by her. And Vera Figner, like many educated people of the time, could not stand card games. This distaste for cards, widespread among the intelligentsia, could be explained by the fact that in those years cards were a social ill in Russia: every spare moment of those with leisure was devoted to cards. They replaced social relations and smothered all other interests and involvements.

Victor and his comrades liked to play chess and from time to time they would even get up a game of whist. Whenever they played cards they would hide like schoolchildren from Vera Figner, making a game of it. One day as they had a game underway, our house guest walked into the room unexpectedly, and Azef exclaimed, "Vera Nikolaievna, look at them! Playing a game of whist in your absence!" Raising the tablecloth he pointed to the cards, which the players had thrown under the table.

Mother was shocked and yelled at Azef. "You ought to be ashamed! You're a real *provocateur*!" Again Ivan Nikolaevich broke into his diabolical laughter.

"*Provocateur, provocateur*!" he repeated between spasms of irrepressible laughter. Mother would say many years later that Azef's laughter was still ringing in her ears. As for Nyanya, who loved all our friends, she never lost her initial distaste for Ivan Nikolaevich and became restless whenever he came into the house.

Later, when we lived in Meudon and Paris, we children became friends with Azef's two sons—Valentin, who was a year older than Natasha and myself, and Leonid, who seemed to us almost an adult. Both were friendly, intelligent boys. Mother was fond of their mother—a gentle, modest woman who worked hard in her own small hat-design studio. Azef had the reputation of a devoted father and husband, as indeed he was—he worshipped his wife and children. As the drama of his unmasking was unfolding, his unsuspecting wife was on the verge of suicide. Her friends and comrades came to her aid and stood by her.

Still in Vyborg, I remember the arrival of Mark Natanson, a man with thin hair and a beard, who wore a pince-nez. He was considered to be one of the Party's best organizers—he had a rather frightening pedantic appearance. He and many other visitors belonged wholly to the world of the adults, and we children saw them rarely. But Ivan Ivanovich Yakovlev, a former army officer and organizer of the 1905 uprising in Odessa, loved children. Wonderfully gifted with his hands, he built us a doll house out of heavy cardboard, with doors and windows that opened and shut, much like that of grandfather Drosselmeyer's in Hoffman's story.

Knowledge of German was considered a must at that time in Russia. While we lived in Vyborg, a young teacher named Hilda Effert was hired for us. She was an Estonian from Revel and her German accent was less than perfect, but she was a fine person, jolly and smart. She fit perfectly within our family.

Mother managed to spend a good deal of time with us, although she was extremely busy with party conferences and with the entertaining of our innumerable guests. She often read aloud to us tales by Pushkin, such as *Ruslan and Lyudmila.* And Victor, who always exuded kindness and joy in our presence, would come to sing to us at night before bedtime. He had a pleasant baritone voice. His favorite song was: "On the sea, the deep blue sea, a swan glides along with her little cygnets, her little children...." Suddenly a hawk swoops down and tears at the white swan, and the water around her turns crimson with blood. I could not stand stories or songs with unhappy endings, and when I heard them, I would bury my face in my pillow and weep. Then Victor would sing a song with Maikov's words: "We brought you the sun, the wind, and an eagle with which to play . . . The eagle has flown home, the sun has gone behind the hill, and after three nights the wind is rumbling back to its mother...." I fell asleep peacefully whenever he sang this.

More than anything else, we children liked to draw, and we always had a supply of pencils, paints and paper on hand. Mother tacked large sheets of paper up on the wall, upon which we used to draw with different colored chalks. Occasionally the adults enacted charades and *tablaux vivants,* which were in fashion at the time. Excitedly, we participated in them. I remember a skit of "Prince Rostislav" who lies drowned at the bottom of the river—a legend in the Russian style by Alexei Tolstoy. Our brother, Vadya, played the drowned hero, while Natasha and I and several other girls our age combed his hair with "golden combs." The stage was hung with strips of blue gauze, suggesting the river's swirling waters. I also remember a scene involving gnomes with bright-colored caps, busily forging Siegfried's sword. We wore little beards made of artificial hairs, which tickled our chins.

Mother was a good deal more feminine than the majority of women revolutionaries in our milieu. She had beautiful copper-gold hair, her white skin was transluscent, and her eyes were light green and they looked blue or green depending on the colors she wore. In her youth she was a bit plump, and she worked hard at keeping her weight down.

We loved Mother with passion and obeyed her unquestioningly—her word was law. Children were never punished in our house—in fact no one ever raised their voice at us. Whenever our friends told us about the punishments to which they were subjected at home, the idea seemed humiliating to us. We were embarrassed and saddened. Our parents did not have to punish us; they made us understand the meaning of dignity, of respect for other people, as well as for one's self, through their own attitude towards us.

-8-

In the spring of 1908, our family moved to France.

The Party considered that Victor's presence was more desirable there than in Vyborg, where his activities were threatened by spies. Many secret agents from the Okhranka managed to slip from Russia into Finland; even then Finland was an autonomous state with its own Parliament and its own currency. In Russia, a series of arrests and raids on Party organizations had begun. Victor went ahead of us, first to a Party Congress in London, then to Paris, where he was to find us an apartment.

I had not yet fully recovered from the effects of scarlet fever by the time of our departure, and the voyage seemed painful to me. Our nurse could not leave with us— her adopted mother was ill and she wanted to visit with her in Russia. She was to join us later in Paris. Hilda traveled with us instead.

I remember that for us children the journey was poisoned by a Frau Bertha, a Baltic German traveling from Finland to France. Not knowing French, this woman had forced herself on Mother, who could not bring herself to turn her away. I have rarely in my life met such a disagreeable person. Elderly and dour, she seemed to think that Hilda and Mother were too young to handle children. She made remarks to us constantly, and could not refrain from sermonizing us. We hated her with a vengeance. I recall how, one day, dragging me on the floor, Frau Bertha was twisting my arm to force me to make some sort of apology. In a helpless frenzy, I was spitting on her long gray skirt with its plush border.

Much later, as an adolescent, I asked Mother why she had permitted Frau Bertha to meddle in our affairs. Mother admitted that she, no less than ourselves, had suffered from Frau Bertha's presence, but neither she nor Hilda had had the self-assurance needed to get rid of her.

Upon arriving in France, we first spent a month by the sea, in Brittany, and then settled in Meudon, a suburb of Paris. There we lived in a small private house with a garden. I remember well how in the fall of 1908 the adults were in a turmoil over the Azef affair. Socialist Revolutionaries from Paris and from SR centers elsewhere kept arriving at our house. Tempestuous meetings were held behind closed doors, and the agitated voices and loud arguments carried all the way to the children's room. Azef's treachery was a crushing blow to the SR Party, one from which it never fully recovered. Many could not bring themselves to believe that Azef had betrayed the Party even in the presence of the most obvious proof. One SR, a young girl, who had had nothing to do personally with Azef, committed suicide. It had seemed to her that all she had lived for—the revolutionary fervor, the sacrifices of the terrorists, the honor of the Party—had been profaned, turned into a sinister farce. Azef, the head of the Party's terrorist organization, was an Okhranka agent!

We attended school in Meudon, even though we did not yet know French. Soon Nyanya joined us. Her own trip had not been devoid of adventure; en route she had met some Belgian nuns who, unable to understand the handwritten notes with which Nyanya had been equipped to make her journey easier, since she did not know French, out of the kindness of their hearts had sent her on to Belgium. As a result of her detour, our nurse brought back with her some coins with holes in them which delighted us —these were introduced in France only later. Right after her arrival, on Christmas Eve 1908, Ariadne was born. Nyanya took care of Mother and of Ariadne, a big healthy baby with charming light blue eyes.

After about a year, our whole family moved to Paris, into an apartment in the 14th arrondissement on Rue Gazan, near the Parc Montsouris. The Kamenevs, who were Bolsheviks, lived in the same building, number 19. They often visited with us. Olga Davidovna Kameneva, Trotsky's sister, a Commissar of Cultural Affairs, was a tall, spare brunette, who had given herself over to the "decadent" style of the day. Her son, Lyutik, was a year older than Ariadne, and they used to play together. We still have one of the photographs taken in the Parc Montsouris: four "revolutionary nannies" are standing in a row—ours, the

Kamenevs', the Steklovs', and the Avksentyevs'—each holding her small charge in front of her.

During our two years in Paris, the three of us—Vadya, Natasha, and I—attended a French school near Place Denfert-Rochereau. To get there from Rue Gazan we had to pass by the "Lion de Belfort," the big bronze lion looking belligerently towards Germany, waiting for revenge. The monument was erected to the memory of the defenders of Belfort against the Germans in 1870-1871. As we walked by the bronze animal with our nurse, we did not suspect that it symbolized the fateful conflict which was to mark our whole epoch and our own lives.

We studied Russian with Mother, and German with Hilda. We continued to live modestly. As in Vyborg Victor contributed to Russian reviews like *Russkoe Bogatstvo, Vestnik Evropy,* and *Sovremennik.* Now it seems hard to believe that a political emigré opposed to the existing regime could be published in Russia in publications tolerated by the Tsar's regime.

Our apartment was once again one of the SR Party centers, where political meetings were held and visitors from Russia and members of foreign Socialist organizations were received. The three of us older children spent most of our time with Russian playmates of our own age. There were many of them in the neighborhood and Parc Montsouris was our communal playground.

In the spring of 1911 our family moved to Italy. To our great regret Hilda did not accompany us. On the insistence of Mother, she had decided to continue her education. She was to become a Russian literature teacher in the upper grades of the Tallin high school. Later, in the fall of 1921, we had a reunion with her there, on our way out of Russia.

In Italy we settled in the little fishing village of Fezzano not far from Spezia. The writer, A.A. Amfiteatrov, a best-selling Russian author who wrote popular novels, was living there with his family. He had begun to edit the Petersburg literary and political journal *Sovremennik.* He had invited Victor to become co-editor of the monthly.

In Fezzano, Mother rented a rambling, ancient villa with high, painted ceilings and gloomy, cumbersome furnishings. An enormous overgrown garden surrounded it and ran down to the sea. It bordered a beach covered with pebbles. Natasha, Vadya and I—Ariadne was only two years old and remained in our nurse's care—spent long hours exploring the wild garden. Every fruit tree in the world grew there. Cherry trees, pear, apple, plum, persimmon, apricot, almond, fig, orange, lemon and tangerine trees were entwined with grape vines, and invaded by tall grass and wild shrubs. It was there that I first tasted a "sweet lemon"—a grapefruit, which was then a great rarity. On a small, grafted tree, oranges dangled from one side, and lemons from the other.

Vadya, who had caught a cold during our journey from Paris, was sick during our first days in Fezzano. As we had been traveling third class, we had had to change trains often, and had spent an entire night waiting for a train on the platform at Turin. Two weeks later Vadya recovered just as quickly, and he was allowed to play outside. Then his temperature shot up again, and it was discovered that he had pleurisy.

Vadya was then ten years old, Natasha and I, eight. Our brother was an intelligent, gifted boy—he drew beautifully, and wrote poems and short stories. He had a great deal of natural nobility. This could be sensed in his appearance, in his thin, handsome frame and black pensive eyes. Among his peers, whether in Vyborg, Paris or Italy, he was looked up to as an authority, despite his gentleness. Adults as well, the old and the young among the noisy crowds that stayed with us all the time, treated him with deference. He never took advantage of us, the younger ones, and we were close friends.

From the very early days of our childhood, our favorite pastime was to clamber up on a couch or on a large bed, and nestled there, to tell each other stories about a family of bears named the Galkins. The prototypes of our heroes were our plush teddy bears of various sizes, white and brown, as well as our several toy monkeys. Their adventures unfolded in the imaginary country of Amishach. The small bears, of course, never obeyed their parents, who brought them up with the help of horribly strict governesses. We would take large sheets of paper and draw the events of the bears' stories, thus anticipating the "comics" which in our childhood had not yet been invented.

We all drew well, but Vadya was the most talented. With incredible speed he could render whole scenes involving several characters, catching their movements masterfully. We invented other countries next to the land of bears, such as the land of "Ruffles" where the women dressed outlandishly, or the country where the people loved dirt, and fought cleanliness with all their might.

Occasionally we chose more realistic subject matter: We would draw "lunatics running." Rushing madly, the lunatics slammed against lamp-posts, toppled benches, tripped up passersby, all the while being chased by policemen and spectators. We spent long hours at these drawings. When Vadya became ill we would sit at the foot of his bed and draw. The only restriction for these sessions was that no adult be around.

As Vadya's health improved during the summer, the doctor allowed him to come on walks with us and even to bathe. We quickly learned to swim. Victor made us big cork lifesavers so that we could swim out long distances from the shore. Some old warships had floundered in the bay, and were covered with a ruddy, dark rust. We would sometimes swim out to them. Normally the Mediterranean is extremely calm; only a few small waves would lap up to the shore.

The town of Fezzano had only a tiny elementary school. Mother made friends with one of the teachers, Signorina Olga Bronzi, who took it upon herself to teach us Italian. She was an intelligent and talented instructor, the lessons were lively, and we quickly mastered the language.

Signorina Olga lived with her mother, the widow of a captain in the Italian merchant fleet. Their home was full of precious objects brought back from many lands: ancient Chinese weapons and armor; a mandarin's silk robe with its small black hat and slippers; a cape decorated with embroidered butterflies and birds; carved ivory trinkets, small Buddhas and priceless vases. The Bronzi's house, otherwise very modest, was stuffed with these intriguing objects but we did not get to see them for a while. Our teacher, although more than hospitable, did not want to invite us to her house at first. She was embarrassed; the standards of living in Fezzano were most primitive. The majority of the inhabitants had no toilet facilities, and the little road leading up to the Bronzi's house was filthy on both sides, left that way by the neighbor's children. And there was no other access to the house.

Mother continued to give us Russian lessons. As for arithmetic, unfortunately we had to take lessons from Victor Fedorov, known by his party nickname of "Victor the Fighter," who lived in our house with his wife and their three-year-old daughter, Galya. The adults valued and respected "Victor the Fighter" for his revolutionary accomplishments. However, he did not have the faintest notion of how to teach mathematics to children. During our first lesson, without any explanation, he dictated the following to Natasha and myself and instructed us to learn it by heart: "Addition is an arithmetical process by means of which, given two or more factors, a new one—the sum—is arrived at." And after that: "Subtraction is an arithmetical process by means of which, given a sum, when one of its factors is removed, the second factor is arrived at." I was to remember these two definitions all my life, though at the time they were completely meaningless to us. Neither of us understood what "by means of" meant. "Victor the Fighter's" lessons were boring, and he blithely established the notion that "the girls have no gift for mathematics." The worst of it was that we believed him. Only later, when we studied algebra in secondary school, did we prove ourselves to be capable math students.

We soon began to take French lessons with a young teacher whom our neighbors, the Amfiteatrovs, had hired for their children. Mademoiselle Marguerita later married Ivan Ivanovich Yakovlev, the SR who had made us our doll house in Vyborg. He stayed at our villa frequently. He and Marguerite had become acquainted there.

From the very beginning, a crowd had been staying with us in Italy—relations, friends and Party comrades. Newly arrived emigrés and escapees from the prisons and places of exile of Tsarist Russia could always find temporary lodgings with us. My mother's oldest half-brother's family, the Sukhomlins, lived with us for a long time. Vasily Ivanovich Sukhomlin was a member of the revolutionary party, the "Will of the People." We loved him and his wife, Anna Markovna. Their son, our cousin Vasily Vasilyevich, was one of Mother's closest friends. Slightly younger than she, he had just graduated from Grenoble University. His beautiful sister, Anya, was there too, convalescing from a case of tuberculosis which had lasted most of her childhood.

Boris Davidovich Katz, whose Party name was Kamkov—a friend of young Vasily Sukhomlin—also visited with us and soon became a great friend. He was then making his headquarters in Germany, having just graduated from the University of Heidelberg. Dark-haired and powerfully built, he was full of vitality and of lightheartedness—he had a sonorous, infectious laugh. Later on he married Evgeniya Romanova, a student of history under the famous Russian historian, Klyuchevsky. Kamkov brought her to our house. A round-faced blonde with green eyes, serious and determined, she was his exact opposite in most things. She taught us history and we came to love her. She quickly took to our style of living and fell in love with our family. Later she was to visit us for long stretches of time.

After the October Revolution, Kamkov sided with the so-called "Left" SRs, who aligned themselves with the Bolsheviks against the bulk of the SR Party. A temporary breach between our families occurred then. Later on, in 1918 on the day of the opening of the Constituent Assembly, during its only session, Kamkov and the other "Left" SRs were supporting the Bolsheviks wholeheartedly against the SRs. They were determined to disrupt the Constituent Assembly by any possible means. Kamkov banged his desk with his fists as loudly as he could as Victor delivered his famous speech while the Red Sailors were threatening him with their bayonets. Yet, how warmly we met with him and his wife in the winter of 1919-1920, when the Kamkovs, pursued by the Bolsheviks, were living illegally in Moscow! This was an unforgettable encounter—our last.

Among the young SR women who had been convicts in Siberia, we sheltered Bobrova, Klapina and Shkolnik while we lived in Italy. We also received the German, Alexandrovich Lopatin. He was a legendary revolutionary, a man with an unbelievable biography, one of the more remarkable men of our times. He visited with the Amfiteatrovs and with us in turn. He had been one of the revolutionaries who had unmasked Nechayev, the nihilist adventurer who served as an inspiration for Dostoyevsky's *The Possessed.*

Lopatin had a fan-shaped white beard. Strong and striking-looking, he had an electrifying presence and was a brilliant conversationalist. Lopatin, who was too independent to join any revolutionary party formally, was a well-educated man and a spellbinding story-teller: he used to tell us about his escape from Siberia in a boat, managing the rapids of overflowing Siberian rivers, in springtime. His was a kindly, masculine and noble figure. He used to play with us children with great gentleness. And as was the tradition within the Russian intelligentsia, he got along marvelously with simple people. He used to say that the affluent Amfiteatrov household was divided into "upper" and "lower" chambers. The innumerable Russian and Italian servants made up the "lower" chamber, and it was there that he found his friends. Our house was more democratic and he liked it for that. In addition to our nurse, there was in our household an old Italian cook who took care of the kitchen, preparing the most delicate culinary delights—she knew the secrets of ancient Italian cuisine. An adolescent girl Gemma looked after tiny Galya Fedorova, "Victor the Fighter's" daughter.

-10-

Not far from Fezzano, along the shore towards Spezia, stood the village of Cavi de Lavagna. It was a favorite with socialist emigrés of various persuasions. Many came to our house to meet Victor and other party comrades. The SRs Kolosov, Ligsky, Filipchenko and Leonovich used to visit, and Ksenya Zilberberg with her daughter, who was our age. She was the wife of a revolutionary executed by the Tsarist government. Ksenya was a small, attractive young woman. She and her daughter were beloved by the SR Party comrades who looked after them.

I remember with great clarity the arrival at our house of Natasha Klimova—Natalya Klimova-Stolyarova—with her husband and her newly-born Natasha, known as Mushka. Mother adored Klimova—they had been friends for many years. Klimova was an inspiration to everyone who knew her. She was beautiful; her dark hair framed her very expressive Russian face and fell back in a huge, loose braid. Her dark blue eyes were luminous and large. Tall and stately, she was full of life. There was something delightfully simple about her face, an earthy quality described by Nekrasov in his famous lines about the Russian woman:

> . . . . The most beautiful woman in the world
> Rose-cheeked, slender and tall
> Beautiful in any clothing,
> Light of hand in any work. . . .

Klimova had joined the Maximalists wing of the SRs,

which had split from the Party in 1905, precisely during the period when so many SRs, turned in by Azef, were mysteriously arrested. In 1908, as a twenty-year old girl, she had taken part in an attempt to assassinate Stolypin, the Tsarist Minister of the Interior, and to expropriate a bank. The police found her and she was arrested and sentenced to die on the gallows. While awaiting her execution, she wrote a farewell letter to her friends, describing her feelings during her last few days. She felt that there was no death—she was only going back into nature; there she would live forever. She experienced each instant so intensely that each was like eternity itself.

Klimova's friends were greatly moved by this letter, which was shown to a well-known religious philosopher of that era, Professor Frank. He in turn brought it to the attention of Russian public opinion. A group of professors signed a petition asking that Klimova be shown clemency. The government commuted her sentence from death to life imprisonment.

Along with other political prisoners, Klimova was detained in the Novinsky women's prison. After three years of incarceration, she managed to organize the famous escape from that prison. She convinced a young warden, Alexandra Vasilyevna, recently appointed to her post, to open the cell doors and escape with them. The plan worked: eleven young women fled the prison and hid themselves in various Moscow apartments, from whence they gradually managed to escape abroad.

Mother recalled with what enthusiasm Natasha had been greeted upon her arrival in Paris in 1908, shortly after the "escape of the eleven." Alexandra Vasilyevna, the prison warden, also came to Paris and subsequently married the well-known SR Fabrikant. Klimova moved to Italy and settled among the Russian colony at Carpi. There she and the SR, Stolyarov, were married. While visiting with us in Fezzano in 1911, Klimova was totally absorbed by her newborn child, swaddling her with the utmost care and breast-feeding her. She used to say: "We are all *babas*!"

This fascinated me. My mother had never laid stress on the physical aspects of maternity. This was due no doubt to the fact that she had married so very early and had had her own children when she herself was little more than a child.

All the adults in our Fezzano villa were very young, and the laughing and merry-making never stopped. While the Stolyarovs were visiting with us, all of us decided to take part in a masquerade sponsored by the municipality of Spezia, and everyone created a costume. Victor dressed as a Viking and unhesitatingly shaved off his beard: he was furnished with an enormous red moustache and a pigtail which came out from under his helmet, a cropped felt hat painted gold, with two cardboard wings pasted onto its sides. A black satin tunic was hand-painted to look like silver chain mail—we, the children, were entrusted with that job. Mother dressed up as a princess of the sea in a light blue gauze dress with a headband decorated with seashells and starfish. She outfitted Klimova with a Greek tunic and a Grecian-looking coiffure, curling and then stacking her thick dark hair high on her head. For Klimova's husband, Stolyarov, she borrowed an ancient Chinese costume from Signorina Olga. Stolyarov was small and had a very Russian face that displayed distant Mongol ancestry. The russet-red mandarin's robe, stitched in gold and decorated with turquoise dragons, fit him to perfection. The little black hat was exactly the right size. Thin moustaches were pasted onto his lip to hang below his mouth, and he put on a long black braid. He looked magnificent as a Chinaman. At the costume ball he was awarded first prize by the municipality of Spezia.

-11-

In 1911, Mother and Victor spent several days with Ekaterina Peshkova, the separated wife of the writer Maxim Gorky, in her seaside house in Alassio. Peshkova lived in the small fishing village between Genoa and San Remo the year round with her son Maxim. Our parents were so taken by Alassio that they decided to move there themselves. They were able to purchase a villa in Alassio. Still under construction, it stood by the sea on land stretching up to the top of a steep hill. Mother still had a small amount of money left to her by her mother, Maria Kolbasina, and it was used for the purchase.

Half a year elapsed before the house was completed, though we had already moved into it. The villa stood at the sea's edge. An unpaved, dusty main road bordered its garden. From there, a path led straight down to the beach. There was almost no traffic along the highway then, except for an occasional peasant wagon drawn by mules wearing red and white straw hats, their long ears protruding; or an important carriage with elegant ladies holding lace parasols, and men in fashionable straw hats known as *canotiers.* Only rarely did donkeys with thin gray legs straggle by on their way to the fields. Enormously weighty bags curved in their small backs while a peasant walked by, mercilessly hurrying them along with loud shouts. Once in a very great while, summer residents rode by on bicycles. And once a day, a small horse-drawn coach passed by on its way to the neighboring town of Albenga.

Crossing the road, which was covered with a thin layer of dust smelling faintly of vanilla, we walked down to the beach along a winding footpath, encountering several marvelous waves of smells—sun-dried grasses, weeds and wildflowers. At the bottom of the path, on the beach, the sea smells were unmistakable, as was the sand of Alassio which had replaced for us the smooth pebbles of Fezzano.

The coast along the Italian Riviera is quite steep; our land rose abruptly in terraces supported by stone walls. It went all the way up to the Upper Way, a Roman road, built by Julius Caesar for his troops. Paved with unbelievably sturdy bricks darkened by time, the road led to the top of the hill above our house where high above the sea on a cliff, stood the ruins of the ancient chapel of

Santa Croce. The terraces were planted with silver-colored olive trees and dark green live oaks, while the ochre-colored earth was partly overgorwn with gray-green thyme.

With the help of our neighbor and part-time gardener, Domenico, Victor planted flowers and shrubs all around the house. I remember how once, alone from among the children, I was taken along by Victor and Mother to Bordighera to a magic garden, the famous Winter Nurseries. We chose two large palm trees, two fan-shaped ones of smaller size, three cypresses, some eucalyptus and mimosa trees, and a few small fruit trees. These were delivered and planted in our garden where they all thrived.

Our house was called "Villa Arianna" in honor of Adya. The house itself was built in the modern manner—straight lines and no extra ornamentations on the facade. It faced the Mediterranean. The upper floor consisted of one large room—Victor's study—with its three windows looking directly out onto the sea. Shelves lined the walls of this room, filled with magazines, political books and pamphlets. Among them were many wonderful editions of the classics: the Brockhaus and Efron Encyclopedia, Pushkin's complete works, Schiller, Shakespeare and Byron. There were also editions in French and German. Victor liked to write standing up, and an upright desk was ordered for him in addition to an enormous regular writing desk. His collection of sea-shells was also displayed in this room. He loved to comb the beaches, walking for hours on end and with our help he was gathering many beautifully-colored shells. Following the beach, he often went as far as the next coastal town of Laiguelia. Our dogs accompanied him, running wildly on the beach.

Victor loved every kind of physical work, and gardening soon became one of his passions. At our nurse's request, and under her supervision, he built a chicken coop on one of the terraces. He contributed further to this enterprise by being the one to clean out the pen. Together with Domenico, he planted a vegetable garden, which soon furnished us with tomatoes, squash and lettuces.

In his relationships with people, Victor was remarkably unaffected and direct. He never became irritated, even when his writing was interrupted by some household matter. He would gladly put down a political thesis or an article on economics for a talk with Domenico. When peasant friends brought us carts of fertilizer, Victor would help unload these even if he was dressed in his summer white suit, grabbing a pitchfork without hesitation.

Thus one day when I was taken to visit the Plekhanovs by Mother, I was quite surprised by their aristocratic style of life. The famous Socialist Democrat philosopher and revolutionary lived not far from us in San Remo. A luncheon at his house was accompanied by great pomp and formality; guests solemnly waited for the entrance of the "leader of Russian Marxism." At the dining table everyone remained silent, waiting for Plekhanov to begin the conversation. This stiffness was noticeable everywhere in the Plekhanov home. It was in sharp contrast with the informality of our own household.

The fact that Victor enthusiastically partook in the day-to-day running of Villa Arianna made our lives interesting and festive.

Victor had always been extremely fond of animals. L. N. Tatarinova, his sister-in-law, had known him since childhood. It was she who told us about how, when Victor was a student in Saratov, he set up his room as a hospital for sick abandoned animals—taking in dogs, rabbits, hedgehogs, birds that had fallen out of their nests, and even grass snakes. Victor fed them and cared for them and his room was full of drawers, boxes and nests made out of grasses and leaves, and looked very much like a zoo. One landlady after another evicted him. In his student days, Victor was always in search of housing for himself and his wards.

Now Victor was full of attentiveness whenever one of us children was sick, recording temperatures, remembering our medicines, and reading aloud to us. But he had one peculiar characteristic. He was always absorbed exclusively in the things of the immediate present. Whenever changes took place and new situations arose, when life took on a new turn, Victor totally forgot people and things he had been involved with shortly before. For him life existed only in the present and there was no looking back. The Russian expression, "one eye looking back but the heart is already ahead," described him perfectly.

Later, when he left Mother, we were to spend many years completely cut off from him. But whenever we met again—and this happened only seldom—our relationship remained as it had been, as if nothing at all had happened, as if there had been no separation, and we had seen each other the night before.

Our house became full of life even before it was entirely finished. Guests fleeing Russia illegally came to stay with us after their escape from prison or hard labor in Siberia. Our parents and Nyanya nursed them back to health and helped them organize their new existences as exiles.

Victor's oldest brother, Vladimir Chernov, lived with us in Alassio for a long time. We loved him dearly, and he was deeply attached to Mother as well as to us, and to Victor. A sensitive and educated person, he knew literature in depth. He wrote lively poetry in both French and Russian, but his greatest passion was the sea. For hours and hours he walked along the beaches gathering shells and rare mollusks which he kept in clear jars of formaldehyde. Vadya, Natasha and I often accompanied Vladimir on his explorations, and together we would walk great distances along the luminous beaches of the Italian Riviera. I remember that I once found a very rare, tiny bright green shell. With what pride I donated it to my uncle's collection! Occasionally our first cousin, Vladimir's adolescent son Misha, who studied in Russia, would visit during the summer. We were close friends despite the difference in our ages. He would tell us thrilling tales of his adventures in the gymnasium which made us wish that we too might go to school in Russia someday.

In addition to their innumerable Russian comrades, Victor and Mother maintained many friendships with foreign Socialists as well. I remember Turati and the lawyer Modigliani visiting us. The brother of the painter, Modigliani was then one of the leaders of the Italian Socialist Party. He once declared that Russian borshch, lovingly prepared by Mother and Nyanya, was in fact an Italian dish—"Italianissimo!"

On occasion Victor participated in the meetings of a tiny Socialist club in Alassio. Natasha and I had a great number of Italian girl friends with whom we would spend long days, often going off on distant expeditions into the hills, accompanied by our dogs.

-12-

Despite its Italian environment, our household remained Russian. Russian was spoken at home, Russian books, periodicals and newspapers came regularly by mail, and friends arriving from Russia linked us with our homeland. Everyday Mother spent time with us: together we read the classics and current Russian literature. We subscribed to Russian children's magazines. Even before our Alassio days, Alexei Remizov was a favorite of Mother's, although he was considered by many as a difficult, avantgarde writer. I remember our reading and rereading his *Posolon* in its first edition. This book remained a great favorite in our family for years afterwards.

Nyanya's harmonious, soft-spoken Russian was part of our world. She was able to give an enticing yet truthful picture of traditional Russia. She told us tales about her childhood in the country, about her encounter with a bear when she was on a walk in the forest, gathering mushrooms and berries. That bear had been busy breaking up raspberry bushes and he had ignored her. Her tales about the Russian countryside were always poetic and unexpected.

Our nurse was generous with her possessions—she

loved to make presents and to receive them. She collected favorite objects in a small wooden trunk, where she kept her most beloved souvenirs: things given her by revolutionaries, some of whom had perished; our childhood shirts and dresses, and those drawings which we had presented to her. At the very bottom lay a hardened piece of black bread wrapped in a snow-white cloth. This bread was holy: it had been blessed by her father as she was leaving home.

Upon our arrival in Italy, long before any of us really spoke Italian, Nyanya understood the local womenfolk as if by intuition. Immediately she became friends with them. She was always up on the latest news concerning their children, whose husband was ill, and who had just become a widow. She always tried to purchase things from the poorest, most run-down stores in Alassio to keep her "old ladies," as she called them, in business. Our villa was about two kilometers out of town. Whenever a certain old man reached our house on his way home from the fields, to make up for the inhospitable barking of our aristocratic English setters, our nurse would invite him in for a cup of coffee and give him, not only a piece of bread to go with it, but something more delicious, like an orange, a peach or a piece of cake: "Just because he is an old man does not mean that he dislikes cake."

Nyanya took care of just about everything in the house—the entire household was in her charge. She did the laundry, cleaned the house, prepared and cooked all the meals, not an easy task given the large number of people in Villa Arianna and Victor's small earnings. She was a magnificent cook, and her small meat pies, her borshch, and her cabbage soup were renowned. She knew how to prepare various economical dishes, and adapted herself with marvelous ease to the material circumstances of a given time and place. The unpredictable numbers and often erratic ways of our guests never disturbed her. Everyone adored her, and there were always volunteers to help her in the kitchen or with other household chores.

Our dining room was located on the second floor of

Villa Arianna. A dumb waiter was used to bring up dishes and plates whenever this room was used. But this was done only on important occasions, such as the entertaining of special guests or a birthday party. In the winter, we preferred to eat in Nyanya's kitchen, and in the summer the garden was a lovely place for family meals. After dinner we usually stayed at the kitchen table while the evening reading began. Volunteers cleared and washed the dishes while Nyanya put them away. Everyone enjoyed this moment. Victor and young Vasily Sukhomlin were tireless, superb readers of Tolstoy, Gogol, Gleb Uspensky and Nekrasov. Occasionally something was read out of the reviews which came from Russia in the mail. Having finished the clean-up, our nurse mended, sewed or crocheted lace as she listened. The habit of doing handwork in otherwise idle moments or while listening to the reading of classics came down to us straight from her. We learned all our sewing and knitting skills from Nyanya.

I have always remembered an episode that must have taken place during the First World War. One day, the adults had read in the newspapers about a sensational case: the murder of a Russian general who was recuperating on the Riviera in San Remo, not far from Alassio. According to the papers, a Russian emigré woman who had disappeared, and whose name was given as Gorizontova, was suspected of this murder. She had worked as the general's nurse.

Most unexpectedly, two or three days later, a woman dressed in black knocked at our front door. Our nurse, who was busy in the kitchen at the time, opened the door. The woman introduced herself as Gorizontova. She said that although she did not know the Chernovs, she hoped that they might help her. She needed money for train fare to Paris, where a job was awaiting her.

Nyanya immediately understood who the woman was. Inviting her to sit down, she went upstairs to Mother with the visitor's request. Mother and other members of the household quickly searched the house, trying to gather the needed cash. It was not easy to find such a lot of money in Villa Arianna—these were difficult times. No one in the family wanted to go downstairs and speak with a supposed murderess. Nyanya was entrusted with whatever was scraped up—enough for a third class train ticket.

With complete naturalness, Nyanya went downstairs and handed the woman her train fare. Then she warmed up some leftover morning coffee and offered it to her. She took the cutlets which were cooking on the stove for our lunch and wrapped them in paper. She carefully tied the package with a string and handed it to the woman for her trip.

After the visitor had left, the adults who had remained in hiding noisily came running downstairs and began asking Nyanya all sorts of questions about her "new friend." When our nurse mentioned the fact that she had given away the luncheon cutlets and that we would have to make do with vegetable soup, everyone laughed heartily: "Nyanya, how could you? Do you realize that you gave the cutlets to a murderess?"

"What is the difference?" our nurse answered, unmoved. "She may well have been hungry!"

-13-

For the first time in her many years abroad, in the fall of 1913, Mother decided to take a three-month trip to Russia, going both to Moscow and to Petersburg. She traveled legally, using an old passport from the days of her first marriage. Nonetheless, she behaved with circumspection, trying to escape the attention of the authorities—the SRs were outlawed in Russia at that time.

In Petersburg, Mother stayed with Sofia Chatskin-Saker, the editor of the Russian magazine *Northern Notes* *(Severnye Zapiski)*. In her early youth Sofia had been the wife of Mother's half-brother Eugene, but this marriage had not lasted because of some deep and tragic incompatibility between Sofia and Eugene.

Sofia Chatskin—Aunt Sonia as we called her—was the only daughter of a wealthy and highly refined Petersburg physician. A widower early in life, Doctor Chatskin had concentrated all his love on his daughter, whom he worshipped. With the help of his sister, he decided to give her a very special education. She was to grow up in great luxury surrounded exclusively with artistic objects aimed at developing her taste. She was only given those books to read that were regarded as having the highest esthetic standards. Her father wanted to screen her from everything that he considered vulgar and unworthy of her. For instance, Sonia was not sent to a Petersburg school; instead professors chosen from among the capital's academic elite taught her at home. Father and daughter traveled abroad, lived in France and Italy, and Sonia knew all the museums and galleries of Europe.

My grandmother, Maria Kolbassin, had been close to the Chatskins. As adolescents, Mother and Sonia had seen each other on occasion. Sonia was four or five years older than Mother. She was elegantly diminutive with beautiful dark brown eyes and eyebrows like finely drawn wings. But the most remarkable thing about her was her voice. It was low and velvety, and yet sometimes it could be almost metallic. She read aloud beautifully, and I have never heard Pushkin's poems sound as magnificent as they did in her rendering. Mother looked upon her brilliant friend with the greatest admiration and longed to introduce her to her brother Eugene, who lived abroad. And indeed, when Eugene finally met Sonia he fell passionately in love with her.

Although Uncle Eugene was not a revolutionary, his older brother, my uncle Vasily Sukhomlin, had joined the "Will of the People" at twenty-three. This was the underground political party which was responsible for the assassination of Tsar Alexander II on March 1, 1881. Vasily—although not directly involved—had been among the members who had been tried for the Tsar's murder and sentenced to death by a military tribunal in Petersburg, in the so-called "Twenty-one" trial. After his sentencing, at the last moment, Vasily's death penalty had been changed to life imprisonment. At first he did time in the Trubetskoy bastion of the fortress of the St. Peter and St. Paul in Petersburg. Then he had worked in the mines of Siberia and spent many years of exile there with his family—young Vasily Sukhomlin grew up in Siberia, until the general amnesty following the events of 1905 freed them all and brought them to Europe.

Uncle Eugene, on the other hand, had not believed in revolutionary action. When the autocratic regime of the Tsar became unbearable to him, in the 1890s, he left Russia and moved to France where he became a French citizen. He studied philosophy and philology at the University of Montpellier which, in those days, was one of the leading intellectual centers of Europe. He had been a friend of Paul Valéry's, who was to become one of France's greatest lyric poets and was also a student in Montpellier. Then the French students in Eugene's group often met in the evening at the home of a well-known, liberal economist, Charles Gide, who was André Gide's uncle. In the collected letters of Valéry, there is mention of the talented Russian student, Eugene Kolbassin.

Having finished the university, Eugene could teach philosophy in the French lycées. In love with the Mediterranean, he had taken a post in Corsica and taught in the lycée of Bastia. When Mother was a young girl, she and my grandmother had often visited him in the south of France and enjoyed long stays there.

It was on one of his trips back home to Russia that Eugene met and married Sonia. Their marriage did not work out, and they soon separated. After several attempts to get back together, they were divorced.

At about that time, my grandmother died. Eugene was heartbroken, as he had been close to her. Seeking diversion, he decided to realize one of his life dreams, which was to travel around the world. He began his voyage by traveling to Norway. Unexpectedly, Aunt Sonia decided to accompany him on the trip, intrigued by the fact that the first part of it would be in reindeer-drawn sleighs. Eugene and Sonia met in Oslo. But after the preparations for the trip were made and all was ready for their adventure, Sonia changed her mind and went back to Russia.

Eugene went off alone, no one knows where. He never returned. Despite all of Mother's efforts, no traces of him were ever found—not in the Bastia school system, nor in the French War Ministry, where, as a French citizen, he would have been registered. Nor did private efforts at finding him ever give any clue as to his fate.

Many years later during the summer of 1921, Natasha and I looked up Aunt Sonia in Moscow; she was all alone, lost, without means of existence. Her husband, Saker, had died. He had been a relative of the young Socialist Revolutionary who had killed Uritsky, the chief of the Cheka in Petrograd in 1918. Sonia had to escape from Petrograd and live in hiding in Moscow. She stayed in dreadful communal quarters established in what had once been the Testov's Restaurant.

We asked Aunt Sonia to move in with us into Mikhail Vinaver's apartment. Vinaver was a member of the Polish Socialist Party, who in 1921 had taken us in. He was tolerated in Moscow as a member of the Russian Red Cross.

With Vinaver's help we were able to feed Aunt Sonia and to give her some clothes. We cheered her up and literally brought her back to life.

Remembering Aunt Sonia, I recall how once she explained to Natasha and me what feminine charm was. She talked about Anatole France's story "The Queen of Sheba," describing vividly for us the Queen's arrival at King Solomon's court atop an elephant. She was followed by a procession of camels, laden with her wardrobe, her riches, her servants and slaves, musicians and jugglers and trained monkeys. And then, the Queen, whom Solomon had come to greet—decided not to get off her elephant after all. For reasons of her own, she declined to meet the king. Instead,

she turned her caravan around and with all the camels, ele-
phants and monkeys, went back home.

"How captivating such a woman must be! What mysterious, capricious charm!" said Aunt Sonia. Only later did
I think of Eugene's disappearance in connection with this
story out of the Bible, retold by a *fin de siecle* French
writer.

Some years after Eugene's disappearance, Aunt Sonia
remarried. She became the wife of a well-known Petersburg barrister, Saker, who was able to spoil her in exactly
the way her father had. She presided over one of the most
brilliant literary salons of Petersburg. She was the editor of
the most refined publication of pre-Revolutionary Russia,
Northern Notes, which printed such writers as Alexander
Blok and Alexei Remizov.

In 1913 the Sakers received Mother enthusiastically.
She was a rare guest from abroad, one with a "revolutionary halo." In connection with Victor's magazine, *Legacies,*
Mother met with the critic Ivanov Razumnik, who was
close to the SRs. At his house she encountered the great
poet, Alexander Blok. She visited with Alexei and Serafima
Remizov. She was delighted to meet them. She had always
disagreed with the rank and file revolutionaries of the time
who considered Remizov to be a decadent and incompre-
hensible author making fun of his readers. At the Sakers,
Mother also met the marvelous writer Mikhail Prishvin,
who was then very young—but then so was that whole
circle of writers and artists.

During the twenties in Paris, Alexei Remizov jokingly
told us that in the winter of 1913 Pryshvin had run to him
and told him excitedly about what was going on at the
Sakers. "They have huge wood-burning fireplaces, white
bear rugs—and Olga Eliseyevna." Remizov, who loved
Mother, appreciated her rare patronymic. He nicknamed
her "Lesevna." It sounds as if it came directly from the
Russian word for forest.

Life at the Sakers was exciting. Aunt Sonia rose at
noon, when it was already turning dark in Petersburg in

the winter. The literary gatherings in the lavish salon with its huge fireplaces lasted until dawn. The weeks passed quickly until, to her great regret, Mother had to leave. The police were beginning to watch the Sakers' residence and to make inquiries with their servants. Mother noticed that she had "escorts" following her in the streets of the capital. Meanwhile we awaited her return to Alassio with impatience, especially Vadya, who had been taken seriously ill. All four of us children missed Mother desperately. We had the habit of running down to the road below our house to check and see whether she might be arriving.

-14-

Mother returned just before New Year's day, 1914. She brought everyone a mountain of presents: handicrafts which one could buy in the Moscow Folklore Museum, toys, books and sweets, including exotic treats like halva, and cranberries packed in powdered sugar. Mother's return filled the house with life and happiness.

All this changed soon, however, when it was found out that Vadya was indeed gravely ill. Local doctors had not diagnosed tuberculosis right away. At first it seemed as if Vadya would soon recover. He often got out of bed and went about normally. Then his temperature rose suddenly and he had to lie down again.

After Mother's trip, the usually rather careful detail of Okhranka agents watching our house became more enterprising. When we were still in Fezzano, our family was often followed under one pretext or another. Agents approached our nurse under various pretexts and started discreet conversations with her about her masters. Nyanya's sense of humor never failed her and she reported to us some of these conversations. She brought the house down with laughter when she revealed having announced once: "My master is a relative of Stolypin; they are all very important people." Stolypin was the Minister of the Interior of Tsarist Russia.

More serious was the fact that agents of the Russian Secret Police had infiltrated the Socialist milieu in Russia and abroad. Thus, shortly before we moved to Alassio, two "fellow Socialists"—Yury and Alexander—arrived at our villa in Fezzano on their bicycles. No one in our family knew them well, but they were engaging. They were greeted warmly and they managed to spend an entire week with us. I still have a snapshot taken during their visit. It has yellowed but one can make out Victor, young Vasily Sukhomlin, and Kamkov receiving the tired travelers with open arms and holding their bicycles up for them as they step into the garden. Yury and Alexander are dressed in the striped sweaters which bicycle riders wore in those days. After the Revolution when the Okhranka archives were opened it was revealed that both were *agents provocateurs* in the service of the Tsarist Secret Police.

Just before the beginning of the First World War, young Vasily noticed that whenever he walked in the center of Alassio, he was being followed. This happened several times in a row, and Vasily decided to take a picture of the agents who were watching him. When he next went into town he took his camera along. His two escorts were following him once again, and when he crossed the main square, he suddenly turned around and sighted them through his viewfinder. One of the agents then pulled a revolver out of his pocket and ran towards Vasily threateningly. This was in the middle of the afternoon, during the Italian siesta, and no one was out in Alassio's main square. But our close friend, Mansueto, a cabman, happened to be passing. Seeing this extraordinary scene he quickly rode up to Vasily, who managed to jump onto the moving carriage. Mansueto jerked the reins, turned into a side street and took Vasily to safety, away from his angry pursuer.

This incident, soon known all over town, made a great impression on the inhabitants of Alassio. They were intrigued by what was going on in the villa where the revolutionaries lived and were fighting the Tsar. Despite this sensational event they remained friendly towards all of us.

Vadya did not get better, and our children's activities slowly became centered in his room. There, we settled down to draw, read and play card games and checkers. During the day, in good weather, he would lie on a chaise lounge on our balcony which faced southwest, looking over the sea and the nearby hills. Sadly, spring went by with no improvement. Occasionally, hope would be sparked and Vadya seemed to get better, but his sickness soon picked up again. He rested on his bed—very thin now—his thoughtful eyes seemingly terribly large. He lost strength, but he did not suffer. He continued to draw and to write poetry and he read a great deal.

A very hot summer followed, but neither Natasha nor I would go on long walks with our Italian friends accompanied by our dogs. Important doctors both Russian and foreign were invited from France and Switzerland for consultations. Doctor Manukhin, who had taken care of Gorky on Capri, came and suggested a change of climate, but in Vadya's state this was out of the question.

The entire household watched over Vadya, trying to help as best they could. Natasha and I would cut the most beautiful roses in the garden and place them in his room. Cecilia, the old woman who helped our nurse in the kitchen, sighed and wiped her eyes on her apron. She told us: "Children, pray to the Madonna, ask for all her Holy wishes. Only she can help your brother." From Russia Aunt Sonia sent him expensive presents and books.

In the last weeks of Vadya's life, Victor was extraordinarily kind and imaginative with him, spending the night in a chair by his bed. In the morning, using a fountain pen with purple ink, he would write down Vadya's dreams in his neat, elegant handwriting directly on the marbletop of his night table. On the tenth of July, 1914, on the morning of a beautiful day, Vadya died. On August second, less than a month later, the First World War broke out. So ended our Italian childhood.

PART III

Return to Russia

When the war broke out, Victor felt that he could no longer remain on the sidelines of the political struggle. He and Mother moved to Paris, where he threw himself into the anti-war movement. In 1915, he took part in the Zimmerwald Conference, taking the position of an "internationalist," or "neutralist" delegate, as opposed to those who called themselves "patriots," and maintained that it was every Russian's duty to fight against the Germans. Hoping for support from German Socialists equally opposed to the war, Victor became the focal point of a small group of Russian Socialists who shared his convictions. They published a paper which spoke against Russian autocracy and the blunders of the Tsarist leadership in those crucial times. This group was completely independent of the "defeatists," headed by Lenin and Trotsky. The Bolsheviks were in favor of actively helping the Germans defeat the Russian Empire in order to bring about the destruction of Tsarism in Russia.

In the meantime, we, the children, remained in the care of Nyanya in Italy. Young Vasily Sukhomlin was living in Milan at the time and came to see us often; he was collaborating on the Italian Socialist newspaper *Avanti*. In 1916 he settled in Geneva to edit the Russian political monthly *Life (Zhizn')*. After Vadya's death, we were distraught and lonely. Mother and Victor spent the winter of 1914-15 in Paris, and came back to Alassio only occasionally. Mother came to Alassio for longer visits, but would soon leave to rejoin Victor.

At the end of 1916 my cousin Anya Sukhomlin-Filipchenko, young Vasily's sister, gave birth to a son, Stepan, her second child; her first one had died of meningitis at the age of three. After Stepan was born, Anya, who had been tubercular, again developed a lung ailment, and Mother went to visit her in the small village of Montecosaro, in the Marche province in central-eastern Italy. There Anya's husband, Doctor Alexander Filipchenko, a fellow SR, worked as local physician, serving several towns. Mother looked after Anya and her child for a whole month. Before she left Anya's husband begged her to "loan" them our Nyanya for a while. Always generous and enthusiastic, Mother promised him to do so.

Upon returning home, using all her persuasiveness, Mother started pleading with Nyanya. She wanted our nurse to go to work for the Filipchenkos, to save Anya's life and that of her little son. Nyanya was reluctant, but with deep sadness she finally agreed and left our home, forever, as it turned out.

I vividly remember Victor walking back and forth nervously while this decision was being discussed in Mother's little study. He was pacing, as he always did when he was distressed. He disagreed with Mother and maintained that one could not release a person such as Nyanya, who had become part of our family. Even to a relative. Even for a while. But Mother adored Anya and she was very obstinate. She prevailed.

-16-

Nyanya left us, and the house became sad, despite the fact that guests were as numerous as ever at the Villa Arianna. Young Vasily Sukhomlin brought his new wife, Nina, to meet us. The young couple settled with us, and so did our great favorite, Dasha from Kronstadt—Julia Zubelevich. At Victor's insistence, she worked on her memoirs while living at our house. These proved fascinating and were successfully published in Petersburg in 1917.

In the summer of 1914, shortly after the war was declared, Kamkov (Boris Katz) arrived at our house straight from Germany. He had been living in Heidelberg for years. There, after his graduation from the University, he had gone to work for a Socialist newspaper. He was shocked by the attitude of his former schoolmates and Socialist colleagues. As soon as the war with Russia had broken out, Kamkov was ordered to leave the country immediately. When he called on his German comrades and asked them to lend him some money and help him obtain a few more hours in Germany in order to settle his affairs, they all refused to assist him. They were German above all. Forgetting all Socialist allegiances and their friendship, they now considered him as a Russian, an enemy of their country.

Kamkov was full of indignation and hatred for German militarism, and for Germany in general, but after some lengthy conversations with Victor and Vassily, he began to calm down. Eventually he came to share their point of view on the war. He, too, became an "internationalist." He spent several months with us in Alassio before moving to Sweden. From there, he went to Russia illegally, on an SR Party assignment.

At this time we had very little money. With the beginning of the war Victor's literary income began dwindling. Our dacha was mortgaged and we lived off our vegetable garden, sacrificing Nyanya's rabbits and chickens one after another. Victor's royalties were just enough to buy a little olive oil, some soap, and our allocation of sugar, which was rationed. All three of us girls were growing quickly and in order to lengthen our dresses bands of fabric were sewn onto our hems with mixed esthetic success. Dasha's artistic mending took care of worn-out elbows. Means of making money had to be found, but what was there to be done in wartime in a small Italian town?

With her medical training Dasha succeeded in finding temporary work in the local hospital. And some weeks before Christmas, Natasha and I, who had always been good with our hands, started making stuffed animals, to be sold as presents for the holidays. We became involved in our new craft and enjoyed ourselves. We stuffed white flannel cats and dogs with straw. A magnificent salamander was made out of orange velvet and decorated with black spots hand-painted with India ink. Natasha came up with a marvelous seal, while Mother made a beaver out of dark brown plush. We also created shimmering butterflies out of silk, painting their wings with watercolors. This enabled us to raise a little money for Christmas.

That winter of 1916-17—our last in Italy—was particularly cold. Our household activities were concentrated in the dining room, where we spread rugs and blankets on the floor. At night, we hung bedspreads over the windows—black-outs had become obligatory. The war was raging and, in Alassio Bay, a German submarine sank an Italian commercial vessel under our very eyes. Unless the windows were carefully screened, our house by the sea acted as a lighthouse—it was visible for miles around.

In the dining room, the inhabitants of the dacha gathered at night. The adults read and wrote letters. There Natasha and I had our Russian lessons with Mother. Sometimes Dasha gave us anatomy and mathematics lessons as well. Adya and her playmate, Seva, the son of the revolutionary Verzilov, who lived with us then, prepared their lessons at the big, round table. After the two youngsters had gone to bed, there was reading aloud as always. Whenever we had enough wood to heat some water, a great treat —hot water bottles—were prepared for all. The upstairs rooms, which now had no heating whatever, were icy.

Fortunately, on the Riviera, Spring starts early and violets and narcissi began blossoming in our garden in February. Russian publications were slow in reaching us, and it was through the Italian newspapers that we learned about the first Russian Revolution. The news was happy: the February Revolution had been bloodless. A democratic Provisional Government had replaced the Tsar's inept, autocratic rule. All of liberal Europe rejoiced. At long last, the tyranny which had oppressed the Russian people for centuries had collapsed.

That for which many of our friends had died had

come to pass. It all seemed like the dawn of a happy new age to the adults at the Villa Arianna. We were going to return to a free Russia; we would at last be able to live in our own country. No one had the slightest doubt that the time to go home was now, despite the difficulties of wartime travel.

Coming from Paris, Victor joined us briefly in Alassio. It was decided that he would start for Russia first, by way of Paris, London and Scandinavia, and would wait for us in Petrograd. Mother would settle our affairs in Italy, pack, and bring us along, using the same northern route as Victor.

Feverishly, we started packing as soon as Victor left. Our house was rented through an agency to an Italian family from Genoa. When we were ready we set forth with Dasha and the Sukhomlins, traveling first to Switzerland by train.

Our older dogs Pichi and Nelo had died of old age not long before. We gave our younger dog—the one who had been named Toutou by Nyanya while she was still with us —to Italian friends. Mother was full of happy excitement. She told us in great detail about the wonderful future which lay in store for us. Studying in a Russian gymnasium would be a new, challenging experience for Natasha and myself.

Despite the mood of elation and the thrilling trip ahead, I was saddened at the thought of having to part with a world I loved. Mother comforted me, assuring me that we would soon return to Italy, but it seemed to me that we were leaving forever.

-17-

Victor had left Italy in April, traveling aboard one of the first ships taking emigrés back to Russia after the Revolution. Soon after his arrival, he was appointed Minister of Agriculture in the Provisional Government. He settled in Petrograd and urged us to join him there as soon as possible.

Leaving Italy, we went to Zurich, where a party of Russian emigrés, anxious to return home, was forming. I remember how the Austrian Socialist, Adler, came to our hotel room and talked to Mother about how she, as the wife of a Russian Socialist official, an internationalist, should consider traveling to Russia through Germany in a sealed train car. He may well have been talking about the very same train that took Lenin back to Russia. His reasoning was that of any left-wing Socialist of that period: "This way you'll set an example for other emigrés," he said. "Socialists must not take sides in the present imperialist war. It does not concern us."

Adler warned Mother that the sea route was dangerous because the seas were heavily mined by the Germans. He said firmly that Mother should not undertake such a voyage with three young daughters. But he was not able to convince Mother to travel through Germany while that country was at war with Russia. Instead, we joined with a group of Russians who were returning to Petrograd through Paris, London, Norway, Sweden and Finland.

The trip was indeed dangerous. Not long before, a ship carrying Russian emigrés had been sunk by a German submarine. Victor had originally been assigned a berth on that boat, but he had given up his place to an older comrade, the well-known and respected revolutionary, Karpovich. Karpovich had perished—there had not been enough life-boats aboard the ship for all the passengers. The SR Ivan Yakovlev, another passenger on board, an eye-witness of Karpovich's death later told us about this disaster in great detail. Yakovlev sat in an overcrowded life-boat, whose gunnels were barely above the water. He saw sailors hit swimming passengers with their oars to stop them from climbing into the boat and overturning it.

During our short stay in Paris, and in London, where we were delayed for over two weeks, Mother befriended a woman of her own age named Ida Samoylovna Pedder. Ida was of Estonian origin. In her youth she had joined the Bolshevik Party. She was married to a violinist named Sermus, also an Estonian, with whom she had settled in Paris. There they had lived in an Estonian colony of artists and bohemians. After the Russian Revolution broke out, Ida had joined with a group of Parisian emigrés who were planning to return to Russia. Her husband was giving a series of concerts in London, and she was to meet him there. From London, they were to make the trip home together.

Wary of German spies, the British government did not announce the schedule of departing ships until the day before each sailing. No one knew when or from which port the boat which was to take us to Norway would leave; nor were we given its name.

One day not too long before our departure, Ida, who was staying in the same pension as we, knocked at our door. Her face was swollen from crying and tears streamed down her cheeks, smearing her mascara. Her light blonde hair, usually set in large curls, dangled mournfully. That day she looked undone. Mother motioned us to go down into the lobby, so that she could talk to her friend alone.

Ida Samoylovna told Mother that her husband had left her for an Englishwoman, giving no warning whatever. The poor woman was in a state of shock, crying and threatening to kill herself. Her life was ending just as everyone else's was about to start anew in Russia. Mother was touched and tried to comfort her.

That evening Sermus, Ida's husband, came to call on Mother and begged her to look after Ida. He asked that we take her to Russia with us. There she would find her old friends, her party comrades, and eventually would return to a normal life. Mother, naturally generous and trusting, promised him that she would take care of Ida.

It was June and the weather in London was beautiful. Natasha and I loved to walk around this new exciting city. Together or with Adya, we spent many hours in the National Gallery. While in the British Museum, everything that was valuable, including statues and bas-reliefs, had been put away in the basement because of the danger of air attacks, the National Gallery had all its paintings on display. But one day we were told that we would be leaving London the following morning for an undisclosed harbor along the British coastline.

I vividly remember our last night in London. The violinist Sermus came to say goodbye to Ida Samoylovna. He was distraught—his face was gray. In the shabby lobby of the pension with its faded armchairs, in the presence of elderly Britishers, he played on his glorious Stradivarius late into the night. From that evening on, his wife became our permanent companion. On the next day we went by train to the distant Scottish port of Aberdeen where, in the dark of night, we were taken aboard an unlit ship. It left that morning before sunrise.

Ilya Ehrenburg, still young, heavy set, and with long, unkempt hair to his shoulders, was a member of our party. He draped himself in a dark green plaid—many years later he described this crossing in his memoirs. During a visit with him in 1962, we reminisced and recalled one incident out of that trip. An Estonian artist by the name of Ruddi, an acquaintance of Ida's, was among the passengers. Though not at all wealthy, he had bought himself a specially designed, inflatable, waterproof suit which could keep him afloat for several days in case of shipwreck. Expecting disaster, Ruddi walked the decks in this extraordinarily bulky, gray-green garment. There was great anxiety among the passengers of the ship. Everyone aboard was issued a life-jacket with a number on it, which corresponded to an assigned seat in a life-boat. Passengers looked out among the high waves, searching for periscopes. Once or twice, panic broke out and everyone dashed to their assigned life-boats.

One of our fellow passengers, a Scandinavian businessman, offered Ruddi a lot of money for his inflatable suit. As the ship sailed along, he kept increasing his offer. But Ruddi would not sell his suit until that blessed moment when a thin line of land appeared on the horizon. However, by that time the buyer, relieved at the sight of approaching land, had withdrawn his offer. His hands behind his back, he strolled along the decks jauntily. Poor Ruddi could not forgive himself for refusing the large sums of money offered to him so recently.

During our crossing, the weather was brisk and cold, but below, in the lower regions of the ship set aside for the returning Russians, the small third-class staterooms were stuffy. We decided at once to sleep on the decks, wrapped in coats and blankets. On that journey, which lasted several days, we were served no hot food except for some tea with cream, poured into enamel mugs. All third-class passengers had been given "Cook Baskets," named after the Cook Company travel agency. They contained dry sausage, chocolates, bread and cheese, and some tea biscuits which were so hard that even Natasha and I, who both had strong teeth, could not bite into them. Our throats dried up, we were thirsty and the tea served in the depths of the ship seemed delicious to us.

But all this did not matter, for we were on the ocean and white gulls flew above us, escorting our ship. In the evenings, wrapped in our blankets, we enjoyed the sunset: on the water, the sun made a wide, bronze-colored streak which ran from the horizon right down to the ship. A new world lay ahead of us; we were going to go to school with children our own age. This pleased and slightly scared me.

I remember our arrival in the small port of Bergen, a town which glistened with cleanliness and smelled of the sea. Right on the street near the harbor stood brand new barrels made of light wood. They were filled with fish. Fresh ones were the color of silver; others, which had been cured, were copper and gold. Neatly coiled beside them were fishing tackle and ropes. This was the last day of June, the white nights were ending, yet it was still complete daylight as we took the evening train between Oslo and Stockholm, where we spent the night. Then our trip was to take us to Russia through Finland.

On the train, headed for Russia, one of our fellow

travelers told us that things were not good in Petrograd. The Bolsheviks had attempted a coup d'etat; they had tried to seize Victor Chernov. Despite the reassurances of our acquaintance, who said that the coup d'etat had failed, we were worried.

-18-

We arrived in Petrograd at night. Victor met us—he was so hoarse that he could speak only with great difficulty: "This is our widely spread 'ministerial sickness,' " he whispered. "There were too many public appearances, too many speeches, too many arguments...."

We got into a large official Ministry automobile and rode along the streets of Petrograd. We drove slowly past the Palace Square, the "guarding lions," evoked by Pushkin in his "Bronze Horseman," along the banks of the Neva and on to the Palace of the Great Prince Andrey on Galernaya Street. The Socialist Revolutionary Party had set up its headquarters in this palace, together with the offices of its newspaper, "The People's Action." It was here that Victor, in his official capacity, received delegates on matters regarding the Ministry of Agriculture.

Victor led us through the main entrance of the palace, up wide marble stairs flanked by stuffed bears on both sides. The white walls, hung with gold-leaf moldings, were decorated with various hunting trophies once earned by the Great Prince. We were met by a tall, severe-looking butler with a black mustache who led us upstairs to two modest rooms which were to be our family's quarters.

Later, Natasha and I tried to talk to this man—one of the servants left from the time of the Prince, who called himself the "Watchman." We tried to get him to tell us his feelings about the Revolution, but he would not say anything on the subject. It seemed as though it did not matter to him for whom he was working in the Palace.

Adya slept on a small couch in our parents' room, and in the other room Ida, Natasha and I shared one wide bed. Days went by and Mother's new friend was making no effort to find her old friends, nor was she trying to go out on her own. She continued to cry, repeating that she was alone in the world with no one to love, that her life was finished. Mother pitied her and did her best to console and encourage her.

Natasha, Adya and I also felt sorry for Ida, as we would for anyone who was plunged into such grief. She was nice to us in a plaintive sort of way. We considered her presence among us temporary. Though we were used to having visitors in our house, we had always wished for a family life without outsiders. But Ida was staying on, though it was clearly becoming awkward. There were too many women around Victor Chernov.

So began our Petersburg existence—disorderly, uncomfortable, and interesting. My sisters and I explored the Palace, walking along the elegent ballrooms, through gilded boudoirs with antique furniture. There were Empire, Louis XV and even mauruesque pieces scattered throughout the splendid rooms. We walked down the long galleries with plate glass windows looking onto the Neva, which was beautiful both at night and during the day.

Our daily life was unsettled. The kitchens were all the way down in the basement of the palace, and we ate, picnic style, at the strangest hours. Tea, which was served to Central Committee Party members, was available to us once or twice a day. Several elderly ladies who had cared for Victor in Mother's absence greeted us with hostility. They tried to keep Mother away from Party work.

There was incessant activity around Victor. A constant flow of people called on him about matters of the Agricultural Ministry. Meetings were held in preparation for the elections of the Constitutent Assembly. Delegations sent by peasants from the far-off provinces had to be received. A steady stream of callers came in with requests, some of them completely unrealistic, such as getting people out of the draft or giving private persons land allotments, or saving estates from State requisition. Certain demands were accompanied by threats. Mother tried to take care of them, screening the serious requests from the impossible or the crazy ones.

My sisters and I walked the streets of Petersburg alone, discovering new places and recognizing the ones familiar to us through books and illustrations. The days continued to be sunny, but after the clear Italian Riviera light, the St. Petersburg sun seemed to us pale and somehow melancholy.

The mood of the people on the streets was anxious; the atmosphere was vaguely threatening. Public meetings held in the streets continued, though the enthusiasm of earlier gatherings had disappeared. People gathered here and there, on street corners, market places and squares. Large meetings were held on the Field of Mars, which had not yet been paved and turned into a city square. The speakers spoke from makeshift platforms haphazardly put together with boards set across upturned barrels. They addressed the crowd with improvised speeches. The expressions on the faces of those gathered to listen disturbed us— they revealed gloom, distrust, watchfulness. Having heard the speaker, the crowd usually disbanded in complete silence.

I remember a one-armed soldier who, standing on a rickety platform, hit his chest with his remaining hand and shouted that he had fought at the front and would go there again if needed. He summoned the crowd to support the war. Somberly, the gathered listeners stared at the ground and then started to walk slowly away.

Long lines stood in front of bakeries and food ration stores. I was struck by the bright blue painted signs which had childishly drawn products on them: golden loaves of bread and biscuits, pink hams, and bottles of milk. After Europe, even after Italy which was then so poor, we were shocked by the threadbare clothing of the Petersburg inhabitants. With their sad, worried faces these people did not resemble the "Revolutionary People" which my imagination had summoned from the headlines and articles of foreign and emigré newspapers during the first days of the Revolution. War was growing more and more unpopular in Russia, yet the street speakers and the newspapers of every persuasion were cautioning against violent changes—from the right, the left, on the front, and in the sharing of lands.

It was clear that Mother, though not wanting to agree with us openly when we offered her our opinions, was quite disturbed about the turn which the Revolution was taking. Victor, meanwhile, did not lose his optimism. When we did manage to see him between official meetings and Party gatherings, he reassured us, explaining to us that, "soon the Constituent Assembly will settle everything." All signs pointed to the fact that the SR Party would obtain a significant majority in that Assembly.

-19-

In the summer of 1917, while we were staying in the palace on Galernaya Street, Nyanya visited us: she was traveling from Italy to Kiev with Anya and her small son. Before going on to Kiev with the Filipchenkos, she was planning to stay with her own family in the Novgorod province. She invited us to join her there. Such a visit had been a long-cherished dream of hers, and of ours as well. How often she had described her village to us! Now she wanted to share it with us, to have us see it, to meet her relatives and friends, to go on mushroom and berry-gathering walks with her.

Mother accepted Nyanya's invitation delightedly. She was anxious to go out into the countryside. She was becoming involved with politics at that moment. Victor, as the Minister of Agriculture in the new Russian government, was absorbed in the drafting of future land reform laws. Mother wanted to investigate the attitudes and the wishes of the peasants at that crucial moment. One evening, we arrived by train at the Okulovka station, along the old railroad built by Nicholas I. We were to spend the night there. The next morning we would take a horse-drawn to Veligory where Nyanya lived.

It was our first night in the Russian countryside. I remember that we spent it in a large gray room with wooden benches built along one of its walls, where we settled down for the night, wrapped in our coats. But no sooner had we turned off the kerosene lamp than we were attacked by bedbugs. Mother lit the lamp again, and did not lie down all night long, trying to protect us from these aggressive insects. Nonetheless, by morning we were full of bites, our faces all swollen up.

The next day it proved hard to find a peasant willing to take us to Veligory: all the horses throughout the region were used for work in the fields during the summer months. But, after some lengthy negotiations Mother eventually succeeded in finding an obliging peasant who agreed to drive us to our destination. On that wonderful August day, we rode in an uncovered wooden horse-drawn peasant's cart along the open rolling fields and the lakes of the Novgorod region, famed for its beauty. Many of its villages stood on the shores of lakes and ponds. White churches with pale green and bright blue cupolas dominated them and were reflected in their clear waters. Once in a while, a master's house with columned porch could be glimpsed in the middle of a large overgrown garden.

The harvest was not yet over, and groups of harvesters and their horses, hard at work, could be seen here and there, silhouetted against the bright summer sky. The fields were full of haystacks, the air smelled of warm straw and of grain.

The driver of our cart explained to us that before February the immense fields which surrounded us had belonged to a single family, the Ryabuzhinskys. We stopped for lunch on the edge of a field. I was embarrassed when the driver refused to share our eggs and cottage cheese because the day was one of fasting—a Friday.

The sun was setting as we started our steep ascent toward Veligory—the "Big Mountains." It was getting dark and the cart was sinking into deep, muddy ruts. We all descended while the driver pushed the cart along, leaning first against one wheel and then against the other. In the muddiest parts of the road, heaps of freshly cut branches had been thrown down to make the ruts more manageable.

When we reached the village, Nyanya and her relatives and friends came to meet us with lanterns. Someone invited our driver to spend the night at his house. Our nurse took us to the *izba*—the wooden cottage—of her best friend, Annushka. Annushka wore a white kerchief and had a face as round and pink as an apple. To me she looked like a symbol of kindly, peasant Russia.

We settled down for the night by the light of a small kerosene lamp. Annushka's *izba* was brand new, smelling of resin and of fresh wood. It was impeccably clean and quite empty. There was only a small iron bed in the main room, with an inviting pile of pillows in embroidered cases on it.

We discovered that a bed was still a great rarity in that part of Russia at that time. Annushka's was her trophy after many years of domestic service in the city. People usually slept on wooden benches which they lined with old blankets and sheepskin coats. They used no sheets. Mother and Adya lay on the bed while Natasha and I settled on the benches attached to the wall of the *izba*.

We went out early the next morning. Veligory, a picturesque small village, was built along the shore of a small lake, in whose waters it was reflected. Beyond it lay a dark, deep pine forest.

Our nurse's family *izba* was old and rather run down. When we called, Nyanya's adoptive mother came to the door to greet us with a mixture of formality and warmth. She was a tall, very thin woman in a white kerchief which covered her forehead. With her was her daughter, Polya, who was pregnant. The two women were surrounded by a crowd of small children. The boys wore only shirts while the girls were dressed like diminutive grown-ups, in shirts gathered at the waist and long skirts with ruffles of faded pink cotton. All were barefoot.

Polya's husband was in the army and the whole family was hoping for his prompt return. Nyanya's adoptive father had long been dead. Pointing out her children, Polya said: "Their bellies are swollen because we eat only potatoes." Indeed, we were struck with the poverty of the countryside—as we were with the patriarchal sense of self-respect and with the dignified manners of its inhabitants. These people were the product of an ancient and beautiful civilization.

Inside the *izba*, the walls were made of unfinished logs. Embroidered linen towels decorated them. There were icons hanging in the "holy corner." On a wooden table scrubbed until it had turned white, the mistress of the house set out a meal of fish soup and baked omelet. For the first time I could see a peasant's earthenware oven, masterfully handled by Polya, who quickly took full-bellied cast-iron pots and loaves of black bread in and out of it.

Nyanya was very happy: at last she was entertaining us in her family home. After lunch we went out into the woods and gathered ripening cranberries and blackberries. The woods were enchanting, just as our nurse described them, but we encountered no bear on our walk.

The absence of men was noticeable in the village. Only elderly men or invalids with bandaged heads or limbs were to be seen. The very few younger ones who could be glimpsed were somber and taciturn. Probably they were deserters from the front.

On our first evening in the village, company gathered at Nyanya's home. Guests eagerly questioned Mother about their immediate prospects, their problems and the future of Russia. At this improvised political meeting we became acquainted with the mood of the countryside. The peasants seemed less tense than the inhabitants of Petrograd, yet they too were anxiously waiting for reforms. The sharing of the land was foremost on their minds. When would the Constituent Assembly gather? More than anything, they wanted the war to end as quickly as possible and their men to return to the village.

On August fifteenth, the day of the Holy Ascension, we went into a neighboring village where every year there was a religious celebration and a big peasant country fair. People—especially the young—gathered from neighboring villages. All were invited. Everyone was dressed up. Sedately, older folk walked around the church and along the slope of the green hill next to it. There were makeshift stalls set up near the church. Salted seeds and nuts were sold there and brightly colored inexpensive candy.

The young girls in their multi-colored kerchiefs and long skirts stayed together. Despite the heat, their favorite footgear seemed to be shiny, black rubber boots. The young men wore bright pink or red sateen shirts, their jackets thrown negligently over their shoulder. They formed a separate group, walking around the girls in a wide circle, exchanging jokes between themselves in loud voices. Then, with the accompaniment of an accordion intercepted with sudden piercing shrieks, they sang *chastushki*, the folkloric Russian limericks. The girls laughed, covering their mouths with a hand or the corner of a kerchief. They all munched on sunflower seeds, spitting out the shells.

-20-

A few days later an elderly peasant, a friend of Annushka's, agreed to take Mother to a village where the SR Party had its headquarters. Mother was away for several days, and she returned worried but full of fascinating tales. She told us that SR comrades had received her extremely well and had arranged for her to visit neighboring villages where she had participated in political meetings.

She recounted how she had been taken past an estate whose main building had just been burned to the ground. Its ruins were still smoldering. Popular wrath had passed rapid judgment there: a few days before, a rumor had spread maintaining the estate's owner had hurriedly sold it to a foreigner to avoid the forthcoming land partitioning laws. An angry mob had invaded the house, breaking its doors and windows, throwing out its furnishings from the second story onto the ground. Then the peasants had set the house on fire. The housekeeper, who had sought refuge in the cellar, was said to have been burned to death.

This was not pillage, but an act of angry revenge. The local SR Party member accompanying Mother did not approve of the wanton destruction of what soon would be national property. He felt especially indignant about the loss of the estate garden which had been ravaged by the mob. "It takes so very long to grow pear and apple trees before they give fruit," he had said sadly. The housekeeper's death struck him as criminal. Mother heard of several other cases of reprisals and destruction through arson. In vernacular it was called: "Sending out a Red Rooster."

Apparently at village gatherings and meetings agitators now appeared out of nowhere. They proclaimed an unquenchable thirst for revenge on the part of the peasants, demanding the well-deserved punishment of their exploiters. Fortunately, there were no important estates in the neighborhood of Nyanya's village, and all remained tranquil there throughout our visit. Shortly before our departure, our nurse suggested that we accompany her to a distant village situated at the edge of a large lake, where her younger adoptive sister, Nadya, lived with Fedya, her thirteen-year-old son. Nadya had been widowed at an early age. The mother and her son lived alone.

To get to Nadya's village we walked through forests and meadows for several hours, until we suddenly came upon a large, quiet lake. It was an extremely beautiful sight and I experienced a moment of recognition, as if I had seen this lake before. Possibly I was reminded of a painting by the famous Russian landscape painter, Levitan, which I had seen reproduced. Boats were pulled up along the shore of the lake and fishing nets lay next to them, drying. The smell of freshly caught fish filled the air and an atmosphere of patriarchal serenity prevailed. Nadya lived in a well-lighted, comfortable *izba*. She was a weaver and embroiderer, famous for her skills. She herself wove bleached fine linen cloth that she turned into enchanting-looking towels and dresses, embroidering them with a variety of ancient traditional Russian stitches. She did this on order—her reputation as a true artist of her craft was well established in the region.

Red-headed Fedya, with milky, lightly freckled skin and blue eyes, was extraordinarily sweet and as good a weaver as his mother. From the first glance at the two of them, one could see the great love linking mother and son. When Fedya left the room for a moment Nadya said proudly: "He is so good around the house! He gathers all our winter wood. He milks our cow and gets our water at the well. But whenever he can, he goes fishing on the lake; you cannot keep him away from fishing. This is really what he loves to do. If only the village boys did not tease him about sitting around and embroidering like a girl!"

Mother left a deposit for several towels with elaborate embroidered designs as well as for a white dress for herself. These were sent to us in Petrograd. Nadya was able to finish the order before the political storm broke out which was to sweep us away. Mother was never able to send her the money she still owed her because of the turbulent times, and the fact that we soon had to go underground. To this day I have in my possession a piece of white linen cloth with an embroidered edge that I had stitched under Nadya's directions during our visit with her—a memento of quiet days spent in the company of gentle Nadya and of her freckled little boy, Fedya. What did the Revolution do to them? I do not know.

By the beginning of September we returned to Petrograd. It was heartbreaking to leave Nyanya. When would we see her next? Of course we had no notion that we would never meet again. Fall was nearing and it had been decided that Mother and Victor would live in Petrograd for the time being, while we children attended school in Moscow, where the climate was less harsh, and the political atmosphere seemingly less tense. Friends had rented an apartment for us near the Arbat, in the old section of Moscow. Once again we were headed for a new city and a new life.

PART IV

The Bolshevik Takeover

We arrived in Moscow early one morning. As the cab drove us from the station to a side street in the Arbat, I was all eyes—this was Moscow! I was surprised to see the small wooden frame houses with their tiny gardens standing right against large apartment buildings. Electric trolleys and horse-drawn carts moved side by side; women in kerchiefs, men in sheepskin coats, and ladies in city clothes walked side by side. Everywhere churches with bright cupolas could be seen, and the air was full of the ringing of their bells. Moscow was sonorous and vital.

Our apartment windows looked onto the Church of Christ the Savior near the Arbat. It was only sparsely furnished, but there was little time to get settled and we had to make do with what was there: school was about to start. It was decided that Mother would return to Petrograd while we stayed in Moscow under Ida Samoylovna's care. Mother promised to visit us in October, and to bring us to Petrograd for the Christmas holidays. But Ida declined to stay with us; she was drawn instead to Petrograd. As a member of the Bolshevik Party in her youth, she knew Lunacharsky's wife and hoped with her help to find a job there.

Mother then went to Dunya Mosolova, a young acquaintance of ours, who had worked as a maid for a Russian family in Alassio before the war. Mother had befriended this warm-hearted, intelligent girl who had been passionately interested in learning. Subsequently the entire Villa Arianna had adopted her. Mother had given her history and Russian lessons, while Vladimir, Victor's brother, had tutored her in mathematics. Dunya, although originally from the Tver region, had gone to Moscow upon returning from Alassio, where she had continued her studies and graduated from high school.

Dunya willingly agreed to take charge of our household in Moscow. She asked Mother whether she could write home and have her younger sister, Frossya, move in with us also. Soon Frossya arrived. She was a pretty, slender red-head, lightly freckled. She had never been to

Moscow; and although slightly scared at first, she happily settled with her sister and all of us in the big city.

For us, too, everything in Moscow was new and intriguing. Natasha and I enlisted in the well-known, progressive Popov gymnasium situated not too far from the Arbat section of town. We walked to school, taking along Adya, who attended the kindergarten there. It turned out that our tutoring in Alassio had been adequate, despite the fact that our teachers had not, for the most part, been professional pedagogues. However, we had certain blanks in areas where we had been without textbooks, notably in geography and physics.

Our gymnasium was progressive in the best sense of that word. Its spirit was free, based on mutual respect and not on rules and regulations. Its students were proud of the confidence which the teachers and the school administration extended to them. The school was co-educational and the students of our gymnasium greatly appreciated this fact. Relations between boys and girls were direct and friendly; flirtatiousness and affectations were mercilessly ridiculed. Students participated in school government— each class elected two representatives who attended teachers' meetings and were allowed to participate in them.

Natasha and I soon felt at home in the Popov gymnasium. During our second month there, we were both elected class representatives. After our isolated life in Alassio, we found ourselves for the first time among our own contemporaries. Their lively young world was exciting to us. We both studied with avidity and every subject seemed easy to us. We often went to lectures and the theater with our schoolmates, who got tickets for us, the newcomers. We even found time to register in the art school run by Natalya Goncharova, the well-known avant-garde painter.

Anna Petrova, our Russian professor, was our class's main supervisor. She was then teaching Medieval Russian, but she also liked to touch on contemporary literature. Like all other Russian schools of that era, the Popov gymnasium had on its staff several teachers with pointed beards—known as "he-goats."

Our teachers of mathematics and physics belonged to this category.

Religion was no longer an obligatory subject in secondary schools as it had been under the Tsars. Nonetheless it was taught at the Popov by a well-known priest, Sergei Solovyov. Sergei Solovyov, a newphew of Vladimir Solovyov, the Symbolist philospher and poet, had been a close friend of Alexander Blok and Andrey Bely, in his youth. His lectures were about the Acts of the Apostles, and were absorbing. Solovyov was such a brilliant teacher that the entire gymnasium attended his classes.

The fact that we had been brought up abroad impressed our schoolmates a great deal more than Victor's post in the Provisional Government. The entire school was involved with the Revolution. For the most part students at the Popov belonged to liberal circles. During intermissions, the schoolyard was a beehive humming with political discussions. SRs, Bolsheviks, Mensheviks and Cadets defended their own views and argued loudly.

In the middle of October, as promised, Mother came to stay with us. Two weeks later the October Revolution broke out. It was sprung with total suddenness, but clearly it had been carefully organized ahead of time. The Provisional Government's military units and the capital's municipal authorities were caught unaware, and soon Moscow fell into the hands of the Bolsheviks.

What took most of us by surprise then had been long planned. The Communist Party was organized in the early years of the twentieth century by the followers of Karl Marx. By 1902 the party had split into two segments, the Mensheviks, who had a moderate political program, and the more radical Bolsheviks, led by Vladimir Ilych Lenin.

As soon as the February Revolution broke out, Lenin, who had been living in exile in Switzerland, began preparing for action—he was determined to seize power in Russia. He left Switzerland, traveling through Germany in a special sealed train put at his disposal by the German government, which was still at war with Russia.

On July 3, 1917, Lenin staged a first armed insurrection in Petrograd, hoping to overthrow the Provisional Government. This insurrection was put down, but a small group of Bolsheviks uniting around Lenin continued their subversive activities. These culminated in the October Revolution, which they excused with a charge that the Provisional Government was sabotaging the forthcoming Constituent Assembly.

There had been an exchange of fire in our neighborhood on the first day of the uprising. The cadets of the Alexandrovsky Military Academy near us tried futilely to defend our section of town against armed Bolsheviks, but throughout the city there was little resistance; no one had expected such bold, speedy action at that moment.

On the very first day of the uprising, the city streets were cordoned off and people ordered to stay home. Our gymnasium was closed. In spite of our protests, Mother set forth for the center of town, where the SR Party had its main headquarters. We spent anxious hours alone with Dunya and Frossya. Apparently, men were firing atop our apartment building. Bolsheviks and representatives of the legal government in turn broke into our apartment. They were convinced that someone was firing out of our windows. They searched the place thoroughly, ran around shouting, but eventually left us alone.

It was dangerous to venture outside, but Dunia and Frossya did go out as far as the small shop across the way, which had remained open. There they were able to purchase some canned food—some fish and stuffed eggplant which sustained us through the siege.

Two days later, Mother returned. She was deeply affected by the lack of resistance on the part of the Provisional Government. It had been difficult for her to reach our apartment. Certain streets were closed off and barricades had been built here and there. She had been stopped on several occasions as she was walking back, but each time she had managed to extricate herself from inquisitive patrols. Sporadic shooting was still going on.

Soon it became known that the Bolsheviks had taken over the entire city. The Kremlin was closed off to the public and the new Russian government settled there. But Mother maintained that the last word had not been said: "All is not over," she kept repeating. "Russia's fate will be settled by the Constituent Assembly."

In the beginning of November, when we returned to the gymnasium, the mood there—both among teachers and students—had changed completely. During intermissions the schoolyard no longer hummed with heated political arguments. If by any chance these flared up, they became at once bitter and even violent. The students from Bolshevik families were delighted. They had become assertive and went around smiling complacently.

At the beginning of the Christmas recess, we set forth with Dunya and Frossya for Petrograd, where our parents were expecting us for the holidays. The trip proved difficult. As we got onto the platform of the Nikolaevsky Station, it was full of people pacing back and forth, waiting anxiously for the train. After a long delay, when it finally pulled alongside the platform, it was already packed with soldiers sitting and lying next to their big canvas bags. With great difficulty we climbed inside a car and settled on our suitcases in a passageway. Huge black boots hung over our heads and, as the train moved, they swung threateningly.

With the Revolution, train rides had become free in Russia; people traveled back and forth along the huge Russian railway network incessantly. Soldiers were returning home from the front, city people were going to the countryside for foodstuffs, while peasants came to the city in search of manufactured goods. Traveling by train was now an ordeal. The trains were always late; often they were canceled altogether. People waiting for them filled the railway stations which were now monstrously congested day and night; whole families were encamped in them for days on end. It was hard to circulate there without stepping on people sitting and sprawling about. Bodies filled every inch of space, obstructing waiting rooms, corridors and passageways. Our trip to Petrograd in the end of 1917 was but the first of our many difficult journeys across a Russia in turmoil.

-22-

In Petrograd our parents lived in a flat belonging to the painter, Bogdanov Belsky, near Millionnaya Street. In that apartment, a series of rooms and the studio were closed off because of the cold. Logs were becoming scarce in town and it was only possible to heat two rooms. It was also getting to be more and more difficult to buy foodstuffs. Dunya and Frossya did the marketing for us, bringing back yellow turnips, frozen potatoes and a bit of fish: herring and sprat.

I was intrigued by Petrograd. So far to the north, in winter it became light only towards twelve noon, and it was dark again by mid-afternoon here. By the end of December the cold became intense. For us, who had grown up in Italy, it seemed quite unbearable.

Petrograd was buried in snow during the winter of 1917-18, the winter which inspired Alexander Blok's *The Twelve.* It was as if the city was frozen throughout, under snowbanks turned to ice. Few people ventured out on the streets; they had begun to fear one another. In front of stores and shops, there were long lines of dejected-looking men and women in black and khaki. In that beautiful, majestic city colors seemed to fade away. Against a background of white snow only khaki and the bright red of flaps, placards and military insignia came alive. The few newspapers which were published warned their readers of night robberies. Along deserted side streets behind dark corners fear itself was lurking. From time to time rounds of gunfire could be heard in the distance. Presumably bandits, or perhaps ordinary soldiers, were robbing the city's wine cellars. Like huge frozen mountains, dead horses lay in the snow along certain streets, left there from the October uprisings.

It was during this winter of 1917-18 that Chalyapin, the great operatic singer, sang in the Narodny Hall, designed even before the Revolution to attract a working class public. There was no public transportation operating in Petrograd; people did not dare walk about the city at night. Because of this, it was possible to buy normally unobtainable seats at the ticket office of theaters just before the performance, thus avoiding long lines and scalpers. Our fearless mother decided on three occasions to take us to hear Chalyapin. Stumbling along unlit streets, crossing windswept bridges, we made our way through snowdrifts. But despite all this, the four of us were happy, with young Adya holding her own as a grownup. If one of us slipped on the ice, the others were there to keep her from falling. Thanks to Mother's intrepidness we were able to hear an unforgettable performance of "Boris Godunov."

Newspapers appeared irregularly in Petrograd. The Bolsheviks were closing all the publications which were unsympathetic to their cause. Whenever an article was printed to which they objected, the guilty paper was suppressed, but it often reappeared under a different name on the next day, until it was closed again for a new infraction. Such was the case of the SR paper *The People's Action*, which successively became *The Popular Cause* and *The Cause of the People,* before it was forbidden altogether.

Because at first the Bolsheviks had counted on winning a majority in a Constituent Assembly, they supported and helped organize the Assembly's convening. As part of their propaganda campaign they accused the Provisional Government of delaying and "sabotaging" the Assembly's opening. The word "sabotage" was especially prevalent in the Bolsheviks' polemics during this period. But Lenin changed his tactics as soon as it became evident that the Political List No. 3, belonging to the Socialist Revolutionaries, would obtain a clear majority, while the List No. 5, the Bolsheviks', was likely to do less well.

The Bolsheviks got their strongest political support from working class Petrograd. When the voting began and the entire country cast itself clearly in favor of the SRs, Lenin decided to take decisive measures against the "Bourgeois" Constituent Assembly, as he now called it. A faction of the SRs, having suffered setbacks within their own party, sought to join the Bolsheviks and were at first demonstratively welcomed by them. They became known as the "Left SRs."

The opening of the Constituent Assembly was set for the 18th of January 1918. Two days before, on the 16th, workers with Socialist convictions and other sympathizers of the Provisional Government organized an unarmed mass demonstration. Both organizers and participants underscored the fact that the demonstration would be peaceful, although on the part of some leaders, feelings differed as to whether such a march could still be safely held in Petrograd. The majority, however, valued the legend of a "bloodless revolution" above all. Socialists were unprepared to believe that other Socialists would shoot at them during a peaceful rally.

Mother took part in this demonstration, first spending that morning at the Central Committee of the SRs getting ready for the Assembly. Before leaving the apartment she made us promise to stay put in the company of Dunya and Frossya. During the days preceding the demonstration and the beginning of the Assembly we saw almost nothing of Victor. He was deep in political work, preparing for the opening of the Constitutent Assembly, a crucial event, and came home only very late at night.

We were in a state of great anxiety throughout the entire day of the demonstration. That afternoon sounds of rifle shots, shouts and the thundering of horses' hooves could be heard coming up from the streets of Petrograd.

When Mother returned at last that night, we found out what happened. Thousands of demonstrators, coming from various sections of town, were converging on the Tauride

Palace, which was their rallying point. They were singing old revolutionary songs and carrying red banners endorsing the Constituent Assembly and promising the peasants a prompt distribution of land. Mother walked with a group of workers and Socialists along Liteyny Boulevard. Suddenly their way was blocked by a Red cavalry detachment. An order rang out: "Back!" and then almost at once: "Fire!" The cavalrymen opened fire into the crowd of unarmed demonstrators. A young man, walking next to Mother, a flag in his hand, fell. Bullets whistled and several women near Mother dropped to the ground. Red stains appeared and spread on the trampled snow around them. The demonstrators turned back and started to run; horses caught up to them, tumbling them down to the ground and crushing them. The Bolsheviks had planned this dispersal beforehand, placing armed troops and weaponry at crossroads, in order to terrify and disband the Assembly sympathizers.

A paradoxical political situation developed in Petrograd. The Delegates to the Assembly, some of whom had been elected by the Bolsheviks, came to the capital from all over Russia; but upon arrival they found themselves in the middle of a city controlled by opponents of the Assembly. They were intimidated and closely watched. The Constituent Assembly was now to open within a hostile, well-guarded fortress. Nor did the Delegates have any military protection. The only regiments who were faithful to the Provisional Government and the Assembly were the Semerovsky and the Preobrazhensky.

The Bolsheviks started using violence and police methods even before the Delegates gathered at the Tauride Palace. The direction of these subversive tactics was left to the chief of the Bolshevik police. The Constituent Assembly's fate was sealed before it ever convened. To stifle it, Lenin was to use all possible means. This included not only the Red Army and the police but also whole regiments of Lithuanian sharp-shooters, briefed and trained beforehand. These Lithuanians, who did not know Russia or the

Russian language and who did not care whom they were to shoot, played a decisive role in this momentous event. Lenin, an amazing organizer and strategist, was also an excellent psychologist. He realized that Russian soldiers, many of whom were of peasant background, might, if appealed to by other Russian peasants, suddenly turn against the Bolsheviks. To prevent such a possibility, Lenin made concentrated use of the Lithuanian divisions. Bolsheviks were to use them time and again afterwards to put down rebellious Russian peasants and workers.

-23-

The first meeting of the Constituent Assembly lasted until six o'clock in the morning of the 19th. When Victor came home it was already daylight. Shaking with anger and exhaustion he told us all that had happened on the previous day and night.

At the appointed time, at about twelve o'clock on January 18, 1918, the representatives to the Assembly had arrived at the Tauride Palace. Liteyny Boulevard, which leads to the palace, and the streets adjoining it, were empty; military patrols guarded them along both sides. Occasionally one heard, "Who's there?" shouted out. The square in front of the palace was filled with machine guns, stacks of rifles and cases of ammunition.

Blocking its entrance, Bolsheviks stood in strength before the Palace. The only remaining entrance was one of the narrow side doors of the Palace. Through it Constituent Assembly Delegates were admitted into the hall upon verification of their identity. Inside, in the vestibule, and along the corridors, armed soldiers and sailors stood guard. They were rude and loud. The Bolshevik armed guards looked threatening. They called out to one another about how nice it would be to try their bayonets on the backsides of the Delegates.

The Assembly Hall slowly began to fill with Delegates. On the sides of the great hall soldiers and sailors ominously took their stations. Throughout the packed gallery which was to be reserved for the public, bayonets stuck out here and there. Uritsky had handled the ticket distribution personally. The "public" in the gallery consisted of sailors, Red Army men and the notorious Lithuanian sharpshooters. Just before the meeting began, the Bolsheviks and the Left SRs—their new-found allies who were to play an important part in strengthening the public image of the Bolsheviks before being destroyed by them—caucused privately in an adjoining room.

The oldest Deputy present, Shvetsov, once a member of the "Will of the People," who had participated in the Revolution of 1905, opened the meeting. As he walked up to the podium, all at once, as if they were acting upon signal, the Bolsheviks, the Left SRs and their armed guards began stamping their feet, banging their fists on the tables, and slamming their desk tops. Nonetheless, Shvetsov managed to declare the Constituent Assembly proceedings open. Two nominations for the Assembly Chairmanship were then put forth. The Left SRs and the Bolsheviks chose Maria Spiridonova, an old SR, who had suffered in Tsarist prisons and had become a leader of the Left SR faction. The SRs and other Socialist parties nominated Victor Chernov. Chernov won clearly, with 241 deputies voting for him to his opponent's 151; he was elected the Assembly Chairman.

Victor told us that it had taken all his self-control to pronounce the introductory speech before the Tauride Assembly. The Bolsheviks and their sympathizers' obstructions intensified as he rose to the podium. Soldiers and sailors came up to him, taking sharp aim at him with their bayoneted rifles. But he did not give in to their intimidations. He finished his speech despite threats, interruptions and the clicking of firearms. He proclaimed that the Russian people had demonstrated themselves to be in favor of Socialism through the recent Constituent Assembly voting.

Political power must be put in the hands of the Assembly, while the Soviets, a controlling force, would become their allies, not their rivals.

After Victor, the Bolsheviks, Skvortsov and Bukharin, spoke to a silent, attentive audience. But when the Menshevik Tsereteli's turn came, the waving of rifles and the interruptions resumed. Lenin was present, occupying the place of honor in a box. To show his contempt of the Constituent Assembly he took a half-sleeping pose, yawned and appeared manifestly bored.

When Victor spoke again and came to the question of land distribution, dawn was beginning to break. An armed sailor came up to him, tugged at his sleeve and shouted: "Your time is up! The guard is tired, time to shut the lights off and go home." Not taking notice of him, Victor voiced the main points of the land reforms; the Assembly then voted on his program. Meanwhile, shouts of: "Enough! Clear the hall!" rose and grew.

At that moment, Victor was given the crushing news. The armored units which had been at the Constituent Assembly's disposal, and were to move if needed for the protection of its delegates, were immobilized. The night before, the Bolsheviks had induced the workers in the army repair stations to sabotage the regiments' armored vehicles. Upon hearing this, the troops of both the Preobrazhensky and the Semenovsky regiments had second thoughts about the wisdom of defying the Bolsheviks. They declined to defend the Constituent Assembly. The delegates inside the Tauride Palace were caught in a huge mousetrap. What form the Russian government would take remained the question on the agenda. Because Victor feared that the Bolsheviks would falsely try to associate in the public mind the decisions of the Constituent Assembly with the notion of restoring the monarchy in Russia, he felt that it was essential to debate this question despite shouts and threats. Through the din of an unruly crowd, he managed to get the Assembly to proclaim a Democratic Federation of Republics—each Republic having total national sovereignty.

The unruliness of the sailors and soldiers grew even wilder. Victor decided to adjourn the Assembly until twelve o'clock noon that same day. It was a gray foggy morning when he announced this. Just before Victor reached the door leading out of the Tauride Palace, an unknown man came up to him and whispered that his automobile was surrounded by soldiers with guns, apparently ready to murder him. The man told Victor that though he himself was a Bolshevik, his conscience could not let him be part of a murder plot. Victor and the man looked out through the glass door at the waiting automobile. Indeed, it was surrounded with armed sailors. Thanking the man, Victor left the palace through another door, and walked home.

Soon after, a rumor that Chernov and Tsereteli had been murdered during the dispersal of the Constituent Assembly circulated around Petrograd. The Bolsheviks proceeded to confiscate and burn all newspapers carrying any reports of the Assembly meeting. Soon afterwards, they were to prohibit all publications except their own. The Tauride Palace gates were sealed, an armed guard ordered to surround the building, thus ending the Russian attempt at democracy.

In his memoirs, Victor wrote: "It was indeed a horrible night, decisive not only for Russia, but for Europe and for the world as well."

PART V

Wanderings through Russia

24

Victor immediately went underground; if the Constituent Assembly was illegal, so was its Chairman. First he tried to disguise himself by dying his grayish brown hair black, but because of the poor quality of the dye available to him, this did not work. Then he shaved his beard. Mother managed to obtain a passport issued to her under her maiden name, Kolbassin, with her three daughters. Ida Samoylovna, who had been living with her Estonian friends, once again moved in with us.

Soon Victor was informed that a group of SRs opposing the Bolsheviks were organizing in the Volga Region. Saratov, where Victor had grown up, had always been an SR stronghold, and Victor decided to go there, taking with him the entire family. Leaving Petrograd, we spent a few nights with SR friends in Moscow, waiting there for a train to Saratov. Accompanying us were Dunya and Frossya, who did not want to return to their remote village, preferring instead to remain with us despite our uncertain future.

It was decided that Mother and all of us would go ahead to Saratov to find a suitable hiding place for Victor, who would remain in Moscow for a while and then follow with Ida. Ida, meanwhile, detailed her talents and experience as an underground conspirator. And she was believed.

On the day of our departure, when we arrived at the railroad station, it was black with people: a sea of bodies swayed around the front of the Saratov train, everyone trying to push onto the train. Soldiers and women wrapped in their gray shawls seemed like a moving wall pushing forward. The cars being used were designed for freight. They were air-tight, without windows. Painted dark red, they displayed a sign on the side which said: "Capacity 8 horses or 40 people." These were boxcars, or as they were called then—"Maxim Gorkys"—because that writer had ridden in such cars in his adventuresome youth. They were heated by tiny wood-burning stoves which stood in the middle of each car, between plank bunks lining its sides. The few passenger wagons of this train were already filled to the limit with soldiers in tall fur hats and armed with rifles.

There were eight in our group; in addition to our family, Dunya and Frossya, Ira, a friend of Mother's from Paris was traveling with us. She was a pianist and had been born in Saratov. After many years abroad she had decided to return home to her family.

We finally managed to approach the open door of one of the boxcars which was already quite full. With some difficulty we climbed onto it. It was very high off the platform. Soldiers who had been sitting inside, upon seeing young women trying to get into their car, gallantly jumped to their feet and helped us to get in and lifted our luggage. We all squeezed into a corner wooden bunk where, by a miracle, there was a crack in the boxcar wall, providing a stream of fresh air. There were no benches in the "Maxim Gorkys," only bunks which took up more than half the available space. People pushed to make their claim for spaces nearest the stove, with its small stack of birchwood. Everyone was cramped; some passengers lay down, others sat, twisting and bending. We were surrounded by unknown bodies which squirmed unpredictably. Hands, torsos, boots, bags, and sacks of food lay in heaps on the bunks. It felt as though one was stuck in whatever position one had fallen into by chance, and that it would be impossible ever again to move. Yet more people with bags and packages continued to climb into our boxcar.

During the first minutes inside the "Maxim Gorky" I felt claustrophobic. I thought that it would be better to get off the train, to lie down somewhere on the snow and quietly to die of cold. But I held my feelings back as best I could, realizing how hard it would be for the others if I suddenly began crying and tried to get out.

Eventually the enormous door of the railroad car was closed. Soldiers standing next to it slid it shut, locking it from inside, thus keeping out of our car the ever-growing mob outside. After a long wait the train started. We began to inspect our own bodies and belongings, discovering that generally we were still whole. Our neighbors began making room for themselves and soon a pattern appeared. Each person began battling for his own share of the space, trying to place his bags and sacks as comfortably as possible. As this happened, I began to notice that personalities were emerging, each traveler developing his own peculiar characteristics. Neighbors began to talk to each other. Soon food was unwrapped and people began to eat. Tea kettles were produced; it would be possible to get boiling water at some of the stops along the way.

As the stove was lit, thick wood smoke began to billow throughout the boxcar, mingling with caustic tobacco smoke. The soldiers were smoking cheap tobacco; they made their cigarettes by tearing long thin strips of newspaper, sprinkling a pinch of tobacco root onto them and deftly rolling the whole into something which was then known as "goat-foot." This all made the boxcar extremely stuffy. Our eyes hurt and we were thankful for the crack near our bunk. Next to us soldiers munched on sunflower seeds, shelling them in their mouths, and spitting the shells out onto their bunks. Some, however, did this operation with greater skill than others. They prevented the shells from scattering around, keeping them glued instead on their lower lip in big clusters.

The Red Army men observed us with a teasing, ironic look; so many young women! We overheard their ribald exchanges. Two soldiers made a clumsy attempt to engage pretty Frossya's attention. She was not flustered, and instead of shunning them, she started a pleasant conversation with them:

"What's your name?"

"Misha and Kolya."

"I am Efrossinya Ivanovna, Frossya for short."

And everything went smoothly. Her cool yet friendly handling of the soldiers completely changed their entire attitude towards her and all of us. Their somehow rude attentions became a romantic flirtation with a pretty red-haired girl. The two soldiers next to us, Misha and Kolya, became Frossya's knights and this greatly eased our trip.

It took our train four days to reach Saratov. Behind the closed doors of the boxcar it was dark, even during the day. Here and there burning cigarettes studded the darkness with their glow. Fortunately for us, Mother had taken some candles along and they proved invaluable for our survival. As time went by, it became more and more stuffy in the car: the air was a heavy mixture of sweat, of smelly peasant hide coats, and of soldier's boots. Undisturbed, most of our neighbors slept soundly through much of the trip, snoring loudly.

The train occasionally slowed down and even stopped. The soldiers, awakening, jokingly called out in unison, addressing our train: "Hey, Gavril! Wake up, hurry on, start rolling!" We listened to their conversation and soon began to know our companions, at least those who were not hostile. When my legs began aching unbearably, I even asked my neighbor's permission to stretch them over his enormous army boots, which he let me do.

Other soldiers, sitting on bunks further away sensed "class enemies" in us. They made fun of us, looking at us condescendingly and aggressively at the same time. One of them, having taken off his gray cap, took out a pocket comb with missing teeth and began combing lice out of his hair onto an open newspaper spread on his knees. Then he killed them under his thumb, looking at me as he did this. I froze with repulsion and closed my eyes as if dozing, but I could still hear the sound of the insects being squashed. I suddenly realized how easy it would be for him to start throwing the lice at me.

The closed train steamed along through the white Russian landscape. It skipped certain stations, stopping at others, God knows for what reason. Taking advantage of these infrequent, irregular stops, passengers got out, and fearing to wander away too far from the train, relieved themselves in the open. The first stop had taken place more than twenty-four hours after we had left; there was little else they could do. The train was traveling through endless snowfields. During a stop, fearing that the train might depart at any moment, people did not even leave the roadbed, women squatting under the train itself. One old woman, dressed in black, with a gray kerchief around her head, exclaimed loudly: "That damn Lenin! Look where he has gotten us!" After such stops, quickly the soldiers helped us climb back aboard. There was a feeling of comraderie among the passengers. Travel ethics were evolved to such a point that there was no question of taking someone else's place in his or her absence.

Whenever the train stopped at stations instead of the open countryside we got boiling water out of a special water faucet installed along the platform. These were not hard to locate; because of the sub-freezing weather, steam rose around these faucets in thick, white clouds. Usually Frossya's new-found knights deftly jumped from our box-car, taking our teakettle along and bringing it back filled with boiling water. Frossya thanked them with a smile.

The soldiers sang a limerick:

A train from the town of Tambov,
Came to the midst of Saratov.
"No further shall I go—
Where is the conductor?

They also sang the then famous song about the chick:

Poor roasted chick.
Poor boiled chick.
Poor little chick, it also wants to live!

It's time to roast the bourgeois.
It's time to pluck him well.
But poor little bourgeois, he also wants to live!

25

We arrived in Saratov early one morning. Mother's
friend Ira proposed that we all go directly from the station
to her mother's house. Hiring two horse-drawn cabs we all
were driven to her home. I shall never forget the hospitality
of her family, particularly the warmth and kindness of her
mother. They were a traditional Jewish family; Ira's mother and her four sons, two of whom were married, all lived
in harmony under one roof.

As soon as we arrived Ira's mother heated the bathroom so that we each could wash ourselves from head to
toe. Next, having put clean sheets on the one big bed in
the house, she made Adya, Natasha and me climb into it.
Then Ira brought us slices of puffy white bread which was
thickly buttered. I fell asleep right away and slept soundly
right up to lunchtime, when the entire family gathered in
the dining room. Mother was placed next to the lady of
the house. When everyone was seated, she turned to Mother and said with a smile: "Isn't it true, Olga Eliseyevna,
that a mother's greatest reward is to feed her children?"

After lunch, Mother went into town and soon found
Ludmila Nikolaevna, the separated wife of Victor's brother,
Vladimir. She in turn helped us find an out-of-the-way,
single-story house for rent. It was situated in a tiny settle-
ment not far from Saratov and known as Guselka. There
Victor could eventually settle in relative safety.

One could still obtain flour, butter and cornmeal in
Saratov. We were able to buy some logs, and our new
house was warm and comfortable. When we first got there
it was snowbound; we cleared our way to the door with
shovels, and uncovered a wooden terrace next to the house.
Around us there was only a white expanse stretching for
miles on end. Only an occasional crow dotted the white
horizon with black.

In March, my sisters and I experienced our first Russian spring. Our house in Guselka was not far from the
Volga River, and we could watch it thaw, as sheets of ice

suddenly broke apart with an enormous crash and floated away. From under these huge, sparkling floes, a mysterious black-blue water broke out in swirls. People from all around came to watch this event, standing on the banks of the river, looking down at this wonderful, elemental spectacle—a promise of spring.

With each day the rushing of the river became noisier and more exuberant, though snow and ice still remained in spots along its banks and in certain coves. All the riverlets flowing into the Volga were full of glittering, joyous water, and soon new young grass appeared along the shores.

Victor arrived in Saratov only a few weeks after we did, accompanied by Ida. He had shaved his beard, and was unrecognizable to the average person. With his arrival, many of his political friends from Saratov, and from all over Russia, began calling at our place. In between the political meetings held in our small house we were able to go for a trip to the Volga village of Chardym, where Victor had a SR friend who was a fisherman. As a rule, Volga fishermen in that region had strong SR allegiances, and they willingly lent us a cottage along the river for our week's visit. We slept on soft, fragrant straw. Every day Victor, who was an avid fisherman, went out in his friend's boat and helped cast and pull the large nets used by Volga fishermen.

I remember one of our evenings on the banks of the Volga. It was getting dark; waiting for the fishermen to return we had started a fire. We had been bothered by mosquitoes and midges all day and decided to put a shovel's worth of dirt on the flame, hoping that the smoke would discourage the insects. As was the local custom, as a protection we all wore hoods of thin netting over our heads, which had been soaked in oil of cloves. When the fishermen returned they were proud of their day's catch, which had been exceptional. They invited us to come down to see the boat; the bottom was a mass of shiny, squirming sturgeons and herrings. Having warmed a large cast-iron pot of water on a stand over the flame of our fire, they asked for onions and parsley. They then cut several sturgeons into small pieces and threw them into the bubbling water. After a while they removed the pot from the fire, setting it down onto the sand near the river. We gathered around it sitting on the ground, and with wooden spoons we ate the delicious fish soup straight out of the communal pot, holding bread crusts underneath our spoon, as is the peasant custom.

-26-

In July Victor, still in the company of Ida, left Saratov, moving clandestinely to Samara. The Volga region was full of political unrest during that memorable summer of 1918. Members of the defunct Constituent Assembly had gathered in Samara where they soon announced the formation of a Socialist government, and Victor was to take part in it.

A few days after Victor's departure, Mother and all of us followed him using the same SR contacts as those given to Victor by his Saratov party friends. At that time, to get to Samara one had to cross the battle lines between Reds and Whites. A large segment of the Red Army under Trotsky's leadership was pitted against the unified divisions of what was known as the People's Army, supporting the Constituent Assembly. The People's Army, largely made up of volunteers, workers, peasants and intellectuals from the Volga region, was headed by Colonel F. E. Makhine. A large Czechoslovak division, made up of former World War I prisoners, also opposed the Bolsheviks. These Czechoslovakians had been mobilized by the Austrian governnment and put to work in factories. Later they had been captured by the Russian armies and brought into Russia as prisoners of war.

Since the beginning of the Revolution, these men had been trying to return to their homeland. But a new Europe was being shaped at the conclusion of World War I. The Russians had made an agreement with Germany at Brest-Litovsk, and they could not free the Czechs without German consent. Trotsky, who had led the Russian delegation, intended to hand the Czechs over to Mirbach, the German Ambassador. This spurred the Czechs into action against the Bolsheviks. They promptly joined the People's Army, opposing them.

This was a time of dramatic conflicts. Victor had always insisted on waging battle against the Bolsheviks without compromising the SR position, but his motto—"No to the Bolsheviks; no to Kolchak"—was becoming untenable.

Soon the powerful Red Army forced the People's Army to retreat north. An anti-Bolshevik conference had met in Ufa, resolving to reconvene the Constituent Assembly once again. But this was quite futile. The right-wing members of the conference had opposed all Socialist tendencies in the future government of Russia. A Temporary Directory was created at this time; full of contradictions, it had no authority, nor any real power. Reactionary forces under Admiral Kolchak's leadership united in the Urals and continued to gain strength there. Kolchak was leader of the White counter-reactionary forces in that region.

The head of the Czechoslovak units was a General Gayda, an energetic and authoritarian man, who was later to lead the Fascist movement in Czechoslovakia. General Gayda signed a pact with Admiral Kolchak. Both men hated the Socialists no less than the Bolsheviks; subsequently Gayda and Kolchak repeatedly plotted for Chernov's assassination—although Victor remained extremely popular with the Russian civilian masses. White officers incorporated into the People's Army also despised Victor for his liberal stand. They too tried to kill him on several occasions. However, thanks to the support given him by Czechoslovak soldiers, and to the solidarity of his Socialist sympathizers, as well as to his own sharp wit, Victor escaped the dangers that were threatening him at every turn.

Once again he went into hiding. With the help of

close friends, he returned to Moscow in the spring of 1919 by way of Samara. But we were to find this all out only much later, during the summer of 1919, when our entire family was at last briefly reunited.

During that August of 1918, right after Victor had left for Samara and we were hoping to join him there in a few days, we said goodbye to our friends in Guselka and Saratov and were once again on our way—now headed for Samara. Frossya returned to her parents, while Dunya decided to stay with us, to face whatever lay ahead.

It had been arranged between Victor and Mother, before Victor's departure, that we would leave Saratov by train. We went a few stations down the railroad line, and got off at a small station not very far along it, where Mother rented a horse-drawn cart. It was to get us to Khvalynsk on the Volga, beyond the settlement of Cherkasskoye. From Khvalynsk we then hoped to reach Samara by way of a river boat. It was very hot as we rode on a low, wooden cart across the wide steppe. We were surrounded by fields of tall moving grass and fragrant silvery feather-grass. Dunya, who had always excelled in practical matters, covered the hard surface of the cart with a thin layer of straw, topped with blankets and coats. The few bags that we had were placed in such a way that we could lean on them comfortably. Nonetheless, the dry clay road was full of ruts and extremely bumpy.

We made it to the town of Cherkasskoye by nightfall. Mother paid the driver of the cart, who left us with our luggage on a quiet small town square. Then, following the instructions given to her in Saratov, she went off looking for the local school. One of the teachers there was an SR and our Saratov friends had advised us to call on her for help. Mother returned quite upset. According to her neighbors, the teacher had suddenly left without saying where she was going. We had to find some accomodation for the night at once as dusk was already falling.

In desperation Mother then tried knocking on doors right in the village, but people were frightened and would not let strangers into their homes. Finally a family named Semenov allowed us to enter and agreed to rent us a side room with wooden benches along its walls, in their own *izba*. They themselves lived in the front part of the cottage —father, mother, grandmother, son, daughter-in-law and two children with old Russian names, Gamalyil and Gennady. Despite the tiny sum we were paying them, they shared their dinner of meat and roasted potatoes with us.

For the night, we spread out all our coats and blankets and somehow made room for all five of us on the wooden benches. However, as Mother was putting Adya to sleep, she noticed that she was burning with a high fever. During the night Adya's temperature went even higher, and she became delirious. We realized that she must have caught the often lethal "Spanish flu," which was then spreading throughout Europe with incredible speed. The next day Dunya fell ill also. There was no doctor in the village, but luckily we had some aspirin with us. The Semenovs' sense of hospitality in the face of our disaster was remarkable.

Mother arranged for Natasha and myself to stay in the *izba* next door, while she took care of the sick as best she could at the Semenovs, putting cold compresses on their foreheads day and night and providing them with plenty to drink. We spent two anxious weeks in Cherkasskoye, but all went well, and Adya and Dunya did not die. When the danger was over and they began to recover, they were so weak that they could barely walk. Mother had succeeded in keeping Natasha and me altogether away from the sick ones. Day after day the two of us had gone for endless walks in the fields surrounding the village. The Semenov grandmother often came with us. One evening, as Natasha and I were walking around the village, we saw a group of Red Army soldiers standing on a street corner talking. Overhearing their conversation, we understood that they were the soldiers of Chapayev, the celebrated commander who had just pushed the People's Army forces north. Now they were headed for Saratov.

Our hosts were quite hostile to the Reds. While we were there, several stray soldiers came into the *izba* demanding milk and eggs from the peasants, not without rudeness. One of them was Chinese. After their departure, the grandmother was terribly worried because a "pagan" had drunk out of one of her mugs. She went out and promptly buried it in the back of her garden.

Mother surmised that the People's Army had made a stand against the Red Army and had been defeated. Perhaps it was better for us to return to Saratov. After much deliberation, full of anxiety and trepidation, she decided after all that it was best for us to try and reach Samara through Khvalynsk as planned. The Semenovs found us a peasant with a horse-drawn cart who agreed to drive us as far as Khvalynsk.

Once again we were traveling in a wagon, this time amidst fields of wondrously bright, yellow sunflowers. Wherever one looked these strong flowers grew, their tall green stalks holding up to the sun balls of yellow fire, each with a pupil of dark, ripening seeds in its center. We observed the way in which these flowers, which reproduce so exactly a picture of the sun, moved throughout the day, following the sun across the sky. By the time our cart began descending towards the Volga, the sun was setting, its rays low on the horizon. Suddenly, as she was making a turn, our driver drove off the road to let a Red Army convoy pass. It was huge—units went by endlessly, the cavalry first, followed by the infantry. The battalions marched in free formation, the men in khaki clothes, looking proud and triumphant. Behind them rode several wagons filled with young women in bright dresses and kerchiefs, their faces wildly painted. These were Chapayev's men. Though the Red Army men noticed us as they marched by our wagon, they did not pay any attention or try to stop us.

When Chapayev's units had at last passed us by, we rode on, going down toward the shining blue Volga river. We had at last reached the settlement of Khvalynsk; soon our cart clattered noisily along its cobbled streets. But here too the SR addresses Mother had been given in Saratov proved fruitless. No SR was to be found at home. As the Red Army was moving in, the supporters of the People's Army had been forced into hiding. Eventually we found a small hotel, and asked for a room for the night. The watchman, dressed in a greasy overcoat, agreed to let us have a room. However, when we went in, we were horrified. We had never seen anything as filthy in our entire life as this room in Khvalynsk. On the tattered wall-paper, squashed bedbugs hung in great blood spots. They looked as if they had been put there on display. In the middle of the room stood a steel spring bed, one leg missing, the large mattress on it torn and its stuffing spilling forth. Dead bedbugs were stuck on the sheets which clearly had been used that very day.

We sat on our bags, exhausted and despairing. Mother announced that she had one remaining possible contact in Khvalynsk, a friend of a friend who had married a merchant named Shishov and settled there years before. She went out to explore this last hope, while the rest of us waited for her in the awful hotel room. The very first person Mother stopped in the street knew the Shishovs and led Mother to a large, good-looking townhouse. Shishov was at home and received Mother enthusiastically. Upon hearing that we were in the hotel, the merchant's wife promptly had Mother fetch us. Red Army men who had requisitioned a room in her house the day before had just left. Now she was happy to have us move in immediately so as to prevent the danger of further requisitions. We were delighted and relieved to leave our hideous quarters for the Shishovs' home.

Shishova was a young woman with a fair, expressionless

face. That day she was nervous and depressed: her husband was away. We assumed that he had gone into hiding from the Bolsheviks. The Shishovs had two children, eight and ten. Their comfortable stone house with its thick walls was divided into many small rooms which were crowded with heavy furniture and had numerous tiny windows.

As she was making our beds Shishov took two brand new satin comforters out of a large trunk. One was pink, the other blue, and they both felt wonderfully soft and expensive. These had been part of her dowry, and they were not to be used every day. Now Shishov greatly feared that Chapayev's men might take these away and decided to let us use them instead.

Her mother, who spent part of her time in her daughter's home, was a character out of a nineteenth century play about provincial life in Russia. To us she was warm and hospitable. She clearly enjoyed the presence of guests in the house with whom she could talk, and who would listen to her long, colorful stories about the past.

"Now, we'll stoke up the samovar and make some tea, and then we will talk."

We had settled at a large oak table. Shishov's mother served us some delicious peasant pancakes made of flour, and dried black bread with jam. From her we learned all about Khvalynsk since the Bolsheviks' arrival. There had been some executions and many arrests, among them that of a neighbor, a wealthy merchant. The interrogators, wanting to find the whereabouts of his money and valuables, had locked the man in a cellar where a real skeleton was hung. Small, glowing coals had been placed in the skeleton's eye sockets to scare the man into telling exactly where he had buried his treasure in his garden. He lasted one night and then gave in, his hair having turned white.

Then the old woman reminisced about her youth. She used to buy herds of sheep in Baskirya for relatively little—by the time they had been driven to Samara across the steppes, they were worth a lot of money.

"You wouldn't believe this now, but I was quite

hardy in those days. Not like my daughter, Katya—I used to herd those sheep across the steppe myself."

Indeed, while Katya was passive and rather dull, her mother spoke an expressive, sonorous Russian and had a lot of spirit. Her stories were full of colloquialisms and of natural wit. When she spoke about a girlfriend of Katya's who had left home to live with a Red commissar, she described her as having, according to her own proud mother, "one foot in sugar, the other in honey." We all liked to listen to her for hours on end.

A few days later, the Red Army withdrew from Khvalynsk. Shishov's mother left her daughter's home. Shishov, meanwhile, gave us ordinary blankets for our beds, returning to storage the satin comforters and other household valuables such as pillows and silver with which she had entrusted us. The fear of requisitions had passed.

Mother, who preferred to retain a certain autonomy and not depend on Shishova fully, arranged for us to cook our meals separately, on a corner of the large stove in the big comfortable kitchen. She and Dunya went to the local market and brought back inexpensive cuts of lamb, which they cooked with vegetables in the oven. Our money was running out quickly. Mother was soon forced to barter with whatever clothes and small household objects we still had with us.

It was obvious that both Samara and Ufa lay beyond the front lines completely outside of our reach at that time. We lived in the hope that some miracle would occur, enabling us to leave Khvalynsk. In the meantime, we enjoyed the beautiful late summer. Natasha, Adya and I loved to take walks along the Volga. A wonderful autumn then followed the hot summer, and we saw the trees turn golden from day to day. The dark blue Volga against the yellowing leaves was indeed an extraordinary sight. With us we had watercolors and a small pad, and we went down to the river to paint river landscapes. I remember the long barges floating slowly by, loaded with dark-green watermelons, so succulent, so inaccessible.

We were now desperate for money, and Mother finally decided to go back to Saratov alone; there she hoped to meet some friends or Party acquaintances and get information about what was going on and perhaps borrow a little money. In Saratov she would try to find us a place to stay until the political situation became stabilized. To pay for her boat fare to Saratov, we sold two of our last dresses. Then she left, down the same blue Volga. Anxiously we stayed behind, waiting for her return.

-28-

A few days later Mother returned. She had tried to find friends who could either put us up, help find us a house, or simply lend us a little money. But her quest was unsuccessful, and for the first time Mother was beginning to lose hope. Then a miracle took place. There, on the main street of Saratov, she met her close childhood friend, Tonya Slep, whom she had not seen since their school days together in Odessa. It turned out that Tonya had married Naum Neiman, a well-known engineer and petroleum expert from Baku. He had recently been assigned to work in Saratov, where the Neimans lived with their three children in a large apartment on Nemetsky Street.

Mother had known Naum in Odessa: he and Tonya had been engaged while still in their teens. The reunion was joyful. The Neimans comforted Mother and immediately suggested that she bring us all from Khvalynsk to stay with them.

According to the housing regulations of those days, the Soviet city authorities had begun "to consolidate" houses, filling all available living space within them through summary requisitions. They were about to assign complete strangers to share the six-room flat occupied by the Neimans. Tonya explained how much they would like to have us be the extra occupants in their apartment.

Life, no less than novels, is rich in extraordinary coin-
cidences and decisive meetings. This encounter turned out
to be the answer to our situation, which was becoming desperate. Mother returned to Khvalynsk to fetch us just as
November had come, which meant that shortly all passenger boat service along the Volga river would stop. However, at that moment occasional ferries still ran, although
they had become unreliable.

We gathered our things quickly. We thanked the Shishov family for having saved us at a most difficult time. Indeed, what would have become of us without their hospitality that summer? I remember vividly the November evening of our departure from Khvalynsk. It was dusk; peasants had agreed to drive us to the dock on the Volga,
which was located far away from the center of town. We
finally arrived at the wooden pier, which extended a long
way over the dark waters of the Volga. We were dressed
warmly, prepared to wait through the entire night if need
be, sitting on our belongings. To keep warm, once in a
while we ran up and down the thick, resounding wooden
planks of the dock.

But we were lucky. In less than an hour, a small ferry-
boat appeared in the distance chugging along the river
towards us. It looked like a toy; it was all lit up, as if out
of a picture postcard. Once our bags were stored on board,
we went below deck, to the warmth of the passenger area.
There were few people traveling along the river at this time
of year, and I was soon able to fall asleep, lulled by the
pleasant, regular sound of the engine.

The next morning we arrived in Saratov and went
straight to the Neiman apartment by horse-drawn cab.
Theirs was a loving, cozy household and we felt its reassuring warmth at once. The Neimans' life had not yet been
shattered by the hardships of the Revolution and of the
Civil War. Naum Neiman was a particularly gentle and
thoughtful man. Valya and Shura, his daughters—sixteen
and fourteen—were pretty and kind. They soon became

excellent companions for both Natasha and me—we were then fifteen. The Neiman girls were as dark as we were blonde. Soon we found that we shared the same intellectual interests. Their younger brother, Misha, was exactly Adya's age and became her friend.

The girls were attending high school, the Saratov gymnasium which had just been renamed "Third Soviet School." There Misha had started first grade. The Neiman apartment was comfortable and well-furnished and it was full of books. Shura and Valya were members of the local library. The Neimans assigned us a small room, where the four of us slept. Tonya was more than happy to give room and board to Dunya as well, in return for household help.

Even before our arrival, their apartment had been "consolidated" by the authorities. Part of it was occupied already by a Madame Bekker and her twenty-year-old daughter. Madame Bekker had an unusual profession—she worked as a matchmaker, arranging marriages for a fee. She had been quite successful at this in Baku and now earned her livelihood in Saratov in the same manner. Every morning, bundled in her gray cape, she went out and spent most of the day about town.

"Where do you find your clients?" Tonya had asked her once.

"Generally, I start by going to doctors' offices, where mature women tend to congregate because of their medical problems. While the doctor is busy and no one pays attention to me, I ask the women in the waiting room whether they know of any unwed ladies, or whether they have any sisters or aunts who might like a husband. This works very well."

Another inhabitant of the apartment was a War Commissar from the Caucasus. He was very short. Dressed in leather riding pants, shiny black boots and an Astrakhan fur hat, he tried to look important. Once, through an open door we saw him take a formal pose in front of a mirror, practicing a prepared speech, with appropriate gesticulations: "Citizens, Comrades and friends, we are living a great historical moment! The All-Russian Party of the Bolsheviks, uniting the forces of the peasants and workers will conquer...." On occasion a voice teacher, who was a Red Army man, came to call on him, and together the two rehearsed revolutionary songs. Roaring stanzas and speeches resounded through the apartment. "This will be our last decisive battle! This will be our last...."

Joyfully, Natasha and I entered the last grade of high school, while Adya entered first grade. We spent the winter of 1918-19 peacefully in a stable, amicable atmosphere.

Foodstuffs started disappearing and fuel became scarce but nobody minded those small deprivations. Late in the winter Mother received news from Victor that he was safe, and was waiting for Mother in Moscow.

Towards the end of winter Mother succeeded at last in leaving for Moscow. Traveling in Russia had become an all but impossible undertaking. To obtain both a ticket and a seat on the train, one had to have an official traveling permit, obtained from Soviet governmental institutions. After months of effort, thanks to Naum Neiman's connections, Mother was able to obtain such a travel pass to Moscow.

Letters from Moscow were not reaching Saratov, and we were long without news from Mother after she left. Finally, through friends, she succeeded in letting us know that she and Victor were looking for some safe refuge where we could join them. Mother asked the Neimans to allow us to stay on with them a while longer, to which they gladly agreed. We had become close friends with Valya and Shura, and our life was a meaningful, interesting one, despite the disquieting news: the Civil War was spreading throughout Russia and abuses both by the Reds and Whites had intensified. That spring, having completed the last grade of the Saratov Third Soviet School, Natasha and I passed our final examinations successfully, graduating from the gymnasium.

At long last in late spring we heard from Mother: she and Victor had settled in a dacha near Moscow, and she asked us to join them there as soon as possible. For a small child, no traveling papers were needed and before long we found an opportunity to send Adya on to Moscow with friends.

Naum's tour of duty in Saratov was coming to an end. The Neimans began to pack: they were going home to Baku. Tonya was reluctant to leave us alone in an apartment filled with strangers. But she had no choice. We said goodbye with great warmth, promising each other never to forget all the good things that had happened to all of us that winter. We did not know that the Neiman's fate would be tragic—Naum, with his technical expertise, and Tonya, with her practical sense, seemed destined to survive under any regime. Yet Naum was a victim of the witch hunt against "engineer wreckers" that took place a very few years later.

Soon Dunya managed to leave also. She had decided to go back to her family in the country. In July an acquaintance of the Neimans who had recently married offered me a pass for Moscow, in exchange for one of the Neiman's rooms. He promised to obtain a similar traveling permit for Natasha in the near future.

While I packed, Natasha moved into a smaller room in the apartment. I was deeply disturbed at having to leave without her, but I trusted that the promised pass would materialize soon and bring her to Moscow. On my way to join my parents, I was sitting near the window in a crowded train compartment. I was daydreaming about my forthcoming reunion with my parents. I knew from Mother's letter that Ida still lived with them. Across from me sat a newlywed couple. The woman was humming a love song about lilacs:

And remembering those days bygone
You tossed a langorous fragrant branch,
You tossed a branch of lilac in my lap.

I have never forgotten this languorous branch of lilac.

It lulled me all the way to Moscow. There in the morning Mother met me at the station, having miraculously received my telegram. We went first to an underground Party meeting place on Trubetsky Lane. The next day we took the Bryansk railroad to a small rural station about two hours out of the city, where Victor was waiting for us.

PART VI

The Dacha in the Woods

We spent the summer of 1919 in the Moscow region, not far from the village of Molodenovo, seven versts from the Zhavoronky station on the Bryansk railway. Our sturdy dacha belonged to a Doctor Lavrov, a person unknown to us. It stood in the middle of a pine forest, close to the steep bluff over the Moscow River. We could easily make out, on the other bank, the low meadowlands which flooded in springtime.

Seen through the pines at the crest of the bluff, these meadows seemed to be bathed in blue mist; they faded into the distance as far as the eye could see. There were frequent rains that summer and the foliage around us remained fresh and green. In the fields, bachelor's buttons, daisies and bluebells grew to a man's height. I had never seen such meadows before. Among the pines, mushrooms began appearing and early in the summer we picked some right next to the house; they were a valuable addition to our unvarying diet of millet, the basic foodstuffs of that hungry time.

About a half verst up the river, beyond a field in the middle of a big garden, stood a house built by Savva Morosov in the Russian Empire style. It was pale yellow with white columns and a wide staircase leading up to a terrace. The doors had been wrenched off and the windows broken. Inside, the printed wall fabric was hanging in shreds. In the drawing room stood a couch with springs protruding through tatters of silk brocade. In the center of the room a concert grand piano had been battered in by heavy blows. The house looked like a forlorn symbol of the Revolution which had swept through that region.

Several other SRs had taken refuge with Mother and Victor, including Vladimir Chernov, Victor's brother, and Ida Samoylovna. One of Victor's friends, Vasily Filipovich, was the permanent resident of the dacha; he had been an SR before the Revolution and was now a convinced Tolstoyan. It was he who had put this dacha at the disposal of his SR acquaintances. This was the brief period of "legalization" of the Socialist Revolutionary Party by the Bolsheviks, which was to end soon afterwards in new persecutions and arrests.

Vasily Filipovich had been born in a peasant family from the village of Molodenovo. He introduced us to his sisters. I remember that one of them, Anastasya Filipovna, embroidered with extraordinary skill; she made icons of silk thread, using the ancient Kiev stitches. Vasily Filipovich, a man of about forty, imitated Tolstoy. He tried to give his own dark-blond, curly beard the shape of the master's, and he wore a shirt of rough homespun linen belted over his trousers. He was gentle and well-wishing, and he spoke readily about his Tolstoyan convictions, trying to impart them to others, especially to females. Mikhail Vedenyapin, another resident of the villa, called him "velvet eyes."

We all loved Vedenyapin, a lively and open man who looked at people with friendly eyes from under his thick, dark eyebrows. Ekaterina Dmitrievna, his wife, was a small, raw-boned, dark-haired woman who was interested only in household matters and in acquiring foodstuffs, a pursuit which was not flourishing in Molodenovo. Valya, her stepdaughter, was my age. She did not like her stepmother very much. Her father had married Ekaterina in Siberia, where he had lived in exile for a long time.

Another young SR, Mikhail Petrovich, was also hiding at the dacha at the time of my arrival there. I do not remember his last name—it was probably never mentioned. Victor told me that he had arrived from Saratov, where he had belonged to an activist cell of the Party. Not long before, he had been arrested by the Bolsheviks along with several comrades and sentenced to be shot. The Bolsheviks had taken the arrested men to the outskirts of Saratov, to the edge of a steep ravine. When the salvo rang out, Mikhail

Petrovich realized that he had not been hit. Instinctively, he fell to the ground and rolled down the ravine, landing among bloody corpses. He lay face down and pretended to be dead. Two men from the execution squad walked down to check that all were dead; Mikhail Petrovich lay still. At nightfall, he climbed up the slope and was able to reach Saratov, where he took refuge with friends. Then, using false papers, he came to Moscow.

Mikhail Petrovich had a beautiful baritone voice, and in the evenings, at the request of friends, he would sing old Russian songs.

The dacha was sparsely furnished with only the barest essentials—iron beds with straw-filled mattresses, tables and chairs. We were able to collect enough firewood and kindling in the forest to light the cast-iron stove in the basement kitchen. Each family lived separately and ran its own household within the dacha.

From the beginning the atmosphere in Molodenovo was oppressive. Within our family, Ida was becoming more and more assertive. She complained less often about her loneliness; with a sigh she now talked about her health—she had always had weak lungs, and was threatened with tuberculosis. Personally, I was shocked by her attitude towards Vladimir Chernov, Victor's eldest brother.

In 1918 in Petrograd, during the generalized arrests of that year, Vladimir had been arrested as a member of the staff of the newspaper *Will of the People*. No arraigment procedures were instituted against him; the Cheka simply forgot about him. He spent a long time in prison under dreadful conditions, without any help from the outside.

Upon her arrival in Moscow from Saratov, Mother had heard that Vladimir was in prison. She and Victor turned to their old friend, Ekaterina Pavlovna Peshkova, who in turn wrote to Gorky—in a published letter of Gorky's dated May 1919, one finds the following line: "I'll pull Vladimir Chernov out of prison yet." And indeed Gorky kept his promise and he was released by the Cheka. In July he was able to travel from Petrograd to Moscow, where Mother and Victor were waiting for him.

As a result of starvation, he had become psychologically ill. Eating was an obsession with him. At the Lavrov dacha, his doubled portion did not satisfy him. Whenever he thought that no one was watching, he would look for food. He searched drawers and shelves throughout the house and in such moments his eyes looked insane.

Normally a mild, refined person, Vladimir often arose during the night and sneaked barefoot into the kitchen. He would light the stove and place a large cast-iron pot filled with water on the burner. Then, out of a sack of millet standing in the kitchen closet, he would scoop up unmeasured handfuls of yellow meal, and pour it into the boiling water. Swelling in the water, the mixture ran out of the pot. The room would fill with smoke and the smell of burning. Hastily Vladimir would devour the uncooked mush, wiping off his beard and his moustache. This scene repeated itself frequently. For the sake of Vladimir's health it became necessary to lock up the household food reserves.

This passing mania did not detract from Vladimir's attractive, educated side. He was aware of his ailment and suffered from it. Once he told me about his prison experiences and about the days following his release, when in a dulled state of mind, alone, homeless and starving to death, he had walked the streets of Petrograd. One incident haunted him. During his wanderings he had seen a small white dog that seemed to have strayed and was sniffing the passersby, looking for its master. In his possessed state, Vladimir lured the dog into a dark courtyard. There, with a large stone, he smashed it to death.

"It was hideous. I sensed what Raskolnikov must have felt after the murder of his landlady. I was delirious. I do not remember what happened next. I do not recall whether or not I ate the dog, but I clearly remember the way in which I beckoned the animal through guile—the guile of a cannibal, tormented by primeval hunger."

Ida's harshness was suddenly surfacing: she lacked

any sympathy or desire to help Vladimir at that difficult moment. She saw him as depleting the "reserves," of the household, thus dooming us to starvation. She kept repeating: "He rummages at night, and with the cleverness of a madman, finds all that is edible. He lies and feigns innocence, thinking only of himself."

When the mushroom season came, Vladimir began picking mushrooms, assuring us that many species which were considered poisonous were, in fact, edible. He brought home baskets filled with large umbrella-shaped "meadow mushrooms" which frightened us because of their similarity to the so-called "death caps," which are lethal. Mother argued with Vladimir, fearing that he might poison himself. So as not to alarm her, he hid his daily pickings. Late at night, he went to the kitchen and cooked himself mushroom soup on the stove.

Ida was indignant; Vladimir not only burned up our supply of wood, but he also risked setting the house on fire. Such activities as watching over Vladimir and trying to hide foodstuffs from him was having an adverse effect on the inhabitants of the Lavrov house. An atmosphere of hostility prevailed. People began locking their bedroom doors at night and the kitchen closets were padlocked. Everyone looked scornfully upon poor Vladimir. I noticed that even nine-year-old Adya spoke critically about Vladimir's sickness. Only Mother showed kindness and concern for him and as a result he did not shy away from her.

"Mushrooms are as nourishing as meat," the hungry Muscovites kept repeating, trying to comfort themselves as they thought of what lay ahead of them. Ida was agitated and spoke about the need to build up our food reserves constantly. Everyone was to gather mushrooms and dry them for the winter. She was irritated when white boleti were served at the dacha, feeling they should be saved for the future. Her incessant talk of starvation destroyed whatever poetic feelings might have existed between relatives and friends coming together after a long separation. "Mushroom folly," Vladimir Chernov called it.

Adya and I took delight in the Russian forest. For us it was full of novelty. Together with Valya, we picked bouquets of ox-eyed daisies to decorate the empty rooms of the wooden dacha. But Ida's unpleasant, deep voice, with its Estonian accent, resounded throughout the house, reminding us of hardships, of the approaching winter and of our complete unpreparedness in the face of it. Hanging in long garlands, mushrooms dried everywhere through the house while Ida sat on the terrace, endlessly threading them onto strands of unbleached thread.

Natasha was still detained in Saratov. The newlyweds who had promised to help her leave shortly after me had not been able to procure a traveling permit for her. Letters sent through the free postal system, a recent innovation, did not arrive. She remained alone, completely cut off from us, without money. I was deeply perturbed—I should have never left her behind alone in Saratov.

-30-

The Molodenovo stud farm which had recently been established stood about a mile and a half from our house. Isaac Babel was to visit it in the thirties—we found this out during a conversation we had years later in Paris, shortly before Babel's death. In Molodenovo, Babel had known Vasily Filipovich's relatives. Babel had said to us—this was in the late thirties—"Now is not the time to write about people, but it is still possible to write about horses, and I am studying them."

Soon after my arrival at the dacha, the wife of the director of the stud farm came by our house. To me, a recently graduated high school student, she offered a regular job for which I was to receive two or even more quarts of milk a day. I was extremely pleased. This was the first job offer I had ever received. I looked forward to making a contribution to our livelihood. But my happiness was short-lived. Ida announced that she herself would take the job. With her lively character and her ability to deal with people, she planned to reorganize the work at the farm and make it a model of efficiency. And, joking on her favorite subject, she added that the first thing she was going to do was to capture the director's attentions; he most probably had never seen a true Parisian before in his life.

I tried to remind her that the offer had been made specifically to me, the high school graduate. Perhaps the director would find it easier to deal with a young person rather than with an adult woman? Moreover, my handwriting was particularly good. But Mother called me into another room, and patiently explained to me why I should yield my place to Ida. Our upbringing by Mother was founded on altruism and a complete lack of self-assertion. One had to understand the other person's feelings, and be helpful at all times. In those years, Mother's authority was unchallengeable for me.

"She is single," repeated Mother, "and entirely dependent upon our family. It will give her great satisfaction to know that she can contribute something to our household."

I stopped arguing. On the next day, in a white dress and high-heeled shoes, her hair set in big curls, her pale eyes accented with black mascara, Ida went off to the stud farm. She returned by dinner time with a can of milk. Her work consisted of recording in a book the vital facts about each horse, its date of birth, its antecedents and characteristics. A record of the farm's yield of milk was to be entered into another book.

The next day, Ida brought back some notebooks in order to line their pages in preparation for the next day's recordings. She started to do the ruling unevenly, smudging the pages. She then asked me to correct her work and to finish it for her. I tried as best I could, but there was no suitable eraser at the dacha, nor did I have a ruler. On the third day, Ida was late for work. Soon she started to refer to the farm in a condescending manner. Her handwriting was illegible, she made mistakes in calculations, and confused items and figures. The job had turned out to be beneath her dignity. Two weeks later, she was told that her services were no longer needed, and we found ourselves without milk.

The rains stopped in the beginning of August and we enjoyed a succession of dry, hot days. The inhabitants of the Lavrov house decided to have an evening picnic, with a big outdoor fire. A few miles away from our dacha lived acquaintances of Vedenyapin, the Rakhmanovs. For the picnic which we decided to hold together with them, we chose a lovely spot at the forest's edge, halfway between their house and ours.

The sun was already leaning to the west, illuminating the tall, ripening, yellow fields when we left that day. Together with Valya and Adya, we gathered bouquets of cornflowers. Having reached the place set for the picnic, everyone formed a large circle around a campsite. Then with dry branches and pine cones we prepared a fire. Each family had brought what they could in the way of food, and we all shared the modest delicacies. When it began to get dark the men lit the fire, which sprang into blaze with a loud, crackling noise.

Mikhail Petrovich was asked to sing. He first sang a solo which resounded through the forest: "With my strong voice, let me not wake my sleeping beauty." A friend of the Rakhmanovs, a young woman teacher, who was wearing a peasant blouse with red and black cross-stitch embroidery, turned out to be a beautiful singer also. Slowly, others joined in. Victor set up a chorus which he directed. I wove flower garlands for Adya, Valya and myself with the cornflowers we had picked.

All through the night the fire crackled and flamed, lighting the far reaches of the forest. The dark trees seemed to recede from us. The singing hushed, the short summer night was ending. Little by little the sky clouded over, and towards morning a light drizzle started to fall. Mother covered Adya and me with a blanket that she had brought along. The forest became cold and forbidding and at sunrise everyone went home through a light rain.

On the following day Mother became ill: she had a violent attack of sciatica. Unable to move, she was forced to lie down flat on her back. Shortly afterwards, she was taken to Moscow.

31-

In Moscow Mother was looked after by our faithful friends, the Logorovs, who lived on Prechistensky Boulevard. It was not easy to arrange for Mother's transportation to their house. Finally, Vasily Filipovich borrowed a cart from his brother-in-law. In it, he took Mother to the nearby railroad station. I accompanied her.

The medical treatment given Mother at the suggestion of the Logorovs' family doctor did little good, and after a few days Victor entrusted me with the responsibility of locating an acquaintance of his, Doctor Dorf, to seek his advice. Doctor Dorf was a brilliant physician and a leading public figure in Moscow. He had once been a Socialist Revolutionary, but even before the Revolution he had given up party work in favor of administrative activities at the Zemstvo—the elective district council in pre-Revolutionary Russia. His good heart and his responsiveness were legendary. Doctor Dorf was paralyzed from the waist down and he moved around in a wheelchair. Despite this handicap, he worked tirelessly. At the time, he was one of those in charge of the Moscow Public Health services. I found his office. He had seen me with Victor on Galernaya Street in Petrograd in 1917, and he recognized me and was very helpful. At once, he wrote a note assigning Mother for treatment at the "Institute for Traumatic Diseases." After much looking, I found the Institute. Its assistant director said that Mother could be brought over on the next day. On the following day, after a long search, I was able to find a cab and take Mother to the Institute.

Two days later, on the hospital visiting day, I went to see Mother, bringing her a small package of sweets and a change of clothes. She lay in a large, crowded ward, with rows and rows of beds. It was filled with the loud buzz of voices. Tormented female faces were everywhere. I located Mother in a sea of unknown people and ran up to her. She had a tired, frightened look. She told me about what had happened at the hospital in the last couple of days. Apparently, during the regular bi-weekly meeting of the lower echelons of the hospital personnel, which included night nurses, cleaning maids, and medical attendants, it was decided that a nurse had the same right to run the Institute as the head doctor: Lenin had said that any cook is as capable of running the government as anyone else. A mutiny had taken place. The night nurses refused to attend to the sick, and even after being operated on, women remained without attention. During the previous night, a nurse, irritated by the requests of the woman lying next to Mother, had struck the patient across the face with the shoe off her foot. The sick in the ward seemed depressed and terrified.

Mother was also upset by the fact that the linen on the beds was of an impossible color. The pillows were wrapped in badly washed soldier shirts instead of pillow cases. I tried to keep Mother's spirits up by promising that I would go to see Doctor Dorf again immediately. The woman lying next to Mother, who had a wrinkled, gray face and dark circles around her eyes, looked at Mother and said, "You look like a happy person. It seems you've been spoiled by life."

On the next day, I went again to see Doctor Dorf. Again the endless corridors, the flights of stairs, the anticipation. I remember the kindly smile on the doctor's face. He listened to me carefully and promised to think of another hospital for Mother. I brought Mother back at once to the Logorovs to await the change.

Then I went back to the dacha for a few days to look after Adya. I found everyone there in a state of alarm. One of the SR comrades had been told by "an unknown source" that the Cheka had information concerning the Lavrov dacha, and that a police search was to be expected shortly. Everyone became agitated. Victor, Vedenyapin and Mikhail Petrovich left the dacha at once in order to hide at the homes of friends in Moscow. Ida also left soon afterwards. Only Ekaterina Vedenyapin, Valya, Vladimir Chernov, Adya and I stayed on in Molodenovo. Before leaving, Victor suggested that in case of police questioning, we should all hold to a similar story: that it was *Vladimir* Chernov and not *Victor* Chernov who lived at the dacha.

We didn't have to wait long. On the morning of the third day, armed Chekists surrounded the dacha. They were dressed in leather jackets and riding breeches tucked into high black boots. Each held a revolver in his hand. One of them swiftly ran onto the terrace. Ekaterina and I walked out to meet them.

"Who lives here? Where are the bandits hiding?"

With her hand, Ekaterina pushed me aside and answered slowly and clearly, with the apparent desire to astonish the Chekists:

"I am Vedenyapin's wife. My husband, Vedenyapin, works in Moscow in the Trade Bureau." This information did not interest the Chekists in the slightest.

"The Kolbassin girls also live here," said Ekaterina. The Secret Policemen were silent. Ekaterina paused and added, counting on a particular effect:

"Vladimir Chernov lives here too." The effect produced by these last words far surpassed her expectations. The Chekists jumped up and began shouting. "Zharno. Where's Zharno? Let's have Zharno!"

They dashed into the dacha and searched through each room, looking behind every piece of furniture, every door. Then they quickly went out again and started running through the woods, calling out, "Zharno!" For a while they darted among the trees, then they disappeared. We did not see them again. Apparently, the search was intended to round up persons other than the SRs. The

Chekists had been looking for a gang of thieves, and when Chernov was mentioned they mistook this name for that of a certain Zharno, the leader of the bandits. The next day, I went to Moscow to report to Victor on the search, and on the fact that there had apparently been a false alarm.

I then went to see Doctor Dorf again. He had found a hospital outside of Moscow for Mother, where electrotherapy and massages were used. If she was not better in a week, the doctor himself was going to arrange her transportation there.

It was then that Natasha joined us at last at the Logorovs! She told us about the spreading civil war on the Volga and about her lonely, claustrophobic life in Saratov during the hot Volga summer. Every day a curfew had forced the inhabitants of Saratov to sit locked up in their houses throughout the long, burning afternoon hours.

One morning just before Mother's transfer to the new hospital, Natasha and I went to Molodenovo. We walked from the railway station along a short-cut through the now-harvested fields. To get to the dacha, we had to cross a small tributary of the Moscow River, the Vyazemka. Instead of a bridge, the river was straddled by two long logs. These logs, one thick, the other thin, were set at different heights. I was scared by this unsteady footbridge, and could not understand why the peasants did not lay three or four additional logs to make the river crossing easier. To me, this bridge was symbolic of the crudeness of Russian life, which seemed at least in part self-imposed. I had once seen a middle-aged peasant look at this bridge doubtfully, then turning up his pants, go down and wade across the stream with his boots under his arms. This time, Natasha and I noticed an old, bearded peasant standing near the footbridge. Frightened but unwilling to take off his boots, he got on all fours and simply crawled onto the other side, along the logs.

As we walked, I told Natasha about life at the dacha and about the various persons living there. I was sorry that she had come to Moscow so late in the summer. The days were becoming noticeably shorter, and now Mother had taken ill.

During my absence, all of its inhabitants had returned to the dacha. Though I had warned Natasha of the difficult situation created there by Vladimir Chernov's mania, she was shocked when she saw Ida's harshness towards the poor man.

I was back in Moscow on the day set by Doctor Dorf for Mother's transfer to the hospital. A friend of the doctor, an administrator in the governmental Health Bureau, came for Mother in a horse-drawn, wooden carriage and delivered us to Khovrino on the outskirts of Moscow. The hospital stood close to the railroad station and had a large garden. The head doctor greeted Mother cordially. We liked the feeling of this new hospital at once. Everything there seemed well-organized and clean. On the way back to Moscow, the horse walked slowly, and the driver and I rode in silence. I remember that he asked me how old I was. I answered that I was soon going to be sixteen.

"Oh, is that so?" he answered thoughtfully. "Well, then you're just beginning life. And life is a riddle."

After my return to the dacha, Natasha and I took turns visiting Mother. For both of us, the hospital seemed a paradise. Mother lay in a room with three well-educated, pleasant women. After the therapy sessions started, her condition improved, and she was able to walk around a little.

Soon we discovered that Adya, too, turned out to be sensitive to humidity—after the years in dry, sunny Italy, the climate of the Moscow region affected her. Her hands and feet began hurting. Mother spoke with the doctor in charge and he agreed to take Adya into the hospital for a period of rest and of therapy. She was placed in a large room in the children's section of the hospital. Both Mother and Adya stayed in Khovrino for several weeks.

The September days grew shorter. Fall was approaching, though the weather remained sunny and clear. Little by little, the dacha was losing its inhabitants. Victor went off to live with his friends, the brothers Rabinovich, on Nikitsky Boulevard. Coming into Moscow from the dacha, we would often meet him at their house. Eventually Vladimir Chernov, too, left. He had found a job as a proofreader in a Moscow publishing house. Fortunately his emotional state was improving.

Yellow leaves began appearing in the forest. There were reddish-pink patches of the maples along the pines. Instead of daisies, we were picking bright, fall branches. Our second Russian summer—the summer of 1919—was ending.

PART VII

The Lubyanka

The good weather lasted through September, when it became necessary for us to think about moving out of the dacha. Party friends helped our family find shelter in a single room in a small house in Moscow occupied by an SR, Sinitsin. The doctor had suggested that Mother not return to Molodenovo, where she might have a new attack of sciatica. It was better for her to stay on with Adya in Khovrino and then move directly to Moscow.

On one of the last days of September, just as we were about the leave Molodenovo, I went to see Mother in the hospital. I always enjoyed the peaceful atmosphere in Khovrino. The patients, wearing their dressing gowns, would take advantage of the sun and walk around the park conversing with each other in quiet voices. Fanny Moyssevna, a doctor's assistant who was fond of Mother, received me warmly. On that particular occasion, she invited me to spend the night at her apartment. She had a habit of quoting an aphorism of Schopenhauer's: "Life is a chain of suffering interrupted only by ephemeral periods of happiness." For me, at that time, spending the night on a soft bed, reading in the evening by the light of an electric lamp were precisely that rare, short-lived happiness.

The following noon, I left the hospital for Moscow, where I was to meet Victor at the Rabinovich's. As always, I was well received by the two brothers and offered tea and food. From there, I was planning to go on to the Logorovs before dark, spend the night with them and then go to the dacha to join Natasha. As we said goodbye, as an afterthought, Victor asked me to run an errand for him the next day before leaving for Molodenovo. I was to go into a stationery store on the Arbat and ask for a certain Zvereva. I was to tell her that the next SR Party meeting would take place on a particular day. This store was a front for secret SR headquarters. Carefully Victor explained to me how to find it.

I walked in the direction of the boulevard where the Bogorovs lived and noticed how mild the weather was. It seemed that the summer did not want to end. Suddenly, I bumped into an old friend of ours, Yulya Chernenkova. She had been an SR, and had lived in emigration in Cavi di Lavagnia in Italy. She had often stayed with us in Alassio. She seemed very happy to see me, and asked me to spend the night at her place. I agreed—the Logorovs were not expecting me—no one would miss me. Yulya brought me to her small room and brewed some carrot tea. We sat down at her tiny table, savoring it. Yulya asked me a hundred questions. We had lost touch with each other since our return to Russia. Together we reminisced about Italy late into the night.

The next morning, Yulya made a delicious breakfast for me. Lighting her small stove, she cut up a fresh cabbage and placed it in a saucepan with salted, warm water. When the water had come to a boil she took out the leaves and served them still crunchy. I ate them with great pleasure, though Yulya had no bread to accompany this meal.

Regretfully, we parted and I went out on the street. The sun shone brightly. I was wearing a dark dress which belonged to Mother and which I had worn for my expedition to Moscow. In this dress, which made me look grown-up, I was too warm. I took off the knitted, tan sweater I was wearing over it. When I reached the Arbat, I glanced at a big, round street clock, and I noticed that it was nearing two o'clock. Soon I had located the stationery store described by Victor. Displayed in its window, one could see blue and red notebooks, pads of various sizes, and pencils set out in a fan-shaped pattern. A few persons stood outside, studying these items, hard to procure at that time. Shoppers entered the store one by one.

From the street, I observed the store carefully. Everything in it looked normal. Behind the main cash register sat a young woman matching the description Victor had given me of whom to approach in the store. After a while I entered and went up to this woman. In a hushed voice I asked whether I could see Zvereva. The young woman jumped up and grabbed my arm above the elbow. She called out loudly: "Comrades, they're asking for Zvereva here!"

I tore free, but three men appeared from the back of the store, where there was a stairway leading to a basement. Two of the men held me firmly on each side, while the third, dressed in a black leather jacket and a snap brim cap, got out a notebook. Looking at me closely, he began questioning me. I realized that I had fallen into a police trap.

"Do you know Zvereva?"

"No," I said. I was telling the truth.

"But you asked for her?"

"I wanted to buy a notebook...."

"Then what do you need Zvereva for?"

"I wanted to buy a notebook."

"Who sent you?"

"I met a girlfriend from school, whom I haven't seen in a long time. She said...."

"What's your friend's name?"

"Tanya Dreiser," I blurted out. God only knows through what powers of association the name of the American writer came to my mind at that moment.

"What's your name and patronymic?"

"Katerina Ivanovna Orlova." I felt that I would soon become entangled in my own answers. Then, suddenly, my interrogation was interrupted by a great outburst of exclamations and a loud call from the cellar.

"Comrade Rothman!" Another Chekist rushed up to the one questioning me. "There's a rotary press in the basement. An underground printing press!"

Rothman let me go and ran downstairs, followed by the two men who had held me. I took a breath. What could I do? I had been caught red-handed. Looking around, I noticed that the store was quickly filling up with people. A Chekist stood by the entrance door. He let newcomers in, but would allow no one to leave. I moved away from the cashier's counter and, unnoticed, started to mingle with the people who had just walked in.

In an effort to alter my appearance, I slipped on and buttoned up my beige sweater. Next, I tied up my hair with a light blue scarf which I had in my purse. Luckily, I do not have any outstanding features. I am of small stature, slender with gray eyes. Nor is my nose in any way remarkable—I do not stand out in a crowd.

The Chekists were overwhelmed by their dramatic find—an underground press! In a state of frantic excitement, they used the telephone, ran up and down to the basement, and conferred with one another. They had forgotten all about me. The record of my answers had not been completed, nor was it signed.

Time went by, and the store was getting crowded. Filled with curiosity, new people kept coming in. All were detained. As evening fell, the electric lights were turned on. I remember that at one point two uninhibited young women opened the door and peeked into the store. Both were snub-nosed and round-faced. One wore a blue dress, the other a violet one, and they had long black ribbons around their foreheads, holding veils reaching to the hems of their dresses. Together, they walked into the store.

"And who are you?" playfully asked the guard at the door.

"We're actresses," the girls said.

"Oh, yes, we know what kind of actresses you are! Do come in, please." The girls tried retreating, but it was too late. The Chekists would not let them out. At that time in Moscow, a campaign against prostitution was under way. Red Army men could be seen carrying long cloth banners stretched between two wooden poles and inscribed with slogans: "Down with prostitution!," "Join in the fight against prostitution and syphilis!," and "Syphilis is a misfortune, not a disgrace!"

It was dark outside when the head of the Secret Police addressed the detained and announced that they were all under arrest. A truck drove up to the store and we were made to climb into it one by one. There were many of us—thirty or forty—and we swayed as one mass as the truck sped along the streets of Moscow. We were taken to the Lubyanka, to what had once been the offices of the Phoenix, one of the Moscow Insurance Companies. The Moscow Cheka was now located there.

-33-

In the dark courtyard of the Lubyanka we were divided into two groups—men and women being separated. Counting us, a Chekist gave us over to a Latvian guard, an enormous, heavy-shouldered woman. With the help of a soldier, she led us to the women's section of the prison. We went down long, dimly lit corridors. At last, the Lithuanian woman opened a door.

We stood on the threshold of a cell filled with women. It looked as if there was no room in it for even one more person. Women of all ages were dashing about. Some were in tears, crying hysterically, others were waving their arms above their heads. It was a scene of despair, like Dante's first circle of hell: "Words of grief, angry exclamations, piercing voices, wheezing, the clasping of hands...."

A wooden plank was set up in the cell, taking up a good third of the available space. Some women were settled on it while others, unable to sit still, paced the cell feverishly. Whenever the door opened, they rushed up to the guard. Shouting, each would try to explain that she had been arrested through a mistake, an accident, and that she had never done anything against the Soviet government. "Write a declaration," the guard would say, pushing away the women crowding around her. Then she left, slamming the door behind her and bolting it from the outside.

I was able to squeeze toward the plank bed. At last I could sit down after those long hours spent on my feet. I

[147]

looked about, trying to assimilate what was going on around me. There were women of every conceivable background in the cell. Some spoke in whispers, some shouted loudly, while others sat in a state of prostration—lips tight, motionless, staring off into space.

Suddenly, a heart-chilling shriek rose above the hum of voices. Women rushed to the center of the bench, grabbing a woman with a carefully styled, blonde hair-do. Her neck was wrapped in a long, blue gauze scarf. "It's better to die. Better to die quickly!" She was crying, in hysterics. Someone explained that the woman was a famous actress, a member of the Arts Theater, who had just tried to hang herself from an old iron hook above the center of the planks. In response to the cries, the guard came in, but seeing that nothing had happened, she walked out again, leaving behind a stack of papers. They were old insurance forms cut into small pieces. "Write down your declarations on the blank side of the paper," the guard had said. "There'll be no supper for you newcomers. Too late."

The arrested women took the sheets of paper, and passing around an ink pencil, they carefully began to write their petitions. Suddenly, a tall, gray-haired woman came up to me. She looked cultivated and had a stern, drawn face. She said softly:

"You are young. Believe me, an older person—don't talk to anyone. Don't believe anyone. Be silent. There are all sorts of people. Don't incriminate yourself—they're only waiting for that. Stay away from them. Look, for example, over there near the door. See the two nice girls who look like students? They're sisters, both prostitutes. But who would have known?" I looked up and saw the two girls. Only fifteen or sixteen. They were pretty, with milk-white skin flushed with pink. Both wore dark dresses with white collars. It would indeed have been difficult to guess their profession.

"Look over there, see the mother with her daughter, sitting on the planks. The daughter is the young one, with her dark hair cut short. They're mixed up in some plot,

something to do with spying in Finland. It's very serious."
The two women she pointed out to me had settled on a
green plaid blanket spread onto the planks. They were silent; their silence separating them from the rest of the prisoners as if it were a wall.

The guard came in again. Walking around the cell, she
picked up the prisoners' declaration and carried them off.
The conversations and movement did not subside. The
writing of the petitions had aroused new, naive hopes
among the arrested. I sat silently, following the suggestion
of the gray-haired lady. I would not have wanted to talk in
any case; I had much to think about.

Hours went by. The Latvian guard came in again and
offered to take us to the toilet. We formed a line at the
door, and she led us in groups across a wide corridor. The
plumbing in the toilet worked poorly and the floor was
flooded. Next to the door stood several pails of water.
When the last group had returned, one of the women cried
out pathetically:

"Do you know what they did with our petitions?
They threw them in the pails. I saw the pieces of paper
floating in the water, the purple ink all washed out. They
are just laughing at us!" These words produced a new burst
of complaints and exclamations.

In the cell the window was completely sealed off with
boards, and it was getting very stuffy. Slowly, exhausted
by the lack of oxygen, by their tears and their shouting,
the women began to quiet down. Outside noises were becoming more noticeable: a truck engine was running in the
courtyard. Then, somewhere near, rifle shots rang out distinctly. Our door flung open and our guard ran in with
another Latvian woman. Their faces were white, and they
held their hands over their ears.

Someone near me explained: "Those are the executions in the basement. To make them less noticeable they
start that truck's engine. It even gets to these two. Shots
ring out loudly in the corridor."

Eventually, the guards left the cell and silence returned.

One by one, my neighbors were falling asleep. Between lying bodies, I was able to stretch first one leg, then the other. I put my old suede bag, bought abroad an eternity ago, under my head. To screen off the bright electric light which hung from the ceiling, I covered my eyes with my blue scarf. And then, a miracle took place. The silent girl with the shortly cropped hair who was said to have been seized with her mother in the "Finnish affair" suddenly said to me across the plank bed:

"I have a pillow; you can take one side of it and I'll put my head on the other." And she placed a middle-sized pillow in a white pillow-case between us, and smiled at me. In her offer I felt a sense of trust. I was touched and thought that all had not been lost, that it was possible to find kindness even in the frightening world around me. We lay down, our heads on opposite ends of the pillow.

The dark-haired girl fell asleep right away. I lay there for a long time, eyes shut, going over the events of the day. The crucial thing was that my presence at the stationery store had not been connected with the discovery of the underground press. What extraordinary luck! I had not been incriminated. In future interrogations I would be able to say calmly that I had walked into the store to buy a notebook and that I had fallen into the police trap by pure accident. It was better to forget altogether about fictitious Katya Orlova and Tanya Dreiser.

I would give my name as Olga Kolbassin and mention the Bogorov's address. I could do nothing else but give the Logorov's address, as that was my official residence. It was my only way out—if I refused to answer questions I would not be released from prison. In the Logorov apartment there was nothing which could incriminate them; no lists of addresses, no forbidden books.

But when would they question me? So many people had been arrested at once, each waiting to be let out! I might have to stay in prison a long time. I would have disappeared, but Mother would think that I was in Molodenovo; Natasha might assume that I had stayed at the hospital, while Victor would believe that I had safely gone back to the dacha. Word that the SR printing press had been uncovered would soon get to him, but wouldn't he think that I had left the store before the police raid? Eventually, of course, it would be Natasha who, alarmed at not seeing me, would go to Victor and start a search. But when?

The electric light penetrated through my light scarf and kept me awake. I tried not to move so as not to wake the girl whose pillow I was sharing. I lay there for a long time, reflecting. Then, all of a sudden, sleep overcame me.

-34-

The Lubyanka Prison came awake again early in the morning. The prisoners woke up, one after another; their grief and fear were reawakened. Excited conversations began again, growing more and more intense as the day progressed. The owner of the pillow got up before and started folding her blanket. She wished me good morning. When I got up, she settled back against the wall near her mother.

An assistant, selected from among the prisoners, helped the guard carry in and distribute white, enamel mugs containing a dark, hot liquid—this was morning tea. Hastily, a few women were getting dressed and fixing their hair: they had been summoned by the authorities for interrogation and they were leaving, filled with hope and fear.

Once again, I reconsidered my situation and held to the decision I had reached the previous night. I would give the name under which I was registered officially in Moscow, Kolbassin. This thought helped me maintain my composure. I began to study my surroundings. I felt detached— it was as if I were a spectator, looking on from the outside. I tried to remember every detail of what was going on around me. I imagined how I would tell Mother, Victor and Natasha about everything I had seen in prison.

It was past noon when we were brought bowls of thin

cabbage soup. As soon as we had finished it, the guard ordered us to get ready immediately, and put on our "city clothes." The prisoners from our cell, including those picked up on the Arbat, were being transported to Butyrskaya Prison. Hearing this name, I was seized with anguish. In the crowded cell of the Moscow Cheka it had seemed that most of the inmates were there by accident, and that upon verification of their identities they would all be freed. But the name Butyrskaya meant a long stay and real prison conditions.

The women quickly gathered their possessions. A few had with them coats and even blankets and pillows. Outside, the Latvian women counted us off. Nearby, the men picked up at the stationery store were also being gathered. Chekists in black leather coats bustled about, while soldiers stood waiting for orders. Once in the street, we were escorted by armed soldiers. An officer walked at the head of the convoy. I noticed what tired, drawn faces the prisoners had.

A bright afternoon sun shone. We walked in the middle of the streets, which were covered with golden, fall leaves. I breathed in the soft, slightly moist air with delight. It was a windless day, and the last foliage was slowly circling to the ground. The soldiers hurried us along. Many women walked with difficulty; some stumbled in their high-heeled shoes.

We walked for a long time through the streets of Moscow. When we came to the Butyrskaya Prison, a tall brick building, the sun had set. Large gates opened up for us and were closed behind us and bolted. In the large reception room the men were once again separated from the women. Everyone was given a small questionnaire, asking the prisoner's name and address. We filled these out and returned them to the commanding officer. The Chekists who had accompanied us began lengthy talks with the prison officials, who were obviously bewildered by the number of arrested persons brought in. For a long time we waited, standing up. Finally, we were divided into groups of four and a guard led us to the cells assigned to us. The commanding officer called at random three other names along with mine. Four of us were taken to cell 14 in the so-called Police Tower—the main building of the Butyrskaya Prison is flanked by two round, brick towers known respectively as the Police Tower and the Pugachev Tower.

We climbed three flights of stairs along a spiral stairway. The guard who led us was also Latvian. She took us into a small, semi-circular cell which was brightly lit by an electric bulb hanging from the ceiling. With a light shove she pushed us into the cell and locked the heavy door behind us with an enormous key. Here we were—four women completely unknown to each other, locked up together by chance.

-35-

I examined my companions in the Butyrskaya cell carefully. The oldest, a brunette with nice features, looked like a well-to-do Muscovite in her forties. The second woman seemed well-educated. She wore glasses. For some reason she seemed exhausted. The third one, a girl of only twenty, was tall and pretty, with fair skin and smoothly combed, chestnut hair. Her face was stiff—she seemed petrified with apprehension.

At first glance these women did not seem suspicious in the least. There was nothing unattractive or forbidding about any of the three. They did not look like prison informers, nor like political activists. Rather, they were average citizens who looked lost, observing one another distrustfully. I relaxed, sensing that I was sharing a cell with three harmless Muscovites. They, however, remained guarded for a time.

Quietly, I studied our cell. It had curving walls except for a straight interior partition which had a cot fastened to it. A brown blanket was folded on its fairly clean mattress.

Very high up there was a single, small grilled window. The walls of the cell were painted black halfway to the ceiling. A dark green latrine bucket was standing in a corner. Attached to the curving wall there was a collapsible table and a bench. An opening closed from the outside, a peep-hole, was cut through the door. Our Butyrskaya cell was not a cheerful spot.

My companions were silent, probably afraid to start a conversation. At last I broke the silence: "Here we are, in a real prison. This seems better than the Lubyanka, quieter and more peaceful. Let us introduce ourselves. I am Olga Viktorovna Kolbassin. I live at eleven Prechistensky Boulevard. I walked into the store to buy a notebook."

The oldest of the three said: "I too wanted to buy a notebook and some pencils. These things looked so inviting, laid out in that store window! I live near the Arbat. My name is Natalya Lvovna Kostaky, which sounds Greek, but my husband is actually Georgian. He's well-known in Moscow Georgian circles."

"I'm from Moscow also. I'm Lydia Matveevna," said the woman with the tired face. "I am a pianist and a music teacher. I thought I'd buy a writing pad." She raised her lorngette as if she were about to inspect a store display.

At the word "writing pad," the third, younger woman burst into tears: "A writing pad! My God, I too am here because of a pad! I wanted to buy one for my husband. What now? I can't do without my husband. He's waiting for me." She started to sob loudly. We understood that her name was Larisa and that she was from a Moscow merchant family. She had just gotten married.

The ice was broken. As we conversed, I sat down on the cot next to Natalya Lvovna. Lydia Matveevna settled on the floor on the blanket, while Larisa opened the folding wall bench. She continued to cry.

"Do you think that we will be shot?" Natalya Lvovna asked in a loud voice.

"We were caught in an ambush—in a mousetrap," said Lydia. "They've arrested so many people that they don't know where to put them. What will they do with us?"

"Oh, damn them and their printing press. We'll get shot and no one will know it."

"They have us locked up and they will massacre us."

I interrupted, "No, they cannot kill us. There are too many of us. We're not involved in anything subversive. We just walked into the store to make some purchases."

"What makes you so sure they won't shoot us? How do you know?" snapped Lydia, the piano teacher.

"I think that if they had wanted to shoot us, it would have been easier to do it at once, in the basement of the Moscow Cheka. Why go through the bother of chasing us across all of Moscow?"

"Well, what a phlegmatic person you are, Olga Viktorovna!" Natalya said. "Do you ever get worried? They will do exactly what they want with us. They will kill us for no reason, or let us rot away here."

"Yes, they might well keep us here for a long time. If only we could know *when* they'll let us out!" I said.

"So you're already set for a long stay? What a patient person you are!"

"What about my husband.... I can't go on without him!" Larisa started to cry again.

I sensed that her weeping might be contagious. I made an effort to control myself. Excusing myself, I used the latrine bucket in the corner. When I lifted the lid, a strong odor of chlorine hit me: at the bottom, a white disinfectant was foaming. The other women used the latrine too.

Then we chatted—about the color of the walls and the fact that the cell had only two corners because of its semi-circular walls. We complained about the cell's black walls. Someone commented that they were painted that color especially to intimidate us. Everyone smiled. But time was going by. Natalya's small gold wristwatch read eleven thirty. It was time to go to sleep.

Natalya settled on the cot, stripped of its mattress. Larisa put the mattress on the floor and stretched out on it while Lydia took the blanket. I was left with nothing. It was straight out of a fairy tale: the lion, the wolf and the fox are dividing their prey according to their respective strengths. In such situations the youngest one, like the little rabbit, gets nothing. I thought about this and it made me laugh inside. I was bolstered by a certain curiosity as to what would happen next. What was life in a prison like?

I lay down on the bare stone floor. It was icy and hard, I wrapped myself tightly in my knitted jacket and placed my handbag under my head. Alas, there was no dark-haired girl with a pillow lying next to me, but I comforted myself, recalling her smile.

Lydia settled down on the floor and pulled up the brown blanket over her head. Natalya unhooked the skirt of her light, cream-colored suit—we had been arrested on a mild, sunny day. Sighing with relief she undid the tightly laced, whale-boned corset which thrust her bosom forward. She then stretched out on the fabric nailed across the bed frame. As for Larisa, she lay face down on the mattress, worn out by her weeping, and fell asleep immediately.

Crooking an elbow, I covered my tightly shut eyes with it; the bulb under the ceiling cast a merciless light around the cell. Everything that happened in the last two days swirled before my eyes. The events of my newly acquired prison experience passed before me—the sound of night executions in the Lubyanka basement, the drone of the truck motor, the bright autumn afternoon filled with slowly falling, golden leaves, and finally the prison gates slamming shut behind us. I was locked up with three total strangers.

I was thinking that if these women were to find out that I was connected with the SRs and, even worse, with Victor Chernov, their leader, they would be scared and become hostile. I would have to lie, or at least be quiet about a lot of things. In their eyes I would be Olga Kolbassin, the daughter of a divorced high school teacher. It would serve as a convenient identity; people usually do not ask too many questions about divorces. We had just arrived from Petrograd; my mother had not yet found work, as the school system was being totally reorganized by the Bolsheviks. I should say nothing about foreign travel, or perhaps admit only to a few faint recollections of an early childhood trip to Berlin, Paris or Italy.

Yes, this would be my story. We had recently arrived from Petrograd and my mother had yet to find a job. For the time being we were staying with friends in Moscow. Mother was ill and was taken to a hospital in Khovrino. My younger sister was there with her. My twin sister was visiting friends in the country. The best thing to do was to stay as close to the truth as possible.

-36-

Lying on the floor of cell 14 in the Police Tower of the Butyrskaya prison I tried to go to sleep, but whenever I dozed off I woke up again because of the bright electric light and the sighs and shuffling of my companions. Towards morning I slept soundly. However, we were awakened early by the prison routine. The cell door was opened and we were taken to a semi-circular landing next to the spiral staircase. There we stood in line in front of the toilets. People hurried each other and pushed: the prison facilities were set up with a single occupant to a cell in mind, whereas, at that time there were at least four persons in each of the cells. The washstand also had a line in front of it. I washed myself without soap, of course, and dried my face with my handkerchief.

When we went back to our quarters the guard ordered us to sweep the cell with a broom made of twigs. The cell was quite clean and there were no signs of bed-bugs anywhere.

That morning I deciphered two melancholy inscriptions on the wall, written in pencil, and standing out on the matte surface of the black paint: "The color of the rose is pleasant, only not in prison...." This was evidently an attempt at writing poetry. In another place, someone remembered the line from Dante: "Abandon all hope, ye who enter here."

The guard, with the help of her assistant, a lively, industrious young woman by the name of Girshpan, brought us breakfast. It consisted of dark brown tea served in enamel mugs and of microscopic portions of sticky, black bread. Burning my lips on the hot liquid, I drank the tea and ate my daily portion of bread with delight. Natalya recognized the grass out of which our "tea" was brewed. She identified it as "chereda" and this is what we began calling our morning sustenance.

After breakfast the young prison assistant went from cell to cell with a stack of newspapers, offering them for sale to the prisoners. Natalya bought one copy of *Pravda,* while I had enough money in my purse for five. Remembering the previous night, I had decided to make myself a sleeping pad out of newsprint. It would be drier and softer than the bare floor. "Paper is a good insulating material," I remembered from a line in a physics textbook. In those days the pages of the newspapers were of an immense format.

No sooner had Natalya opened her *Pravda* than she exclaimed loudly: "An explosion on Leontiev Street! A terrorist attack by the left SRs! And here is an editorial by Steklov!" She began reading the article aloud. Steklov was demanding that all of Moscow's inhabitants be "forced, as through a sieve, in order to find the guilty."

"That's what happened. We got stuck in a sieve! Because of the SRs! No wonder I have always hated the SRs! They're far worse than the Bolsheviks! With their 'bloodless revolution' and their 'land to the peasants' they have allowed the mob to go wild. And now it's bombs and printing presses for them while we are the ones to be arrested!"

Natalya was shouting loudly. More restrained, Lydia

wholeheartedly agreed with her. I said nothing. Larisa, curled up on her mattress, stared into space with her beautiful, expressionless eyes.

"Now it's the firing squad for us. After all, we were caught right in the SR printing shop!" Natalya screamed.

I looked over my overwrought companions in the light of day. Natalya was a bourgeois Muscovite without much education. Lydia seemed quite characterless, but of course, it was possible that she was being secretive, just as I was. She was clearly not an SR, but she could have other motives for silence. Who would know? As for Larisa, she was indifferent to anyone outside of herself and her husband—they were newlyweds. I recognized that my companions could have been much worse. None of them seemed to be ready to hurt or denounce anyone.

I also sensed that, compared to me, they were unsophisticated in political matters. Within the context of prison experience, it was as if I, who had grown up in a family of revolutionaries, was much older than they. Instinctively, I realized that it was a lot better for my own survival to try to help them, rather than to probe my own inner fears. I had to stop thinking about myself and about what lay in store for me. Deliberately, I attempted to comfort my companions. I clearly remember my conscious decision, which was to influence the course of my whole life afterward.

I tried to soothe the two older women, especially Natalya, who was whipping herself into a state of frenzy. As far as Larisa was concerned, she lay in a state of prostration: she was not going to listen to anyone. I said:

"I am convinced that we will be helped out by the fact that there were so many of us arrested on that one day. Evidently things got hopelessly mixed up. Just think, four prostitutes were picked up along with us, and they too are imprisoned here. I saw two of them being arrested. Do you remember the girls with black headbands and veils in the stationery store? No one will believe that they are SRs and would throw bombs! The Chekists will have a hard time making sense out of all this confusion. What they might do is detain us here for a while to give themselves time to sort it all out." I was suddenly seized by anguish at the thought of endless days spent in this cell.

"If we could only find out how long they're going to hold us here," I said. "Two weeks? A month? It would be easier to wait it out if we knew. Each day would bring us closer to freedom. We can draw a calendar on the wall and, as each day goes by, cross it off. That's what prisoners have always done."

"You've gone mad with your inventions out of the *Prisoner of Chillon,*" cried out Natalya. "Are you counting on staying here a full month? What a strange person you are!"

We all fell quiet, sinking into the unexciting reading of *Pravda.* Soon lunch was brought to us. It consisted of a watery soup made from gray millet, with a few green droplets of hempseed oil floating on its surface. Natalya could not stand its taste and with her spoon transferred the oil from her bowl to mine. After lunch we napped, each woman on her own "bed," and I on my newly bought newspapers.

For dinner we were given cabbage soup with pieces of meat of dubious origin. Our daily menu was based on these two soups usually served alternately. Sometimes the cabbage soup contained herring heads. One day, we were served lentils, which we ate with delight, though cautiously, as there were many grains of sand and miniscule stones mixed in.

Going to sleep that night, I painstakingly wrapped my legs in pages out of *Pravda,* pulling my stockings over the paper. Under my dress, I also wrapped myself in sheets of newsprint. I spread the remaining newspapers on the floor. I felt warm and dry right away. I fell asleep thinking that I was being warmed up by wood pulp from some lovely, far-off forest.

In the morning, it became evident that a certain trust and sense of solidarity were developing among the prisoners in cell 14. Larisa remained aloof, but the three others were able to laugh at the comic side of the situation. Natalya had a good sense of humor and gave amusing nicknames to the people and objects around us. Her bourgeois attitudes also became more noticeable as time went by. Since I was a new arrival in the city, she described to me, in great detail, life in Moscow in the pre-Revolutionary days:

"First of all, there was the phone. I rang all my friends in the morning, or they rang me. We would confer about parties, about the theater, discuss our guests and make plans. We would gossip. Then I would sit down while the maid—that bitch—would lace up my boots. Do you know that during the first years of the war, high boots, all the way to one's knees, were in fashion? I had a pair like that. Dresses were wide and short. I was thinner of course, and my maid would lace my corset very tightly. I looked sensational."

The way she referred to her servant amazed and shocked me. But I decided to say nothing. My progressive upbringing would become evident if I were to open my mouth. An argument would follow and that would be awful in our small quarters: it was as if we were all four in a train compartment on a voyage of indefinite duration. I sensed that Natalya might have recognized in me someone alien to her world. Consciously or not, she wanted to provoke me. I decided not to give in.

On one of our first days in the Butyrskaya Prison, as Lydia was held up at the wash basin outside the cell, Natalya quietly asked me:

"Say, don't you think that Lydia Matveevna is Jewish? Maybe that's why she doesn't talk about her family. She's not typical looking, she is just a brunette, but I don't know for sure. Most likely though, she's Jewish."

This time, breaking my restraint, I said to her that I could not care less whether Lydia was Jewish or not. "I try to judge people by their individual qualities and not by their background. Mother has always told us that anti-Semitism is dreadful."

[161]

"Now wait, what are you saying? Why use that word? said Natalya. "Why, many of my husband's and my own best friends are Jewish."

Five monotonous days went by. Nothing at all happened to us. No one was called in for questioning. The newspapers, our only source of information, were brought to us every morning. There seemed to have been no further terrorist acts in Moscow. And one evening—it was in the evenings that we were most depressed, feeling the full weight of uncertainty upon us—Natalya said to me:

"Listen, Olechka, I want to say something—and I hope you will forgive me if, from now on, I call you Olechka: my daughter is a year older than you. I now agree with what you said on our first day here, about knowing exactly how long we will be here. I would be happy if I was sure that, in a month, I would be freed. Do you know what—let's make one of those calendars on the wall."

Using a folded newspaper as a ruler and a hair pin, I scratched out a square on the wall and drew thirty smaller boxes inside it. I wrote the days of the month into each small square and marked the Sundays with a special sign. From then on, before going to bed, we crossed out the day that had gone by.

-37-

During one of our long evenings in cell 14, when, in anguish, we could not go to sleep, I suggested that each of us, in turn, recount a story from a book we had read or an event from our own or someone else's life. My companions agreed to this willingly. On the following evening, after we had settled down, each on her own bed and I on my layers of newspaper—which had by then become quite thick, what with our daily reading of *Pravda*—Natalya, as the eldest, began her story. It was an account of a trip she had taken abroad with her husband.

At first our story telling was not very smooth: we were shy. But, little by little, we gained self-assurance. Soon each of us told stories so well that the listeners were spell-bound. Ahead of time, we prepared in our mind the story that we were going to tell when our turn came.

I knew many poems by heart—the Russian classics and some modern poetry. I also had recently read Knut Hamsun and Ibsen. These made up my repertoire while Lydia recounted the Symbolist plays of Maurice Maeterlink, notably in *Palleas et Mélisande* and *Les Aveugles*. Together we remembered Mélisande finding a crown in the impenetrable forest, and also the scene when her long hair is hanging from the window of the tower. Natalya told us about the theater, which she loved, especially the Moscow Art Theater.

"Olechka, you must be sure to see Kachalov in his great roles. The way he plays the Baron in *The Lower Depths* by Gorky: 'In the mornings, I drank my coffee with cream!' He is also marvelous in all of Chekhov's plays. You will be enchanted with the sound of his voice.

Even Larisa joined in. She described her Moscow childhood and a pilgrimage she had taken to Kiev's holy monastery, the Pecherskaya Lavra. This helped her come out of her shell. But more than anyone else, it was Lydia who livened up our nightly sessions. She must have liked the Symbolists for a long time, but had had little occasion to discuss them.

My "phlegmatic side" stopped irritating Natalya. Instead, she complimented me on my good upbringing and praised my mother for it. However, her picture of Mother bore little resemblance to reality. She saw her as something of a Puritan, someone rigid who had brought up her daughters sternly.

"I would so like you to meet my daughters," she often repeated. Natalya maintained that I would be freed first because of my age, and she asked me to remember the following: go to her husband and tell him where she was. To get her released, he should go to Tsivtsivadze first, who could in turn approach the Bolshevik Enukidze. Her address was No. 1 Povarskaya Street.

One day Larisa told Natalya in confidence that she was pregnant. Soon this news became general knowledge. We all tried to bolster Larisa with encouragement and small attentions.

"But my husband doesn't know about this," she would say through her tears. To divert her, we suggested that she choose names for the child. We too would come up with suggestions, both for a boy and a girl.

"I like all names," said Natalya, "except for two, which I cannot stand: Vladimir, for Lenin, and Victor, for Chernov. You must share my feelings...." I remained silent, though I was greatly tempted to tell her where my patronymic name came from. But I resisted this impulse.

Once, after lunch, we were unexpectedly taken on a ten-minute walk outside. We followed long corridors and walked downstairs, ending up in a miniscule courtyard surrounded by the tall walls of the prison's main building. One could see the small grilled windows of the cells, but no one could have been looking out, as the windows were placed too high for prisoners to reach. We walked around, one following the other, exactly as depicted in the famous painting by Van Gogh, which I had not yet seen at that time. I breathed in the fresh air greedily, knowing that our guard would soon lead us back indoors. After that, we were taken on a short walk every two or three days.

On the tenth day, in the evening, we were finally called for questioning. The interrogator sat behind a desk overflowing with papers. As I walked in, I gave him my name. He reached for my file and asked me a few questions. I told him that I had stepped into the stationery store to purchase a notebook. To my intense relief the interrogator did not pursue the questioning. He made me sign a statement, and the guard took me back to the Police Tower. When everyone was back we discussed our interrogations. My companions were very excited. They worried about their depositions and talked about them endlessly.

On the following day, the prison assistant, Girshpan, offered us stationery and envelopes, requesting that we write to our relatives. We paid her a few kopeks for the paper—the postal service was free at that time. Here was an opportunity to let my family know where I was. However, I hesitated to write to the Logorovs and compromise them with a letter postmarked from the prison. But what else could I do? I had vanished and my entire family and the Logorovs themselves must have been worried on my behalf. I had already had to give the Logorovs' address to the interrogator. I decided to write to Natasha in care of them, asking her to bring me a change of clothes, a towel, a book and, if possible, some kind of handwork to keep me occupied.

Days began to drag again, monotonously, with the morning "chereda," the day's newspaper, cabbage soup, perhaps a walk, and long tales from the evening "Scheherezades." Thanks to the story telling, we had come to know each other and got along well.

Once, late at night, when I was already beginning to fall asleep, I heard Natalya's whispering:

"Lydia Matveevna, I am very worried that there will be a search of my apartment and that the Chekists will break into our safe. I was so careless! No, no, don't think that I have gold or illegal papers hidden there. No, I placed a distasteful book in the safe, something obscene. I brought it back from Paris. Like a fool I did not tear it up. I was buying magazines at a stand before getting on the train, and this book was in my hands. I took it and paid for it: it had seemed a curiosity. But how disgusting it turned out to be, how loathsome! The French.... When I got home I put it in my safe, knowing that my daughters would not get to it there. Now I am afraid that it will be found—what a disgrace for a respectable woman!"

I listened, and laughed inside, but it was too late to open my eyes and reveal that I was not sleeping.

"The French—they are awful," continued Natalya. "My husband and I once went to Paris, leaving our children with my sister. My husband took me to see Montmartre at night. That's where they have the famous cabarets." Natalya spoke in French: " 'Do you understand?' Well, we walked into one cabaret called 'Hell.' The outside looked like a cave with red lights, devil horns, and large, twisting snakes of papier mache crawling over the entry. Inside we were greeted by a tall devil. Settling us on a couch near a small table he said: *Madame, mettez ici votre adorable fesse, et vous, Monsieur, votre gros pétard.'* Do you understand? Young girls with horns served us. They wore trousers like hairy devil-legs, while their bosoms were naked." Natalya went on to describe her Paris adventures in whispers. I soon fell asleep on my newspaper bed.

-38-

Fourteen days had gone by since our arrest. On the fifteenth day, as it was getting dark, a guard came into the cell and told me to get my things ready—I was free!

I quickly combed my hair, took my bag and put on my sweater. I said good bye to my companions. But even before I was led out of the cell, another guard came in and told Citizen Kostaky that she, too, was being freed. We both embraced Lydia and Larisa, making wishes for their quick release. We followed the guard down the narrow stairs and the long, dark corridors.

We were taken into the interrogator's office. He showed us our documents, which had been seized at the time of our arrest, and told us that they would be kept in the prison authority's custody. In their place he issued us temporary identity cards. In a week, we could exchange these for our documents. He presented us with small slips of paper bearing the prison stamp above our names. Then we were led to the prison gates. Natalya cried out happily as she recognized her husband waiting for her at the prison door. A well-dressed man in his forties, he was very tall, thick set and looked distinctly Georgian.

"I have a carriage here, my dear," he said. "Let's go home. I found out this morning that you'd be freed." Natalya introduced me to her husband and said a few very warm words about me. She offered to take me as far as Povarskaya Street near the boulevards. I got into the carriage and sat across from the Kostakys in a jump seat. Natalya conversed with her husband in a hushed voice while I, leaning backward, looked at the dark sky and the bright, distant stars. The weather was balmy and I was filled with happiness and relief. On the corner of Povarskaya we said goodbye and I disembarked.

"Run along, hurry up," called out Natalya as the carriage drew away. "It's getting late. Don't forget the curfew."

I soon reached Prechistensky Boulevard. Under the shining street lights, the pavement looked golden. Fallen leaves crackled beneath my feet. I rang, and Madame Logorova let me in.

"How wonderful! Here you are. We were terribly worried. My goodness, if this had happened to my Shura...." I told her in brief about my experiences. When she heard that I had been released on a so-called "wolf's ticket"—a prison pass—she became upset. She was afraid to let me spend the night with her—she was alone at home that night. The rest of the family was away in the country. I did not try to explain to her that, since I had had to give the Logorovs' address as my own, there was nothing illegal in my presence there.

"All of Moscow is being searched day and night," she said. "If they were to come up suddenly, and here you are with that paper.... Better run quickly to the Rabinoviches'. You will still make it before the curfew."

Having run down the stairs, I hurried along the deserted streets. It was a long way to the brothers. Out of breath, I reached the Rabinoviches' apartment house. I climbed to the third floor and rang the bell in our pre-arranged manner. Yevgeny, the younger brother, opened the door. He showed no sign of pleasure at seeing me. Somehow embarrassed, he led me into the living room where his brother and Ida Samoylovna were sitting. Ida had a white shirt on her knees that she was sewing.

"When did they let you out?" asked Yevgeny.

"We thought you had decided to stay in prison forever," said Ida. "You requested some handwork! Here, I was mending one of your shirts. I was preparing a parcel for you." Upon hearing that I was straight out of prison, and that I had a "wolf's ticket," the two brothers, with Ida's energetic assent, absolutely refused to let me spend the night at their house.

"You see, Victor might come in at any moment. If there was a search and they found you with your "wolf's ticket" here, it could be the end for Victor. "Go on at once. If you run you can still make it before the curfew to the Logorovs'," Yevgeny said, looking at his watch. He led me to the door.

I wanted to tell them that I despised them for their cowardice. Blood rushed to my temples, but a feeling of pride made me hold back. I turned away in silence and walked out, slamming the door hard behind me.

I ran back towards the Logorovs' apartment house on Prechistensky Boulevard. My heart was beating madly and I was gasping for breath. At that time, according to Moscow regulations, the front entrances of all residential buildings closed tightly at ten-thirty, and and remained locked throughout the night. Running up to number eleven, I saw the janitor locking the building next to it. But I had time to slip into the Logorovs' entrance. I rang the bell and said to Madame Logorov that the Rabinoviches had not taken me in, nd that I was *forced* to spend the night with her. There was nothing else I could do anyway, as the downstairs door had already been locked.

Madame Logorova, who may have felt badly at having chased me once, this time showed only kindness. She made me undress completely in the kitchen. Wrapping my things in a newspaper, she brought me some clean clothes. She took a big zinc tub off a nail and prepared a bath for me. She then carefully soaped and scrubbed me, pouring water over me. Afterwards, she helped me get dressed, as I had little strength left to do anything.

She then took out a large, black frying pan and heated some cold boiled potatoes with a piece of lard for me. This was filling and delicious. When I had finished, my hostess said, trying not to alarm me, that she had heard that Mother was very ill in Khovrino. An abscess had developed in her throat, which was about to be operated on. It was imperative that I go to see her at once. Logorova promised to wake me up early the next morning.

She settled me on a sofa for the night, but I could not fall asleep. The news of Mother's illness, my wild running along the boulevards, the transformation of the friendly Rabinovich brothers into creatures disfigured by fear, all these impressions kept me awake. I, who had expected a triumphant return to freedom, who had wanted to boast that I had outwitted the Chekists, who had counted on sharing my adventures.... I was destroyed.

The next day when I walked up to Mother's cot in the surgical section of the hospital at Khovrino, she was delirious and did not recognize me. She moved her hands as if to brush something away from her face and kept saying:

"Take that dog away, it's licking my lips. Do chase it away; don't let it lick me. Where are Natasha and Olga? Please ask them to take this dog away."

Two hours later the operation was performed. The surgeon, a tall man in a white robe, came out of the operating room and told me that the operation had been successful. Mother was saved. He had been able to puncture the abscess which had threatened to choke her. Coming to after the anesthesia, Mother continued to say strange things. It was only after a long period of sleep that she recognized me.

I stayed overnight with Mother's friend, Fanny Lvovna, and told her that once again, after that chain of sufferings referred to by Schopenhauer, I was again enjoying a brief moment of happiness resting in her room. I spent all of the following day in the hospital. Adya and I sat at Mother's bedside for many hours. Then I went straight to Molodenovo.

I had a sense of relief as I walked from the railroad station towards the Lavrov dacha. The weather had not yet turned cold. I breathed in the fall air, scented by mowed meadows and fields. The last flowers had disappeared, but the leaves on the trees shone bright red. Above the Vyazemka, a light mist rose. This time I got across the river fearlessly, running swiftly along the fallen logs to the other side. Twilight was falling as I reached the dacha where I found Natasha alone, and not in the company of Ekaterina Vedenyapina, as Mother had assumed.

"When Vasily Filipovich left the dacha a few days ago to attend a conference of followers of Tolstoy, Ekaterina did not want to stay on without a man in the house," Natasha said. "One morning she went off, taking a milk pail with her. She said that she was going to the village to get some milk, and would return shortly. But she never did. She must have felt uncomfortable at the dacha alone with me. At the same time, she did not want to leave her belongings without someone to watch over them. This may be why she did not ask me to come with her when she went off to Moscow."

I was impressed by my sister's fearlessness—staying alone in the depths of the forest at night! Natasha explained that she had become so disgusted by the cowardice that some of the adults around us were showing, that a feeling of scorn had replaced all fear in her. Of course, at first it had been terrifying to be alone in the woods when the pine trees creaked in the wind, and an owl screeched nearby, but she had gotten used to it. She had been alone at the dacha for four or five days.

It grew dark, and the forest was noisy, swaying like the sea. There was only a little kerosene left in the house, so we went to bed early, continuing our conversation in the dim moonlight coming through the window. I told Natasha about all that had happened to me in detail since we last had seen each other. It was very late when we heard a noise. To me, it sounded as if someone had walked in at the other end of the house.

"Oh, that is only a kitten playing," Natasha said. "He has scared me before." But it was not a kitten; we heard heavy steps resound throughout the empty house.

"Who's there?" I shouted. The door opened, and to our great relief, Vasily Filipovich appeared. He had just returned from his conference. He seemed delighted to see us.

"Forgive me for scaring you—it is so very late," he said. "I've frightened you! Are you really here alone? Why don't you get up and come to my side of the dacha? I will make you some tea and you'll tell me your adventures."

Vasily Filipovich's room was cozy. The Tolstoyan symbols, a scythe and sheaves of wheat, hung on the wall above the bed. Our host lit a cast-iron stove and placed a huge enameled teapot on it. The table was covered with a homespun brown tablecloth. On it Vasily Filipovich put out a honeycomb and some rye cookies made by his sisters. He brewed real tea for us.

When he asked her why she had been all alone at the dacha, Natasha recounted how Ektaterina Vedenyapina had gone off to fetch some milk a few days ago but had never returned. Vasily Filipovich did not want to criticize the wife of his old friend Vedenyapin. Not without a certain unctious tone, he said that the human soul was a mystery, and that it was not right to pass hasty judgments about people. "Tolstoy points out that a man's soul is complex," he said. "It may present itself to us in very different ways according to circumstances."

When he had finished Natasha remarked that, when she left, Ekaterina Vedenyapina had carried off two heads of cabbage from our reserves. At this, Vasily Filipovich could no longer restrain himself, and forgetting his didactic tone, he burst into laugher: "Well, Ekaterina Vedenyapina is no better than a nanny goat. We'll bear it in mind;

better not let her near a cabbage!"

Natasha and I spent several days together in the forest before moving back to Moscow. One morning, with the help of Vasily Filipovich's relatives, we transported our few possessions to the station and left the dacha on the banks of the Moscow River forever.

PART VIII

The Cheka Ambush

Mother recovered; our entire family moved into one room in the small house by Moscow's Yauza Gates. Again, Ida was living with us. The Bolsheviks had intensified their hounding of SR Party members and of all those who were suspected of opposing their policies. From day to day we expected to be discovered by the Chekas.

December 24th was Adya's birthday and we had wanted to celebrate, no matter what. I do not remember where we got our miniature Christmas tree, but I recall that Natasha, Adya and I made decorations from pieces of colored paper which we had somehow collected over the weeks. We had cut dolls out of thin cardboard and dressed them with shreds of fabric. We also made butterflies and birds and we glued together a traditional garland of multicolored paper. A star was cut out of a cardboard box.

As a present for Adya's tenth birthday, Natasha and I sewed her a dress out of a small piece of beige flannelette which we had bought at a second-hand market in town. We decorated its pockets and collar with embroidered red berries.

Soon after our Christmas party the inevitable occurred: we found that we had lice. The Muscovites called them "semashkas" in honor of the Commissioner of Public Health, N.A. Semashko. One of us must have caught them in a line somewhere and brought them home. Lice were the scourge of those times; not only were they disgusting, but they also were a carrier of typhus.

On the open markets one could buy "medicinal" amulets made of cloth held by a narrow tape, which were supposed to protect against lice. The words "shield" or "armor" were printed on these amulets in violet ink. We had worn them around our necks, but, needless to say, they failed to protect us.

Now that we had caught lice, there was little that we could do to get rid of them without hot water, without soap, without the possibility of changing our clothing. We checked our clothes for lice at night and in the morning, especially around the sleeves and collars. We killed the lice by squashing them. Whenever we had the possibility to heat an iron, we ironed our dresses, turned inside out. But nothing helped. My body was on fire. I felt sick and feverish; I shuddered with revulsion. We were getting desperate. To lie down in a clean bed with clean sheets, without the necessity of "inspecting" one's clothes, seemed a remote, unreal dream.

Every night when we were ready to go to bed, Mother shut off the light for fiteen or twenty minutes. During this time Adya would fall asleep, along with those of us who were tired. Then Mother turned the lights back on and those who were not sleepy could read quietly. Sometimes the electricity went out, but we did not use our kerosene lamp: we were saving the little kerosene we had for some extreme emergency.

Lying in a crowded space or down on the floor with the lights out, my body swollen from the lice bites, I imagined an enormous, sparkling crystal. I was inside the crystal, on top of a column reaching to the stars. The dark blue night sky shone through the crystal's transparent walls. Starlight was refracted through its polished facets, and formed a rainbow. This imagined vision of harmony would calm me, and I usually was able to fall asleep.

Finally, in early January, in the middle of the night, we were searched by the Cheka. Victor had been writing that evening and, instead of hiding his manuscript under a board of his table, as he usually did, he had left his papers spread out. Ida had gone off early in the day to visit friends with whom she was spending the night. We woke up to the sound of loud voices outside our door. The Chekists had knocked on the front door and our neighbor, Sinitsin, in our "consolidated" crowded house on Yauza Gates, had let them in.

We jumped out of bed, not turning on the light. Our first thought was to help Victor run away. Luckily, our window, which was insulated all around with rubber edging, could nonetheless, be opened freely. Just in case, we had not sealed it in the beginning of the winter.

Rapidly Victor dressed and pulled on his sheepskin coat. He grabbed some of his belongings which were lying about, and jumped onto the sidewalk from the second story window. But, no matter how much we rummaged in the dark, we could not find his hat. Victor stood below our window, asking us to throw down his manuscript to him. We refused; he could not go about Moscow in the middle of the night carrying with him a work which was political dynamite from the Bolsheviks' point of view. We were frantic—we could not locate Victor's hat. It was extremely cold that night and a hatless man was likely to attract the attention of the patrolling Soviet militia. All our women's hats were too small for Victor.

After a couple of minutes Mother slipped out into the hall, acting as if she had just awakened. She closed the door behind her. She said to the Chekists, who were about to knock on our door: "The children are asleep; please do not wake them up ahead of time."

In those days, according to the law, before starting a search in a given house, an uninvolved witness residing elsewhere had to be produced by the Cheka. Someone had just been sent out to find such a person. In the meantime, there was a great commotion in the hall. Three Chekists stood there with the three Red Army men. At the sound of voices our neighbors, the other Chernovs, had come out of their quarters.

Taking advantage of the confusion, Mother made a sign to the other Chernov's wife, asking in a whisper for a man's hat. Our neighbor, who had always been friendly to us, understood immediately and, going back into her room for an instant, she brought out a deerskin cap with long flaps. Without being noticed, Mother took it from her. Opening our door for a second she handed me the cap behind her back. In the darkness I took it and threw it out of the window to Victor. He pulled it over his large head, and I thought I could hear the hat's seams burst. But Victor was staying on, looking up at us with reproachful eyes. He was begging us for his manuscript. His dark figure stood out sharply against the snowy street.

"Please Victor, go," we implored him. "They are about to start the search," and we slammed the window shut. Through the glass panes we could see Victor shrugging his shoulders and slowly disappearing in the darkness.

Natasha and I hid Victor's manuscript in the usual hiding place under a board in his desk, and jumped back into bed, as if we had just been awakened. That night it was my turn to sleep on the floor. Adya too pretended to be still asleep. The first Chekist to walk into our room was a tall, young investigator wearing a gray overcoat and a snap brim cap. We were to find out later that he was the notorious Chekist, Kozhevnikov. This was the beginning of his specialization in SR affairs. He was excited at the thought of investigating the whereabouts of Victor Chernov himself. Sitting down heavily on a chair, the man waited for his comrades and for the witness. Natasha pulled her coat over her shoulders and sat up in bed. She addressed Kozhevnikov:

"Do you get paid well in the Cheka?"

"Is it that you want to work for us?" the inspector asked in a friendly manner.

"Oh, no, I could not," Natasha said seriously. "I still have a conscience."

"Do you think we at the Cheka have no conscience?" asked Kozhevnikov.

"Why do you then go around searching people in the middle of the night and often execute innocent victims?"

Kozhevnikov began a speech about how the Cheka was guarding the Revolution, how it fought only against counter-revolutionaries, speculators and saboteurs. Natasha argued with him; he became involved in the discussion, which remained reasonably amicable. During that time I got up and put on my clothes. Unnoticed, I went about the room putting away the objects which might have indicated the presence of a man in the house.

When Mother came into the room from the hall Kozhevnikov asked her:

"Where is Chernov? Are you his wife?"

"Chernov and his wife live in a room on the other side of the house," she said calmly. My name is Olga Elyseevna Kolbassin, and I live here alone with my daughters. You've made a mistake."

Upon verification, it turned out that indeed, a young Chernov family did live next door to us. Chernov was still a very young man; certainly, he did not resemble the head of the Socialist Revolutionary Party. The Chekists were confused.

After a while two other men in leather jackets came into our room. They brought along a witness, the janitor's wife, an old woman bundled up to her eyes in a gray, knitted scarf. She sat in the corner of the room on a stool, completely uninvolved throughout the proceedings. She yawned and swayed sleepily on her stool as the Chekists conducted their search.

Kozhevnikov continued his conversation with Natasha, while the two other Chekists went over our books and papers, looked through our suitcases and searched the closet, where some men's clothes were hanging. However, in those years, people wore whatever they could get, and any kind of clothing at all looked normal in an average household. Fortunately I had been able to scatter Victor's shaving things away in different places throughout the rooms.

The Chekists checked inside our stove and searched the drawers of the desk, but luckily they did not try to lift up its top. They went on searching for a long time without finding anything suspicious. Obviously, a mistake had taken place because of the Chernov name. A mix-up, perhaps. In any case, their hopes in regard to spectacular SR arrests were not realized.

A large, leather briefcase lay out in the open on our dining table, containing Mother's notebooks. She was then teaching adults a course in history and literature at the "Zhelyabov People's House" near Taganka Square—on occasion Mother had taken me along with her to the People's House and I had helped take care of younger children who had come along to the House with their parents.

"Comrade Kolbassina, we will take this briefcase along with us," Kozhevnikov said. "Do not worry about it. We will soon return it to you with its contents."

After the Chekists left, Mother suddenly remembered that the day before, she had put her wedding ring, which had slipped off her finger, in that briefcase. She had never been superstitious; but this incident with the ring she took to be a bad omen. Of course, neither the briefcase nor the ring were ever returned to her.

-40-

The day was beginning to break. We all had sleepless, gray faces, our beds were unmade. After the search, our room was in disarray. Having conferred with his men at length, Kozhevnikov had departed. Though his findings had been inconclusive, he had posted guards in our house— they were to watch over us. Out of the three Red Army men who had come with the Chekists, two were remaining. The soldiers' orders were to detain whomever came to see us.

From then on two soldiers at a time guarded us at all times. They were supposed to be relieved every two days. In their long heavy military coats, they sat outside our door in the wide hall which led to our own back entrance, leaving the Sinitsins undisturbed. Whenever the guards were changing, an officer of the Cheka accompanied them.

I especially remember the second shift of men who watched over us. These were ordinary soldiers who seemed primitive, almost wild. The older of the two, dark and with a short, thick beard, was about thirty. The other one, still very young, a country boy with light hair and tiny blue eyes, seemed perpetually sleepy. Headquarters had forgotten about them. One, two, three, four days went by, and no one came to replace them. They were becoming starved, and it was now up to us to feed them.

A small barrel of sauerkraut gotten through a miracle by Natasha and Adya stood in our hall. My sisters had gone to Molodenovo late in the fall. From a family of peasants, friends of ours, they had bought a row of cabbage, still uncut, sticking out of the frozen earth. A peasant woman had agreed to cut and salt the cabbage for us. She had brought it to us in a barrel on a sleigh not long before. This had been a great help to us during the lasting famine.

"Little ladies, won't you give us some cabbage?" the guards begged, looking straight at us with trusting, hungry eyes. How could we refuse? Mother dished out two plates of cabbage. Soon the soldiers finished off the barrel.

One night, both men were seized by some kind of irrational fear in the unlit hallway where they slept. They began to force our door. Alarmed, Mother blocked the shut door with the desk and the table. Then by the sounds of their voices, which came through the barricade, we understood that the men had no harmful intentions. On the contrary, they were seeking refuge with us from the grips of their childish fright.

On the fourth day of the men's turn of duty, Mother suggested that they telephone the Cheka headquarters. As he was departing, their officer had left with the bearded soldier a piece of paper with his name and the letters M.Ch.K., the Moscow Cheka's initials, printed on it. They were to call him if anyone was seized at our house.

We had a telephone in our room, but we used it rarely. Whom would we call? Anyway, it was a miracle if the operator managed to connect one with one's party. Sometimes it took a half hour or even a whole hour before the operator answered at all. When she did, one had to say the number one wanted quickly and clearly. Then one waited for the connection, often without any result.

Feeling sorry for the hungry soldiers, Mother showed the bearded man how to use the phone. He got the bedraggled piece of paper out of his pocket, carefully straightening it with his fingers. He read it aloud to himself, and then carefully took up the phone. After a long wait, the voice of the operator came on and he said:

"Please, give me the Mmm, Chchch, Kkk."

Not understanding, the operator asked him to repeat his number. Again and again the soldier repeated: "Mmmm, Chchch, kkk...."

Mother told him to speak up and to pronounce clearly: "Em, Che, Ka," but the man only glanced at his piece of paper and smiled proudly. Finally he said: "What are you talking about— 'Em Che Ka'? Don't try to fool me. There are only three letters written here, and you are trying to get me to say many more letters than that."

The soldier continued to ask for the M.Ch.K. in his own way, and it did not come across. Soon, the operator gave up on him. Finally, on the fifth day, the replacements did come, and two new soldiers were posted at our door. The officer in charge felt badly about having forgotten about his men, and flew into a rage at the bearded soldier. It was useless to bother with the other sleepy boy—as always, he was nodding off.

"Why did you not call Headquarters?"

The poor soldier explained that he had tried to call but that the operator had not wanted to connect him to the Mmm, Chchch, Kkk. The officer shouted at him: "Don't you know Russian? What are you? A Greek? An Armenian?"

"Us? We are from Kaluga," the bearded soldier answered seriously, in a hurt voice.

None of the soldiers watching us turned out to be too intimidating. The Soviet Special Police force had not yet been established, and these were plain Red Army men. They had not been through any special training. They were simple, decent human beings, and despite their awkwardness, they were not rude or mean to us.

As our provisions ran out and the vigil continued, Mother was able to convince the guards that we had to have food—otherwise we would die of hunger. In any case, we were not arrested. The orders were only to detain those who tried to see us. Why not let the girls go out to shop, one at a time? A soldier could accompany them. Adya, a small child, simply had to have a walk. Finally, the guards agreed to let us go out one at a time, with Adya. They did not want to accompany us—they were embarrassed.

In case of a further search, Mother considered it dangerous to keep Victor's manuscript in our room. It was decided that, on the next trip out, I would hide the manuscript under my dress and take it to an old friend of our family, Doctor Freifield. He was a former SR who ran a large hospital not far from Yauza Gates. Perhaps he would agree to hide Victor's memoirs in his apartment, which was in the hospital building? He lived there with his wife.

Doctor Freifield, who always had liked our family, and who once let us have hot baths in the hospital, was terrified when I appeared in his office. Knowing that I had come from a house which was being watched by the Cheka, he refused to take custody of Victor's manuscript. Instead, he asked me to leave immediately. I came home, indignant by this show of cowardice. It was only later that I understood that one should never ask a favor which could cost a person his security and that of his family. At that time I could not imagine the steady, cruel persecutions which were to befall all those who had had dealings with the SRs.

Back home, taking the manuscript out from under my dress, I replaced it in the hiding place, covering it with school pads, some of Mother's notes and old newspapers.

That winter there were enormous snowfalls in Moscow. One day they blocked our back entrance completely. Under the watchful eyes of the soldiers, obligingly we cleared a path through the snow, using a wooden shovel. Enormous drifts stood on each side of a passageway which was supposed to bring visitors to our door and entrap them. The shift of soldiers was replaced again and again, but no one called on us. Apparently word about the ambush had reached the few friends who might have visited us.

One thought was worrying us: What about Dasha? How would she know of the danger of visiting us with all the traveling which took her away from Moscow? And then, one evening, we heard a knock on the front door. It was a soft knock, yet we heard it clearly from our room. Someone had come to visit.

Natasha and I walked into the hall as calmly and self-assuredly as we could. Natasha moved swiftly towards the door while I stood in the middle of the hall and tried to screen it from the soldiers. I asked the men some question in a very loud voice in order to distract their attention for a second or two.

Natasha opened the door, and there stood Dasha. Our sweet Dasha was bundled in a dark scarf with icicles all over it. She was carrying a knapsack on her shoulders and a pocketbook in her hands. Seeing Natasha, she stopped on the threshold of our house. Natasha said quickly:

"Go away, Dasha, we are under a Cheka watch! There are guards here! Victor has run away and no one has been arrested so far." She slammed the door in Dasha's face.

For a split second I had seen the expression on Dasha's face change. She then turned away quickly and rushed down the passageway. The soldiers pushed Natasha aside and threw the door open. Dasha had disappeared.

"Who was that woman?" they demanded.

"Our cleaning woman," Natasha said. "She comes and washes the dishes once in a while. You would have detained her, and she has children at home. I told her to run away."

"Ran away! Too bad, we would have loved to take a shot or two at her! What a grasshopper she must be!" And the two laughed heartily. It was obvious that they would make no report of this incident to their superiors.

We saw Dasha a few weeks later, when our guard was

removed. She told us how she had walked to our house from a distant railroad station, after a long train ride in an overcrowded train. She was carrying a heavy knapsack. Hungry, tired, she was walking towards her corner in our room—the warm spot near the back of Sinitsin's stove. When Natasha had opened the door and told her that there were soldiers inside, she had started running. Only a few steps from our entrance door she had fallen head first into a drift, landing in the fluffy snow.

"There I was, lying in the snow, and I began crying. I cried and cried," Dasha said. "I could not stop crying. It was all too much—the Cheka's ambush, my own exhaustion, and hunger—all these things suddenly overcame me."

After a very long while, Dasha had gotten up and pulled her knapsack back over her shoulders. She picked up her handbag and walked slowly towards the not too distant Taganka Square where her good friends, the Butkeviches—two nice women and their mother—lived. Natasha and I were soon to meet them also and to benefit from their hospitality.

-41-

The watch over us was lifted. After two long weeks, one day the officer in charge of the guard came to pick up his men. This time he did not replace them with a new shift. For a while, we still felt as though we were being watched. Whenever we left the house, we always looked carefully to see whether we were being followed. But we were not.

We became even more cautious in our contacts with people. Victor had moved around the city, staying in different people's apartments every night. For a time he had lived at the Rabinovich brothers. When he finally decided that it was safe to return home, he continued to be circumspect. Before entering the house near Yauza Gates, or leaving it, he studied the surrounding area slowly and meticulously.

Soon after the guards were removed, Ida returned to live with us. There had been one advantage to our ambush: Ida had been away and we had a respite from her presence. She had not been the heroine of that event; she could not claim to have saved Victor's life.

On the first night of her return, she began complaining about the fact that she had dedicated herself completely to our family, and yet she still felt somehow left out. She was not reproaching anyone in particular; she had never really counted on gratitude. Soon, very soon, we would be rid of her. She was unlikely to last through the spring. A few days before, a doctor friend had examined her and found her to have an advanced case of tuberculosis. She had to have plenty of nourishment, so as to build up her strength, but she would rather die than accept an extra portion of food from us. Ida usually talked in such mournful tones in Victor's absence. Mother always rushed to comfort her, assuring her of our devotion to her.

That night Ida began weeping. She lay on the bed, her faced turned to the wall. She got up only after Mother had assured her once again of how indispensable she was to all of us. Mother said that, without Ida'e energy to pull us through, the entire family would have perished long ago. Ida cried for a long time. She covered her face with her hands, and tears rolled down between her fingers.

After a while, she told of how she had fainted on her way home. When she had fallen down in the street right on the path, on the hard-packed snow, charitable passersby had picked her up and carried her to our door. Every day she was getting weaker. She suffered from dizziness, and often lost consciousness altogether. For some reason, however, these fainting spells always occurred without witnesses. No one from our family was ever around when they happened.

Ida did not hide her regrets about the fact that, as a Bolshevik Party member and a close friend of Lunacharsky's wife, she had not, in due time, accepted some important post with that party—she could easily have become the Commissar in charge of the Arts. She had chosen instead to lend her support to the family of Victor Chernov. She did not add that, in the beginning of the Revolution, when Victor had been a member of the Provisional Government, it had looked as if he might next become the President of the Russian Republic.

From time to time, when Ida was out, Natasha and I told Mother frankly what we thought of her. In our opinion Mother was fooled by Ida's caprices and fibs. We pointed out that her friend was acting out scenes from Dostoyevsky's *A Friend of the Family*, that Mother's naivete was ridiculous: "How can you believe that she is so completely dedicated to us? Don't you see that she is only using your kindness? You have been sheltering her; we are sharing our room and food with her. Why doesn't she go out and live on her own? Why doesn't she work?"

Mother answered, using the very words of the good uncle in *A Friend of the Family:* "If a person owes everything to you, then you're *obliged* to be generous to him or her. Ida has nothing of her own; she is completely dependent upon us. That is why she makes such a point of what she has done for us. You must understand and pity her."

"In your view, she is dedicated and suffers for us. She is selfless, she is a martyr. In fact, she is our benefactress—just as Foma was the good uncle's savior in Dostoyevsky's story. Don't you see that she is seething with frustration and anger because she cannot tell everyone that it was *she* who saved Victor during the search? That is why she's upset. Foma, the intruder, the self-appointed household tyrant, also gets upset in Dostoyevsky's story whenever he is not at the center of events."

Little by little, as the winter advanced, Mother's eyes began to open. Perhaps she started at last to sense that her friend's intentions in regard to Victor were not as pure as she would have us think. She stopped comforting Ida during her fits of complaining and weeping. Ida began to go out on occasion with some new friends of hers who worked in the Aviation Chemical Research Center. She stayed out overnight more often.

One memorable evening, she returned full of excitement, explaining in a loud voice, her Estonian accent more pronounced than usual, that she had been offered a job through an engineer friend of hers. The work involved a new Production Bureau which was being set up in the northern city of Vologda. The purpose was to reorganize the Russian local industries. Ida had accepted the job and was leaving in ten days.

Mother, who loved to travel under any conditions and was, throughout her life, always ready to launch into new adventures, was sincerely happy for her friend.

"How marvelous! I have often heard Vologda described. It's an ancient Russian city full of handsome log houses with extraordinary carved shutters. In Vologda, the local craftsmen make marvelous handmade objects out of wood, as well as embroidered cloths. It is one of the areas of Russia where the purest Russian is spoken. Many Russian revolutionaries were sent into exile there in the past. I heard about Vologda in my childhood from them."

"You must be sure to dress warmly on the trip," I said. Natasha and I were trying hard to hold back our feelings for fear of showing how happy we were at the thought of Ida's leaving. Victor was not with us that night; he continued to move from apartment to apartment for fear of arrest.

We were barely able to fall asleep, we were so delighted. In low voices, Mother and Ida Samoylovna continued to talk about the ancient city of Vologda. Adya was already asleep. I lay under my covers, holding my breath, my heart beating fast. I was overjoyed.

The next morning Ida slept late, her face turned to the wall, her head covered with our plaid blanket. We got up quietly and inspected our clothing for lice, though their number was fortunately diminishing. We then washed ourselves with cold water and got dressed. Ida did not stir. I went outside to start the samovar which had been set the night before with slivers of pine wood.

When I came back with the boiling samovar, Ida was still lying down, but muffled crying could be heard from under the plaid blanket. Her crying was interrupted by gasps for air. Mother walked up to her side of the bed and bent over her with solicitude.

"Idochka, what is the matter?"

Ida sat up in bed and wiped the tears from her face. Her hair was all messed up and wet, and her face was indeed pitiful—her strongest weapon.

"How can you even ask what is wrong? Of course, nothing is wrong—for you! Now at last I know how you feel about me. My trip to Vologda makes you all very happy. You are lettting me go off, alone and sick. And Olechka is so pleased that she tells me to dress warmly! It did not occur to all of you that someone in my condition should not be working at all! In the middle of winter! Do you know what? I never got any offer for work—not in Vologda, nor anywhere else. I was only testing you. Now I know your true feelings towards me."

This scene was so very similar to the famous departure scene of Foma Opiskin that Mother, naive as she was, simply could not go on playing the role of the good uncle. Ida had overdone it. Mother was deeply disturbed. Nonetheless, she held herself back and said only:

"No one is chasing you out into the cold, Ida. Go on or stay here, do whatever you want. But as to your 'testing' us, I consider it unworthy of you."

Ida stopped crying, seeing that her acting had gone too far. I brewed some carrot tea and we drank it in silence. I felt sorry for Adya. As a rule, we tried to protect her from adult quarrels. What could a ten-year-old girl think of what was going on? Ida had never been disagreeable with Adya, as she often was to Natasha and myself. In fact, she often remarked with a sigh that no mother could possibly love a child as much as she loved Adya.

Ida sat on the bed and placed a mirror against its iron

headboard. She placed the lighted kerosene lamp on a stool at her side and started warming her curling iron. Setting her hair, she made up her eyes, got dressed and left without saying a word to us.

She returned at night, and we went back to a seemingly normal existence, sharing everything with her as always. But openness disappeared from our relationship.

PART IX

Off to Bashkiria

In the end of January, Victor mentioned the possibility of moving us all to Bashkiria in the southwestern lowlands of the Urals. A few members of the otherwise banned Socialist Revolutionary Party were able to get positions in the agricultural and economic organizations in that remote area, which had become, in 1919, the first autonomous Soviet Republic. The Chairman of the Republic Bashkiria, Validov, was well-known; he was said to be energetic and enterprising. Agricultural cooperatives in the spirit of the SR Party program were going to be set up in that region, rich in natural resources. For this, new people were needed in Bashkiria.

To stay on in our room in Moscow was dangerous: the Chekists had made their way there once, and could again appear at any moment. We had a noose around our necks, which could be tightened at any moment. Victor and Mother decided to accept Validov's offer. Ida was also to go with us. Validov was soon due in Moscow. I remember going on an errand to some huge government building to find out whether he had come yet.

Validov finally arrived in Moscow and came to see us. He was of average build and looked vaguely Mongolian; he wore a para-military overcoat and a white sheepskin cap. Victor would abstain from all political activity. He would work in his own field, but nobody would know who he was. I do not remember to which city in Bashkiria we were invited to go, but to get there we were to travel first to the capital of Ufa. The wife of an important cooperative official, a friend of Validov's, was soon to arrive in Moscow. She was to help us with our travel permits.

We awaited her arrival with impatience. It seemed to us that any change at all in our lives at that time could only be an improvement. The prospect of work or of a teaching job seemed a miracle. I remember that I was afraid of only one thing—of the cold. People had said that in the winter Bashkiria often had temperatures of 50 centigrade below zero and that the winds there were terrifying. Soon Vera Ivanovna—I do not recall her last name—did in fact arrive in Moscow. She was a small woman with smoothly combed hair. She was energetic and seemed quite efficient, although she was in a fairly advanced stage of pregnancy.

As far as our trip was concerned, Ida decided that Mother and all of us should go ahead with Vera Ivanovna, and that, as a security measure, Victor should follow in a few days—under her aegis. Once again she convinced everyone of her great experience as an organizer. In the meantime, Mother, with the help of Vera Ivanovna, would find us lodgings in Bashkiria. It would all be safer for Victor.

Vera Ivanovna agreed with Ida's plan, impressed by her organized, forceful approach to practical problems. Our departure date was set; in a few days a special train for Bashkiria was leaving. We began packing.

I was not at all sad at the idea of leaving our room. Although at times we had been happy there, with our readings at night and with the unforgettable, unexpected visits paid to us by Dasha, Ida's presence had been a dreadful strain. In new surroundings, something had to change. Perhaps she would no longer be living with us.

As we were about to leave I suddenly regretted the fact that I had seen so little of Moscow while we lived there. I had not gotten any real sense of the city, despite the fact that over our months there we had walked great distances on foot. In those days, I was always on guard. I had gotten into the habit of pulling my head in and walking swiftly, never stopping or lingering or even looking up. I usually covered my face with a scarf. I had at the time a light-weight coat which was stylish, light-blue, and my young friends had envied me. But it attracted attention; people noticed the "girl in the light-blue coat." I would have gladly traded it for something more neutral, and warmer. Now, as I was preparing for our trip, I was sorry that I had not paid more attention to the houses and streets of Moscow. I had been afraid to go into churches or explore public squares.

We easily put together our few possessions and books, collected our pencils and paints. Using rope and leather straps, we tied pillows and blankets within our plaid blanket. Our clothes fit into the brown suitcases which we had purchased abroad. They were roomy and sturdy.

A difficult task was to wash and dry a change of clothes for the trip. Mother was working on formalities connected with our departure, and went with Vera Ivanovna on endless bureaucratic errands. Natasha and I were put in charge of the laundry. Our supply of kindling and wood was running out, and there was no time to try and procure some more. We were unable to heat the water for washing. Instead we scrubbed the laundry in cold water on a board over a basin, using pieces of soap substitutes. We then rinsed it in cold water. Wringing it out, we hung it over two ropes which criss-crossed our room. The laundry dried slowly. The room became humid as a result of the washing and we both began developing rheumatic pains. Our hands, our elbows and shoulders ached.

On the eve of our departure, in the middle of January 1920, we agreed to meet with Victor at the Rabinovich brothers in their apartment on Nikitsky Boulevard. This was to be our farewell evening in Moscow.

Having finished our packing, the four of us left the house in the early evening. Ida had been out during the day and was to drop by at the Rabinoviches. Holding each other by the hands, we walked along the dark streets and then along the Kremlin walls, which seemed trimmed with white fur. The towers were topped with huge snow caps. Icicles hung from them; they shone brightly in the winter moonlight. The Kremlin stood in all its imposing beauty—I was never to see it again looking as majestic. Nowadays, since gardens have been established at the foot of its walls, it has lost some of its stern grandeur.

Leaving Red Square, we slowly crossed a slippery bridge, holding on to each other. There was no one around, no cars or passersby. I remember that my entire body ached. I walked along barely sustained by the thought that the Rabinoviches' apartment would be warm.

The younger brother, Yevgeny, opened the door for us. As he greeted us, he said that Victor was already there. The brothers' living room was icy; the cast-iron stove had not yet been lit. Victor, who was good with fires, offered to start it. He settled on the floor and stuck some paper and kindling into the stove. But no matter how hard he tried, the logs would not burn. The paper went out, the kindling was charred, yet the fire did not catch.

Victor, lying on the floor, tried to get the fire going by blowing into it. Finally, shortly before we left, he thought to check the flue, which he found blocked with half-burned wood. He cleaned it out, and the fire began crackling and the pipe humming. But it was getting late, we had to go. We were taking the train for Bashkiria the next day.

Victor, who had always been extremely kind to Natasha and me, his adopted daughters, said goodbye to each of us very warmly, although we were parting only for a few days. Ida walked back to the Yauza Gates with us. She had not yet packed.

Dasha came by the next day and took us to the station after an early lunch. Ida did not come to the station with us; she still had things to do around the house, but then she was joining us in Bashkiria almost at once. We said goodbye to Sintsin's wife, explaining to her that we were leaving a few things in our room, to be picked up later. Ida's suitcase and the samovar, which belonged to friends, were to be collected by Dasha and Ida after we left. We did not see Sinitsin himself—he was not around that day.

We loaded our things on a sled and set forth for the Kazan station at the other end of town. It was cold, our faces were numb, but we walked ahead swiftly. We pulled the sled in twos, taking turns. Thus we reached the station by nightfall. We were lucky to find a porter. With his help we found the train for Ufa and the compartment where Vera Ivanovna had already settled. Besides her and our family, there was no one around. The train was due to leave late that night.

Vera Ivanovna was pleased to see us arrive early, as had been agreed; she admitted to having felt very nervous that afternoon. We began settling in, putting up our three suitcases on the compartment shelves. We had not yet unwrapped our blankets when a train employee walked through the car, announcing that the train's departure was delayed due to snowstorms. It would not go for at least a day, he said. He asked that everyone get out of the compartment as he had to lock the train. However, we could leave our things behind—they would be safe in the locked compartment.

Vera Ivanovna said that she would go spend the night with friends in town. Mother decided that it was best for Natasha and me to return with Dasha to our room at the Sinitsuns, while she went with Adya to our old friend, Vasily Leonovich. This was an elderly SR whom we had known in our early Paris days. He now lived near the Arbat. Mother hoped to meet Victor at his apartment. At around noon on the next day, we would all meet on the train again.

I was exhausted by our packing and by the cold. My shoulders ached under my heavy winter clothing. And here, once again, we had to go out into the icy evening! Dasha tried to cheer us up on the way to Yauza Gates. Winter was coming to an end, and in the spring she would visit us in Bashkiria. We reached our house and knocked on the Sinitsuns' front door.

Sinitsun's wife opened the door for us. She looked extremely upset as she let us into what had been our hallway. She said nothing, but we saw our belongings, which we had left behind in our room, heaped in a disorderly pile in a corner of the hall. The samovar lay on the floor as if it had been violently thrown there. Dasha wanted to open the door to our room, but instead it was flung open from inside by Sinitsin himself, who stood threateningly on the room's threshold. He shouted: "You again? Enough! I will not let you into this building again!"

Dasha tried to explain to him that the train was held up for some hours by snow drifts and that we had come back only for the shortest time—to spend one night in our room.

"This is no longer your room!" Sinitsin screamed. "Enough of this! You poisoned my entire winter, and I will not let you in again. Go away, immediately!"

Dasha said as calmly as she could that he had no right to kick us out of a room which was still legally ours.

"I spit on your rights!" he shouted.

"You will answer for this before an SR Honor Committee," said Dasha.

This made Sinitsun lose his temper completely: "I have nothing to do with Party judgments! I am kicking you out of my house! I have the right to do that! And if you do not leave at once, I will go to the Housing Commission and tell them in detail what sort of people you are. I will turn you in!"

His heavy face trembled with anger, he seemed to get drunk on his own vociferations and on his power over us. He ran into his room and went out again, wearing his fur hat, his fur coat trailing behind him. He rushed towards the door, but Dasha blocked his way.

"I am off to turn you in!" he screamed, pushing her aside.

Here—and this thought still pains me—I burst into tears. I could not stop weeping. I cried despite the feeling of burning humiliation that the tears brought on. Dasha embraced me by the shoulders, she took Natasha's hand and we went out, walking past the snow bank into which she had fallen not long before.

It was extremely cold, and my tears were freezing

to my lashes. Dasha decided to take us to spend the night at her friends the Butkeviches, who lived close to Taganka Square and had taken her in when she had to flee from our house during the ambush.

It was past midnight as we climbed several flights of stairs and knocked on the Butkeviches' door. One of the sisters, a coat pulled over her nightgown, opened the door. The mother and her two daughters had just gone to bed. I remember the concerned, gentle faces of the two sisters— the mother was already asleep next door. They helped us remove our frozen coats and wrapped us in warm clothing. They gave us something hot to eat and drink. Quickly, blankets, old coats and dresses were spread on the floor. The three of us lay down on this makeshift bedding and fell asleep at once.

The following morning, when it was still dark, the two sisters left for work. Their mother started the samovar and insisted that we drink some tea before setting forth. When we left their apartment it was daylight—an overcast, frigid day. On our way to the station, walking past an open market, Dasha had us stop by a woman selling a liquid puree made of potatoes and carrots. The woman ladled the puree out of a tall tin can into white enamel mugs. This warm food seemed God-sent. Our courage was revived.

-43-

At the appointed time, around noon, we went back to the station and walked into our train compartment. Mother and Adya were already sitting there, their knees covered by an enormous raccoon coat, something like a Siberian great-coat. It had been given to them for the trip by Victor. Vera Ivanovna was settled in the opposite side of the compartment in the corner near the window. A thick blanket and a pillow, dressed in a clean, white pillow-case, lay by her side. She wore soft slippers and had wrapped herself cozily in a warm, dark plaid shawl.

The train was slightly heated, and after the fierce cold outside, it felt quite warm. Apparently, the train was not leaving until nightfall. Dasha nestled herself in a corner and dozed off in the warmth. Natasha and I got our books out of our suitcases and read by the quickly vanishing daylight. Then, exactly as on the previous day, a train employee walked along the train, announcing that the train would not leave that evening because the tracks had not yet been cleared of snow. He added that this time passengers would remain in their compartments. No new time of departure had yet been set.

Evening had come. I sat in the corner, on the corridor side of the compartment. From the station a little reflected light was falling on my book. I was reading George Sand's *Indiana* in French. The exotic South Sea island, where the heroine was living amidst palm trees and tropical flowers, transported me into another world. The station was quiet. Even though the train stood still, this did not matter to me, as long as we were not rushing off into the cold again. Vera Ivanovna, upon hearing how Sinitsun had acted the night before, said sternly to us:

"Now sit still. Do not go off anywhere. Otherwise you may get into real trouble."

Meanwhile, Mother could not stay put. On an impulse, she decided to go back to Vasily Leonovich's apartment—she had agreed with Victor that in case of further train delays, she would meet him there again. Mother was preoccupied; she evidently regretted having left Victor in Ida's care. I begged her not to go. After our experience the previous night, I was frightened. It was as if something threatening was hanging over the frozen city of Moscow. Natasha joined in: "Please do not go; stay with us! The train may leave unexpectedly. Then what would we do without you? Please stay!"

Clearly Vera Ivanovna was unhappy with Mother's decision to leave. She expressed herself vehemently on this matter, and then became silent, pretending to read a book, yet one could sense that she was seething with anger. Mother pulled on her fur hat, she raised the fur collar of her wide, purple coat, and tightened a leather belt around her waist as a protection against the cold.

"Why are you all in such a panic?" she said. "You are supposed to be my brave girls! Take Adya for example, who does not complain about my going. She and I, we are the 'animals full of gaiety'." She added, quoting out of a children's book which Adya loved. "And besides, Dasha will spend the night with you here."

Mother left. I continued to read. Indiana had gone back to France, but her proud straightforwardness and honesty were not appreciated by her worldly French cousins. In the opposite corner, Natasha was reading Balzac's *Cousin Pons.* Adya, who had wrapped herself in the raccoon great coat, had fallen asleep against Dasha. Vera Ivanovna was going to bed; she put out the compartment light. I continued to read by the dim light of an outside lamp, but sleep was beginning to overpower me, and I shut my eyes.

Suddenly, the sliding door of the compartment opened with a jolt. Against the lighted rectangle of the door the tall figure of a Red Army man could clearly be seen. He wore a belted overcoat and a white fur hat. We jumped up and turned on the light. He was a well-built young man with a pleasant face.

"Are you the Kolbassins?" he asked. "Comrade Leonovich has told me to find you. Your mother has been held up at his apartment in the Arbat."

"Who are you?" we asked.

"I'm from the Secret Police, but I am also a private friend of Comrade Leonovich's. Your mother asks you to inform your father of the guards posted at Leonovich's. There is an ambush at his place. Do make sure that he does not go there. You are to warn him of this in person—all right?"

My mind spinned. Mother had fallen into a Cheka trap, but Victor was not yet arrested. This could only be a provocation.

"This is a provocateur," Natasha was whispering in my ear. Vera Ivanovna's face was covered with red spots. She got up, glanced angrily at us, and shook the soldier's hand, thanking him warmly:

"Thank you, Comrade! Thank you!"

The soldier disappeared.

"Vera Ivanovna! They are trying to entrap us," Natasha and I cried together.

"This is very peculiar," Dasha said. "A Red Army man employed by the Secret Police suddenly showing up as a friend of Vasily Leonovich's! It's too strange a coincidence—it cannot be."

"Now, you too!" Vera Ivanovna suddenly screamed at Dasha, losing her self-control. "You are all so careless—so stupid! You cannot sit still! Instead, you do foolish things and imagine provocations! Why did Olga leave? Obviously she has fallen into the hands of the police! And now... now, listen girls! I am the one in charge here from now on. Don't you dare walk off anywhere! I am going to deliver you to a place where you will be safe, where you will not harm me or yourselves. And you will wait there until everything gets cleared up. They may let your mother go at once. We will leave Adya here with your friend Dasha. They will not touch them. As for you two, Natasha and Olga, get dressed and follow me! I've had enough unpleasantness."

Vera Ivanovna was on the verge of hysterics. As a result of Mother's arrest, her trip back to her husband could be delayed. Natasha and I both felt a sharp sense of guilt on Mother's behalf. This feeling obligated us to remain in Vera Ivanovna's care, to obey her.

Quite irrationally "the person in charge" had one thought only—to get off the train and to lead us away with her. Was she trying to protect us, or was she afraid of careless words on our part in case of an arrest? Or, more simply, had she lost her head? Her lack of judgment overwhelmed us, but for us there was no arguing. Vera Ivanovna

[202]

was putting on her fur coat and her hat, throwing her plaid shawl over her shoulders. She ordered us to get dressed at once. She explained to Dasha that, for the time being, she was leaving her luggage on the train; she would return for it the next day. She seized her handbag and grabbed us by the hands, literally dragging us out toward the station exit.

A strange thing happened even before we left the station. Although it had taken us a good half hour to get going, the Red Army man in the white fur hat, who had presented himself as a friend of Leonovich, stood by the station gates. We bumped into him, and he smiled and said that he had gotten turned around and was now looking for a direct way to get back to the center of town. I took Vera Ivanovna by the elbow and said in a very low voice:

"He has waited for us here. He will follow us to see where we are going. They are hoping that we will take them straight to Victor. Don't you understand that they will do anything to seize Victor? Let us go back to our compartment." But Vera Ivanovna would not listen. Straightening her shoulders as if she was confronting the enemy, she asked the Red Army man in a ringing voice how to get to the Sadovaya ring of boulevards from the station. She even told him which one of the boulevards she wanted.

Stepping aside, trying to remain inconspicuous, Natasha and I tried to convince her in muffled voices that the soldier was sure to follow us. The best for all three of us was to go back to the train. If we went with her into town the Cheka was likely to arrest us at our place of arrival. As potential links to Victor, we might not be taken if we went back to the train compartment. In the meantime, she would be able to depart for Bashkiria. Or else, she could leave us on the train and seek shelter on her own. She would only compromise herself and give in to a provocation, if she walked around Moscow with Chernov's daughters.

Upon hearing the word "provocation," Vera Ivanovna once again became hysterical. She reiterated her accusations against Mother and ourselves, saying that we were silly and irresponsible. Now she was screaming again. Though it was true that her acquaintance with our family had gotten her into trouble, it was not the time for a scene. My sister and I, in desperation, decided to give in to her.

Now we were walking briskly along unfamiliar streets, headed God knows where. I could not orient myself at all. It was evening, and the buildings seemed dark and forbidding. Each rare street light threw a dim light over snowy streets and empty crossings. There was not a soul to be seen anywhere. All of a sudden, as we passed an apartment house, I noticed the figure of the Red Army man in the tall fur hat. It stood out sharply against an orange background—that of a lit janitor's door. I made a sign to Vera Ivanovna. Upon seeing the soldier, for the first time she seemed to share our doubts. Once again we suggested that we go back, but instead of turning back or stopping, she squeezed our hands harder and hurried along. She would not reason; she was moved along by panic.

Now we were rushing along wide snowy streets, which I failed to recognize altogether—had we reached Sadovaya yet? The moon shone, the sky was absolutely clear. It was fiercely cold and our footsteps on the snowy sidewalk sparkled in the moonlight. Finally, we made a sharp turn and walked along a narrow side street lined with enormous snowdrifts.

"Vera Ivanovna! Where are you taking us?"

"Don't ask! Shut up! I'm taking you to a safe place, where you will wait this out."

"But we are being followed—don't you see? We are bringing Chekists with us. Think about the trouble which we will cause to whomever we visit!"

Vera Ivanovna did not argue. She slowed down slightly to catch her breath. At this moment, on the opposite sidewalk, footsteps resounded. Clearly, someone was walking right behind us on the opposite sidewalk. We were on the lighted side of the street and the moonlight was so bright that the buildings cast dark, rectangular shadows onto the snow. This made it difficult to see anyone on the other side of the street.

When we reached the next corner, we saw clearly a bundled female form, a big woman in a gray, tightly closed overcoat, with a black scarf tied crossways in her back, in the peasant manner. The snow squeaked under her felt boots. She was not trying to hide herself from our view. She was like a vision out of a dream. As if under hypnosis, we walked on. Once, Vera Ivanovna tried to lose her by making a sudden right turn down a small alley and then a left turn at the following corner. But the woman was there all along, walking right behind us on the opposite side of the street.

If it had not been for what we had just gone through —Sinitsin's performance, our hunger and exhaustion, the cold, which pressed our foreheads and froze our faces, transforming the reality of this second night of wanderings across frozen Moscow into some kind of wild nightmare— Natasha and I would probably have had the good sense and the strength not to argue further with Vera Ivanovna, who had obviously lost her head. Instead, we would simply have sat down on the sidewalk, right on the snow, and refused to go further. But a strange confusion had seized me. The women who was following us was not real. Behind us, she advanced ominously. All of a sudden, the rhythmic crunching of her felt boots on the snow made me think of a folkloric poem which had scared me in my childhood. The bear in the story mutters:

Quiet, quiet, quiet, quiet.
Through the linden forest,
Through the birch tree forest,
The water calmly sleeps,
The earth is sound asleep.
Even the village is sleeping,
Only the old woman stays awake....

At last, after walking down another side street, Vera

Ivanovna signaled to us that we had arrived. We quickly dashed into an inner courtyard. The big woman walked heavily past its gate. Within the yard, Vera Ivanovna found the right entrance. She guided us along stairs which were quite familiar to her. Only when we were safely inside the apartment building did she tell us that she was taking us to an old friend of hers, a certain Khovrin. He had been an SR, but had long before left the Party. He had known her when she was a child. She said that he suffered from a heart condition.

For the last time, Natasha and I tried to dissuade her from imposing us on her friend, but it was too late. Vera Ivanovna was knocking on the door, first softly, then with all her might. We waited on the landing for several minutes. When Vera Ivanovna began shouting, the door opened at last. Khovrin—we were never told his first name—was busily fastening his clothing. He led us into his kitchen. He was an old man, very thin, with graying hair.

Taking her friend aside, Vera Ivanovna explained in a low voice the reasons for our sudden intrusion. I cannot say that our host looked enthusiastic when he heard our story, but neither his tone of voice nor his gestures betrayed any displeasure or fear. He was stoic about our intrusion.

The night was ending, but daylight was not yet breaking. Khovrin had us settle down in the kitchen. On a narrow, uncovered table, he heated a samovar. Using dried carrots as tea, he poured each of us a cup of hot liquid. Suddenly it seemed as if we had broken away from a deadly dream. The apartment was not heated, but it seemed quiet and warm after a night spent in the streets. The copper samovar, the steam rising above our cups, and Khovrin's calm, slightly muffled voice, all this belonged to the real world, and I began to regain consciousness.

PART X

The Second Arrest

An hour had not gone by before there was a strong knock at the door. Khovrin went to the entrance hall. After a short conversation through the door, he let in three Chekists. The first one to walk in was our old acquaintance, Kozhevnikov. He was dressed in the same gray overcoat he had worn during the search in our room near Yauza Gates. He sat down on a kitchen stool, put a folder filled with papers before him, and began the usual questioning. His men, dressed in leather jackets, stayed in the hall. One guarded the front entrance, the other stood before the kitchen door.

Kozhevnikov once again was disappointed. Khovrin's gaunt figure, his dry, clipped answers, demonstrated at once that he was not Victor Chernov. The Chekist then interrogated Vera Ivanovna, who gave him all the facts about herself. Then he turned to me:

"Your first and last names?"

"Olga Ivanovna Kolbassina," I said.

"Where is your father?"

"He and my mother were separated long ago. We have lost touch with him. As far as we know, he may not even be alive."

I spoke without hesitation. Natasha repeated the same things in the same assured tone. Perhaps Kozhevnikov would think that there had been a mistake made once again by the Cheka.

"Why did you leave the train?" He turned to Vera Ivanovna.

"It was getting cold. Didn't I have the right to go to friends and take the girls with me?"

By the end of the interrogation, the morning was breaking. Another gray, gloomy Moscow day began. Kozhevnikov stood up, gathered his forms and announced

that we were all arrested. At this moment, poor Vera Ivanovna must have understood her foolishness. I felt terrible,
thinking that this pregnant woman, only a distant acquaintance of ours, was being arrested because of us. What made
me feel even worse was the thought that they were taking
also the elderly Khovrin, who was so obviously in poor
health.

This feeling of guilt has not left me to this day. I do
not know what happened to Vera Ivanovna. Later, when
we met Maxim Gorky's first wife, Ekaterina Peshkova, in
Germany in 1922, and again in Paris in 1928 and 1936, she
told us repeatedly about Khovrin. Despite our assurances,
she could not bring herself to believe that Natasha and I
had met Khovrin only once, that we were not acquainted
with him.

Peshkova reported that after he had spent a month in
prison following our visit, Khovrin was freed. But with each
new wave of arrests undertaken under the new heads of
the Cheka—be it Dzerzhinsky, Yagoda or Yezhov—Khovrin
would be rounded up, along with all those who had been
previously arrested in connection with SR affairs. He
would be thrown back into prison for a few weeks or
months. Peshkova, who often tried to intercede on behalf
of her former SR comrades by appeals to the Bolshevik
authorities, recounted that he jokingly came to call us "my
young godmothers."

In 1957, after thirty-five years of life in emigration, I
saw Peshkova again in her Moscow apartment. There she
told me that, to her knowledge, *all* former SRs had perished. All of them. Two or three might well be hiding
somewhere, but this was unlikely. Personally, she knew of
no survivor. I hoped that Khovrin, with his weak heart,
was able to die in the peace of his apartment, rather than
behind prison walls or in a camp.

On that gray, freezing morning we were all forced to
go downstairs and get into a large truck which was surrounded by Red Army men with rifles. They were waiting
for us at the building's entrance. There was quite a display

of military force all around—the Chekists had obviously hoped to capture Victor Chernov himself. Without much ceremony, we were seized and pulled onto the truck. We stood up in the open, holding onto the truck's sides as best we could while it sped towards the Lubyanka, along the uneven Moscow streets.

This time, we were taken to the ominous All Russian Cheka Division at the Lubyanka Prison—in the Fall, I had dealt with the more innocuous local Moscow Cheka. Its entrance, up a few stone steps, was right off the street. Two armed soldiers guarded its door. Inside, Kozhevnikov and his men turned us over to the commanding officer on duty and disappeared. We were officially placed under arrest and told to sit down some distance away from one another. We settled on a long, wooden bench along the wall of a narrow room which had formerly been the reception hall of the Russia Insurance Company. The window facing the building's main entrance still had its stained glass windows. They featured a gray bird, a Phoenix, symbol of that company, which was shown against a background of orange flames. Below it, there was the inscription, "I revive through fire." Its prophetic meaning was clear, and Natasha and I were not able to keep from smiling at the irony of that inscription.

We waited for a long time, sitting in a strong, icy draft created by the door that Chekists would continually open and close as they went in and out of the reception hall. Most were dressed in black leather coats but a few wore street-clothes. At last, we were called one by one to a tall control-desk to fill out our forms, giving our first name, patronymic, family name, year of birth, social background, and occupation. Then we were separated. The soldiers turned me over to a guard, an enormous Latvian woman. She led me along corridors and down numerous stairs. Suddenly, as the corridor made a turn, I caught a glimpse of Mother. She was pale, her face was swollen. We rushed towards each other but the Latvian prison matron pushed Mother away. Holding me firmly by the hand, she led me further. Finally she opened the door of a large, dusky room.

I saw women sitting on wide wooden benches all around this cell. Each one of them seemed surrounded by a wall of loneliness. One could see by looking at their eyes that these women feared one another. Those who paced back and forth in the cell also seemed alienated from the others—one could sense it in their movements. I remember one prisoner who must have been on duty. She was a dark-haired woman in her thirties who dragged a pail of soapy water and a mop behind her. She was scrubbing the room's wooden floor. She went in and out of the door freely. In a loud, unnatural accent, she sang an ugly song:

Oh, you are chasing me away,
And your heart feels no pain....

I do not remember whether or not we were given any-thing to eat that day. When the guard called me, it was eve-ning again. I had no watch with me and I had lost all sense of time. Once again we walked along endless corridors. This time, we stopped in front of an unpainted door. The guard unlocked it with a huge key and pushed me into a small, windowless cell—these are now called "boxes" in Soviet prison jargon.

This "box" was dark inside, except for a tiny bit of light which came through the cracks of its door. I managed to feel my way to a wooden bench along one side of the cubicle. As I sat down, I realized that there was someone right next to me. I heard a woman's nervous breathing. The woman spoke and I recognized at once a distinctive, scratchy voice, familiar to me since childhood. It was that of Iya Denisevich.

Iya was the younger daughter of an SR Party mem-ber, Anna Yakovlevna Denisevich. Mother knew her whole family and was a close friend of her middle daughter, who was her age, and the wife of the SR A. Foldman. She was also the sister of my future husband's stepmother, but that relationship did not exist then.

Iya had always moved in SR circles; she had lived abroad with her mother. At the beginning of the Revolution, Dasha had heard that she had married a Cheka investigator, Berdichevsky. We had not seen Iya for several years.

"Is this Olga or Natasha?" Iya asked in her unpleasant, scratchy voice. "I've never been able to keep you straight. So you, too, are waiting for questioning?"

"Iya, do you work for the Cheka?" I asked.

"No, of course not! I took a clerical job in the Moscow Cheka solely to be able to help out our SR comrades. My own case is not serious, a trifle, and I will be freed shortly. This will be my last questioning, only a formality. And your mother—was she arrested too? How awful! I have certain connections. I might be able to help her. Obviously, they're looking for Victor. I'll go warn him right away, as soon as I am freed. Your mother gave me your address not long ago; we met by chance on the street. But I forgot your street number. What was it again?"

"Iya, you're working for the Cheka." I fell silent and ignored her pleas for friendship and her assurances that she only wanted to go over to Victor in order to help him out. I turned away. But our *tête à tête* was soon ended as the guard came to pick her up, as if to take her to an interrogation.

I was left alone. My eyes slowly became accustomed to the darkness. I heard voices and footsteps outside my cell door. Anxiously, I attempted to clarify things in my own mind. Obviously, Iya had been placed with me in order to try and find out where Victor was hiding. From this, I could deduce that the Cheka had not yet caught him.

Suddenly there was a noise; the door was unlocked and a different guard appeared at the door. She took me by the arm and led me out of the cell. After the darkness, the electric lights in the corridors burned my eyes. I tried to shield them with the palms of my hands. Going down a flight of stairs, we walked along a carpeted corridor: we were approaching the officers of the interrogators.

The woman stopped before a white double door which was guarded by a soldier. The soldier opened it and the guard disappeared. I was left alone on the threshold of an enormous, luxuriously decorated room. As I walked in, I saw very little at best—I was blinded by the blazing lights.

This room had surely been the office of one of the former directors of the Russia Insurance Company. I could make out the crystal chandeliers hanging from the ceiling and shining with their glittering, many-faceted ornaments of glass. An oriental rug covered the floor and white bear skins lay on top of it. Near the walls, comfortable armchairs were disposed. Three writing desks were arranged around the room, with spaces left between them. An interrogator sat behind each desk.

At first I could not make out the Chekists because of the glaring lamps which stood in front of each of them, their beams directed towards the center of the room. Huge mirrors hung all around the room from the gilded moldings which ran around the white walls. A secretary sat ready at a typewriter set on a small table. I was politely asked to sit down on a stool in the middle of the room, in a spot where the three powerful light beams converged.

When my eyes became somehow accustomed to the light, I was able to make out Kozhevnikov's face. He was sitting behind the desk on my right. By listening to the way the interrogators addressed each other, I was able to figure out who the other two men were—the personalities of the Cheka investigators were well known and often discussed in those days in Moscow. Directly in front of me was the famous Latsis, and to the left sat the equally notorious Romanovsky.

Of the three, Kozhevnikov clearly played a secondary part. He seemed to have been assigned to do the basic work on the Chernov case. Obviously, he did not wield any great influence. Even his outward appearance was somehow rough. He wore the same gray overcoat, now open, and his cap was lying next to him on a chair. Papers were laid out before him; these were probably the records of our earlier questionings. He was checking something out as he leafed through them.

The investigator Romanovsky was known in Moscow as a sadist as well as a drug addict. He was about forty and was dressed in civilian clothes and wore a tie. He was balding, but his enormous head still had a thick fringe of ashen-gray hair in back. He was deathly pale—there was something lifeless about him. His colorless eyes peered forth from behind blue shadows.

As he sat right across from me, and despite the brilliant lights, I was able to study Latsis' colorful appearance. He had reddish hair and a bright red beard, both carefully groomed. His skin was very white, suffused with a pink blush. Solid and heavy set, he assumed the manners of a *grand seigneur* as he sat back in his armchair and stroked his beard with his well-manicured hand. He wore a signet ring and a gold chain bracelet. His movements were deliberately slow, and he spoke in an exaggeratedly ingratiating tone. The expression of his light green eyes was cold and piercing. He wore a sleek khaki field jacket over a snow-white shirt and tie.

As I sat on my stool in the glare of the lamps, under the crossfire of the interrogators, everything around me shone—the crystal desk set, the gilded trinkets on Latsis' table, his ring. The mirrors multiplied the glitter all around me. Although I did not catch my own reflection in them, I was quite sure that I looked pretty miserable. I was feverish and shivered, even with my blue coat on. My uncombed hair was tied in back with a black ribbon, which had begun to fray. I had Mother's gray boots on, which were too big, and I was wearing an old pair of Victor's socks. My face was frost-bitten after our two nights of walking about in the snow. My eyes teared both from the lack of sleep and the blinding lights. All this made me feel humiliated. In those years I did not yet know that although I am not tall, if I straighten my shoulders and raise my head, this alters my own conception of myself and gives me self-confidence. I was to learn this much later, when we lived in France under the German Occupation and I had to hold my own with German officers and soldiers when my husband was arrested.

Latsis led the interrogation. Kozhevnikov asked me only some routine questions and I gave him the same answers as I had that morning.

"Is your father from the nobility?" Latsis asked.

"I don't know. But weren't social distinctions abolished by the Revolution?"

"But your mother was from the gentry in the Tsarist days, wasn't she?"

"Yes, she was."

"That's what I thought," Latsis said, running his hand through his red beard. "Tell us now—were you present when your mother and Victor Chernov parted? Where was that? At the apartment, perhaps?" Once again he ran his fingers through his beard; it was obviously his favorite gesture. He then fixed his cold eyes on me.

"I don't know what you are talking about," I said.

"What a shame that you do not remember! Comrade Iya Denisevich has given us the rundown on your family."

"Well then, why don't you ask Comrade Denisevich?"

Latsis broke into uninhibited laughter. He got up from his desk and moved to an armchair which was closer to me. He crossed his legs.

"You see, my dear, there's quite a difference between you and your sister Adya, a true daughter of Chernov's. Not an adopted daughter. Chernov is not at all from a noble family. He is from the people, and he has the solidity of the people. You say all class distinctions have been removed. Yet, your sister who is a true daughter of Chernov is so much more open, so much more talkative than you. Such a noisy little grasshopper. Why, she told us everything about her father."

Latsis smiled, then Kozhevnikov; finally even the hollow cheeks of Romanovsky broke into a smile. They seemed pleased—were they taking a holiday from more serious and bloody deeds? Knowing Adya, a reserved and sophisticated child who understood perfectly our predicament in regard to secrecy, I marveled at Latsis' lack of insight when he called her a "noisy little grasshopper."

"Remember, please," Latsis slowly continued. "Chernov is our enemy, but at the same time he is our friend. We have a love-hate relationship with him. And I think all we'll have to do to straighten matters out is to have a talk with him. In an hour or so of good conversation we are certain to understand each other. You see, there's only a difference in methods between us. He is a Socialist and so are we, and we agree with him on many points. If he would only try and take a step in our direction, we will quickly solve our misunderstandings. We'd like to meet with him for a friendly chat. Do you understand? Please pass this on to him."

"What high school did you finish?" Romanovsky suddenly asked.

"The Saratov School—in the Third Soviet District."

"Why did you go to Saratov?"

"Because of starvation elsewhere."

"And where did you live before?"

"I lived in Moscow with my mother."

"But didn't you study under the name of Chernov? Comrade Denisevich told us that Kolbassina was your mother's maiden name. What is your father's name?"

"I don't know."

In the next room I heard someone talking on the phone loudly. They were spelling a name clearly, letter-by-letter:

"...Sermus, S-E-R-M-U-S. Ida Sermus."

This was certainly a strange occurrence in a chain of extraordinary events, culminating in this eerie session in the interrogator's office at the Lubyanka. I know only that I was not having a hallucination, and also that I was asked no question whatever about Ida.

Latsis began again. "Your sister told us that your father gave your mother his fur coat for the trip...."

"She said no such thing. You are lying!" I interrupted.

Latsis burst into jovial laughter. "For such a well brought up girl, what language! You mean, of course, that you all said goodbye to him on the train." He added this sentence as if by chance.

"I did not say goodbye to anyone."

"Where were you going?" Romanovsky asked.

"To the country—out into the provinces, anywhere."

"Comrade Denisevich told us that your nurse had always lived with you. Where is she?" Latsis asked. "Was she traveling with you?"

"I don't know where she is at the present time."

"Now, that is not very nice—to forget your old nanny like that. This is bad, very bad...," Latsis said, laughing.

"And Comrade Zubelevich"—he meant Dasha—"was she also traveling with you?" Romanovsky asked, turning over some papers. "She is here with us too and we will have occasion to have a chat with her."

Their questions were endless. Latsis used a mildly prurient, playful tone as he asked about the imaginary scene between "Mother and Father" as Victor was seeing us off at the station. He was always coming back to the notion that it was essential for the Bolsheviks to meet Victor Chernov in order to work out certain important points. To my surprise, no one asked me anything about Vera Ivanovna or Khovrin.

At last the interrogation ended. For a while the secretary continued to bang on his typewriter. When he had finished, he handed me a copy of the testimony I was to sign. I insisted on reading it before signing it, but I was too tired to do this properly. My eyesight was blurred and the letters jumped all over the page. I had the feeling that the entire questioning had been full of fabrications and intrigue, that the bulk of the investigators' information had clearly come from Iya Denisevich. I signed the protocol and was put into the custody of a guard and dismissed.

The night was ending, my second night without sleep. I felt a deadly fatigue. I was despondent. What bothered me most was that I had not been able to read the transcript of the testimony carefully before signing it. The Chekists could have introduced any number of names into it, names of individuals I had never mentioned. Nonetheless, I had signed it and that was irreversible.

-45-

As I was taken back by the guard along long corridors, I was in a daze—I could barely walk. At last we reached a cell lit only by a dull light. As I entered, the door was slammed behind me. Women were sleeping on the wooden benches all around the room. I managed to find a spot near a wall and sat down with my legs folded under me. The excitement and anxiety of the interrogation faded at once. In my mind, I went over the questions I had just answered. In retrospect, I thought I could have handled some of them much better. I could have been more firm, more ironic, more scathing. I was not pleased with myself. I was perplexed with Latsis' preoccupation with "noble origins"—I did not know then that he was writing a book, in which he maintained that the element of "guilt" is only secondary in police investigations, and that the major, deciding factor is the individual's "background." I worried about Mother and my sisters. Outside, it was slowly getting lighter.

As morning approached, another prison guard, a snub-nosed Latvian, came into the cell. She spoke little Russian and expressed herself mostly through her hands. I was able to make out that she wanted me to follow her. As she took me down the stairs, I heard the same ugly song somewhere in the distance.

Oh, you're chasing me away,
And you're not sorry at all....

We went past the reception desk on the ground floor

and walked along a corridor to the left of it. At the end of a small passageway there was a door with a guard standing just outside it. He opened the door and I saw Mother, Adya and Natasha settled on the wide, wooden bunks. I rushed towards them. The guard locked the door behind me. The four of us were together again, without anyone else in the cell! We embraced one another. In muffled voices, we began recounting what had happened to each of us after our arrest. I was struck with the expression on Mother's face. There was an unusual, deep grief in her eyes.

Soon, the door opened and a soldier brought us tin cups filled with a dark liquid, which we took to be tea. He also brought in a chipped enamel plate with three carefully measured portions of raw, black bread. Each portion, weighing one-eighth of a pound, had an additional fragment of bread, the size of a domino fastened to it with a small stick. The Red Army man counted us off, pointing his thick finger at us: "One, two, three," he said. "Children don't count," he added, pointing to Adya.

During our entire prison stay, the child continued not to count and the four of us were given only three portions of food. I do not think that there was anything spiteful in this omission. Rather, in accordance with prison regulations, children were not to be arrested. It followed that they did not exist in prison and therefore did not eat. The rations were micoscopic and that circumstance aggravated our acute state of starvation.

Mother told us how she had fallen into the Cheka's hands. An ambush had been set in the Leonoviches' apartment. But who could have been privy to Victor's going there? Who had informed on them? These questions are likely to remain forever unanswered. But it must be noted here that, years afterwards, in emigration, the eminent Osip Minor, one of the Party's most respected figures, maintained that Ida Sermus might well have been involved in this affair, which turned out to be highly propitious for her future.

Mother recounted for us that, as she approached the

building where the Leonoviches lived, something intangible put her on guard. She looked in all directions. The small side street off the Arbat was empty. Everything seemed quiet. Instead of following her instinct, she walked up to the apartment and knocked on the door, using the agreed-upon, special knock. The door opened instantly. The Chekists were waiting for her. They had probably watched her through the shutters. She was immediately surrounded by armed soldiers who took her to a back room, where she had to wait for several hours. Then she was driven off to the Lubyanka. She was concerned about Victor. But she was somehow reassured when she was placed in a dark cell with Iya Denisevich. It was probably the very one where I had spent a couple of hours with her. Iya offered Mother to go to Victor after her own imminent release and per- sisted in trying to get Victor's address from Mother. Mother then realized that he had not yet been arrested. The ques- tions asked of her during the interrogation further indicated that Victor was still free.

Much later, Victor told us that he had gone to the ar- ranged meeting place, and had apparently arrived there be- fore Mother. Before walking into the building, he looked around. He noticed on the snow fresh tire marks and num- erous footprints made by heavy boots leading into the house. There was no one around. Quickly Victor turned away and walked down the first through street and fled.

Adya had been seized on the train; a large group of Chekists had come for her. Dasha was also taken, but they were separated at once. A complete stranger in the next train compartment became indignant at seeing that a ten- year-old girl was being led away alone by Secret Policemen. She tried to escort Adya, but of course the Chekists would not allow this. Adya was driven to the Lubyanka in a pas- senger car, and handed over to the authorities in the recep- tion hall. There she sat on a bench for several hours with- out moving. Finally she became angry; she got up from her bench and said loudly: "What is this? Since you have ar- rested me, you must give me something to eat!"

Her demand amused the guards on duty; they all laughed. The officer in charge directed a man to feed Adya, and she was brought a plate of lentils. Later she was taken to Latsis' office. He kept asking her the same question over and over again:

"Dear little girl, did you see your Daddy hand your Mommy his fur coat? Was it on the train or was it back at the apartment?"

Adya answered coolly that she had no Daddy. She did not move from this position in any way, despite Latsis' repeated attempts at trapping her.

Natasha had also gone through a long interrogation with more or less the same questions asked me. She had handled herself magnificently and her spirited attitude bolstered all of us. Putting together what we had said in our interrogations, we began exchanging our impressions. We pondered certain questions: what had happened to Dasha? Soon we even saw the humorous side of certain questions.

Our quarters, a small office converted into a prison cell, were dark. The full-length window, grilled with solid bars, looked onto an inner courtyard. A bare light bulb hung from the ceiling; it burned day and night. Wide wooden bunks filled about half of the cell's space. In one corner, to the left of the door, stood a half-circular white ceramic stove. It was not lit and the room was icy. The floor was so cold that we sat on the bunks with our feet curled up under us.

After lunch, which consisted of gray-colored cabbage soup with herring heads and liquid wheat kasha with a greenish drop of hempseed oil, a soldier brought in an armful of logs and tried to light the stove. However, the damp wood burned poorly. The toilets were far away from our cell. The guard posted outside our door escorted us up a flight of stairs to use them. A relatively clean lavatory with a small sink, was enclosed by a glass door, the panes of which had been broken. As we used the bathroom, the soldier stood guard, observing us with complete indifference.

On our third trip to the bathroom, we found that the

broken panes of the door to the lavatory had been replaced by sheets of pink blotting paper tacked in their place. The paper was full of ink spots. Along a diagonal, in bold letters, the name "I. Denisevich" and "Iya Denisevich" was printed in reverse. We were all taken to the bathroom in one trip, and one by one we read this amazing sign. There was no doubt left in our minds: Iya worked for the Cheka. It was as if she herself had said this in writing.

Dinner consisted of the same soup, but in a more diluted form. We settled down on the bare wooden benches, and because there were no blankets, to keep warm we snuggled up to one another. We must have looked like the Menshikov family in Berezovo in the famous painting by Surikov. The color of my blue coat, purchased in London, made me think of the girl in a blue skirt reading the Bible in a corner of that painting. We fell asleep trying to shield our eyes from the blinding light bulb above with our elbows.

When I opened my eyes in the morning, Mother was already awake. She had had a painful dream, and she told it to us in detail. Victor and Ida had gotten on a departing train. She was trying to get on it with them. The train, moving slowly at first, started gaining speed. Mother ran after it, but she was unable to get on. Instead, she had fallen into a deep snowbank. The train had disappeared from sight. This dream depicted a drama which had subconsiously troubled Mother for a long time, but she was able to perceive this clearly only after the shock of her arrest. Mother was in a state of despair.

After our morning tea we began to examine our room more closely. The wallpaper had been torn off, but on the uneven plaster there were recently drawn signs and drawings. Among these was a roughly sketched ink caricature of a soldier in profile. He was dressed in uniform with his decorations and epaulettes, and was wearing his military cap. Under this was the inscription—"The Devil General" and a poem:

Nobody here can force me

To pick up a rifle and fight.
Pick one up yourself, brother
And go to the front alone.

A deserter had been locked in this cell sometime before us. The most bothersome aspect of our new lodging
was the ceiling light. It prevented us from sleeping. Even
during the day it hurt our eyes. After lunch—the same raw
cabbage soup cooked with horse bones and the same liquid
kasha—we asked the attendant if he could give us an old
newspaper, or else buy one for us if we gave him the money—we still had a little travel money left. We hoped to
make a paper lampshade out of the newspaper. That evening the soldier returned with an armful of logs and a
newspaper. He tried to light the stove again but the logs
barely got warm, hissing and dripping with sap. However,
the newspaper made an excellent lampshade for the naked
bulb over our heads.

Toward the end of the day, the door suddenly
opened, and Iya Denisevich came in. She walked in timid-
ly, and stood a bit to the side. Not looking directly at us,
she once again tried to get the address of Victor's hiding
place from Mother. She insisted that she wanted to go to
him and to our SR comrades and give them a message from
us. She knew they were after Victor and she wanted to
save him, she said. She had to have his address at once,
while there was still time.

Iya was dressed in a stylish coat with a big collar, decorated with a fringe of black monkey fur which ran down
and around the coat's hem. Her fashionable fur hat was
pulled below her eyebrows.

"I've forgotten where you all live," she persisted in a
stubborn, annoying tone. "You can never write an address
down these days, it's considered dangerous, yet I have such
a poor memory! What was it again, Olya?" She had always
called Mother "Olya."

"Are you not ashamed of yourself, Iya?" Mother
asked.

But Iya seemed so very sad, the whole thing was so depressing, that we did not have the heart to call her an *agent provocateur* to her face. She repeated the same questions again and again, as if she had been wound up. We turned our backs to her and ignored her, but she insisted, waiting for an answer. Finally she gave up and left. We sighed in relief. "She is probably under a lot of pressure from the Cheka," Mother said. "She must have seen at once that we do not trust her."

-46-

The following morning began well. Our three suitcases, which we had left on the train, were unexpectedly delivered to us. Each one of them was stamped with bold, dark red letters: V.Ch.K., for the All Russian Cheka. This was a miracle; now we could change our clothes, put on warm things if we got cold, and most important, have our books. Our blankets and pillows had stayed on the train, as had my copy of *Indiana*. As for the raccoon fur coat, Latsis had probably kept it as a memento of Victor Chernov, and of his talkative young daughter. In any case, the great coat, along with Mother's leather briefcase, which Kozhevnikov had taken earlier that winter, were never returned to us.

We began to get settled. We took out all our clothes and spread them at night on the benches. During the day we folded them up and sat with our legs crossed, our backs against the suitcases. We disposed our books on the bench in a row. Just to look at them made us happy.

We had a one-volume edition of Lermontov in a green cover. It was an old edition which had many pages of illustrations—four pictures on each page. The drawings were naive but very expressive. Under each, two lines of text were quoted:

"In front of the altar, in the flickering of candles, she

recognized a familiar voice within the holy chorus...."
and

"He put his entire life into one kiss, into one moan...."

We also had a copy of the *Divine Comedy* in Italian, in a gold-leaf parchment binding. Natasha and I had been familiar with it since our Italian childhood. Later, as I read the interpretations of the *Comedy* put forth by experts on Dante, I was surprised to see how accurate we had been in figuring out many difficult parts of the text.

We also had some French books with us: Anatole France, who was extraordinarily popular in those years, not only in France, but also in Russia; a Balzac anthology; an anthology of French poetry; and the collected short stories of Guy de Maupassant in Russian.

We had no Pushkin, but each of us knew a lot of his verse by heart. At night, when our eyes were tired of reading, we would recite his poems, as well as those by Tyutchev and Blok. Adya had an extraordinarily retentive memory and she knew by heart several lengthy poems by Alexey Tolstoy.

Our greatest good fortune, our incredible good luck, was that we were imprisoned together, without anyone else in our cell. We were able to talk freely, as long as we lowered our voices. Who could overhear us? Our thick plaster walls had no openings or cracks in them, we could see whoever stood under our window, and the soldiers outside our door were completely illiterate. Listening devices and tape recorders had not yet been invented.

We were able to do what we wanted with our endless hours of leisure. We could read to ourselves, or read aloud, or sleep, or simply rest. Our relationship with the soldiers on guard was relaxed and friendly, just as it had been with those who had guarded our room near Yauza Gates. The Latvian guardswomen, on the other hand, were professional prison personnel. They were less pleasant than the soldiers, but fortunately they did not appear very often.

The food remained the same, almost inedible. We remembered the verses quoted by Dostoyevsky in his *The*

House of the Dead:

> They have poured me out some cabbage with water,
> As I eat it, my ears are ringing....

Sometimes, despite our hunger, it was impossible for us to eat. Once we were given the usual horsemeat soup, but instead of meat, pieces of jaw, complete with long teeth, were floating in it.

The stove continued to draw poorly. Once, when the weather was colder than usual, Mother spoke to the soldier who guarded us. He went to the commanding officer with our complaint. Soon, the officer himself came in, a tall man dressed in boots and a fur cap, carrying an axe. He introduced himself, and got down on one knee next to the stove. Very gracefully, he chopped the thick, aspen logs into small slivers. After he left, we were able to light a fire in the stove and to keep it going by mixing the small pieces of wood with the larger logs.

We collected what little money we still had and asked one of the soldiers on guard to buy us some food, although this was against regulations. But there was little we could get. It was impossible to get bread without the proper ration cards, and potatoes would never cook on our stove. We remembered the carrots we had eaten raw when we lived near Yauza Gates. Our guards were able to find some carrots for us from time to time. They would smuggle them in, wrapped in newspaper. No one ever denounced us. This kept us from contracting scurvy.

Once, a Red Army man unlocked our door, and a young woman walked in. She was short, unassuming, simply dressed. She handed us a plate with an untouched meal on it, some millet pudding and a piece of bread. Shyly, she explained that she had something else to eat and that she wanted to give us this meal. She departed and we never saw her again.

In the evenings we usually read aloud, and this kept our spirits up. Once, Mother was getting ready to read us

Maupassant aloud, and she was holding his collection of stories in her hands. A soldier walked into the room with an armful of logs for the stove. He glanced at the book in Mother's hands and looked surprised. Laughing, he said: "Comrade, is Maupassant appropriate for family reading?"

"Maupassant has written many different stories," Mother said with a smile. "Why don't you sit down on the bench and listen, comrade?"

The Red Army man sat down on the edge of a bench. Mother read a remarkable story about two fishermen, who were executed by the Germans during the occupation of Paris in 1870. The soldier sighed and shook his head. He seemed deeply impressed: "So, this is how it was!" he said, and left, wishing us good night.

Thus the days passed. We were never taken on walks. We did not see the sunshine, even during those days in February when it might have been shining over Moscow. Nothing happened in the narrow courtyard outside our window. Occasionally, the dirty snow was packed down by a soldier's heavy boots. The window was frozen shut, and our only ventilation was through the stove and the door. Luckily, as happens to most women in time of starvation, our menstrual bleeding stopped. Because we did not walk, except for our trips to the toilet, we became very weak. It was so cold that we always stayed bundled up, without moving. Unfortunately, we were unacquainted with Prince Kropotkin's *Memoirs of a Revolutionary.* His experience with isometric exercises done with a chair would have been an inspiration and an incentive for us.

Mother was worried by the state of our health. She wanted to write the director of the prison and thereafter to start a hunger strike unless we were let outside to exercise. But we managed to convince her not to do this. Such a protest could easily lead to a worsening of our situation. What if we were separated, or put in a large, overcrowded cell? Mother's idea of going on a hunger strike seemed a horrible idea to us.

We often thought of Italy and of the happy years we

had spent on the Mediterranean. It seemed as though a century had passed since we had left Alassio and our house by the sea, surrounded by a garden bursting with white roses.

Four weeks went by. The days were supposed to be getting longer, but we did not notice this in the confined surroundings of our cell. February was ending. We were completely cut off from the world. We had no idea of what had happened to Victor. The news of our arrest probably had not reached the Political Division of the Red Cross and our friend, Ekaterina Peshkova. At that time members of the Political Division of the Red Cross were allowed to visit political prisoners. They brought them packages from their relatives. We did not hear from anyone, and it seemed as though we were completely forgotten.

Then one day, late in the morning, we heard voices outside our door. A soldier opened it and a small woman in her middle fifties walked in. She introduced herself to Mother as Divilkovskaya, the wife of the editor of *Izvestia.* She had heard that a ten-year-old girl was in prison and Dzerzhinsky, the head of the Cheka himself, had given her permission to take custody of the child. Along with other members of the new Bolshevik ruling class, she lived with her family in the National Hotel on Red Square. Divilkovskaya told us that she too was a former emigré; she had spent many years in Switzerland.

Worried as she was about Adya's health, Mother accepted Divilkovskaya's offer at once, and Natasha and I quickly started collecting our sister's belongings. We filled a small suitcase with her dresses, shoes and books. In the meantime, Divilkovskaya sat down on the bunk next to Mother and spoke with her in a loud, animated voice. She said: "All of us disapprove of the Cheka's methods. In our circle, we call the Cheka the "Excess-ka." This did not sound amusing. Divilkovskaya asked us no personal questions whatever.

Mother inquired whether she knew how long we would be kept in prison. What were the reasons for our arrest and detention? Could not Divilkovskaya help us find this out? Divilkovskaya answered that we were being held as "hostages." She added that she would try to obtain custody also of Natasha and of me.

Adya's things were ready. I buttoned her gray, artificial fur coat, and tied a patterned woolen scarf over her hat. She put on her mittens, which Natasha had made for her not long before out of small loose pieces of material. We said goodbye. Mother thanked Divilkovskaya with all her heart.

We were relieved that Adya was being taken out of prison and into the fresh air. She would be leading a more normal existence. No doubt she would be given sufficient nourishment. But we also had some doubts. Staying with strangers could also be a painful experience for Adya. However, Divilkovskaya seemed to be a decent person and this was reassuring. Mother began hoping that Natasha and I would also be freed soon.

PART XI

The Hotel National

With Adya's departure our life became empty and sad. With her around, we all had tried to remain cheerful and this in turn gave us the strength to face the immediate hardships of prison as well as the prospects of the future. Time dragged on monotonously. At first, after Adya's departure, we hoped that Divilkovskaya would think of letting us know how she was, and perhaps send us some provisions, but nothing happened. We were worried about Adya. Two weeks went by in this way. Without any news of her we did not know what to think.

But Divilkovskaya had not forgotten us. One day in the first half of March, she came into our cell, accompanied by the officer in charge of our prison section. She had brought some papers with her. They were permissions for Natasha and me to be released into her custody. These were officially stamped. The officer checked them, looking them over carefully, and then told us to get "our things ready for release." Divilkovskaya sat down on the bench next to Mother, while Natasha and I gathered our clothes and packed a suitcase. She said that Adya was waiting for us in the car outside.

It was difficult for us to leave Mother behind. We had gotten used to living in close proximity, sharing everything, bolstering each other's spirits! How would she manage alone? We were both deeply upset as we parted. Mother, however, was happy at seeing us freed and encouraged us to go.

We found ourselves outside. It was a sunny day; icicles were falling down on the ground from the roofs with a tinkling noise. Frozen puddles sparkled, their black ice creaked and shattered under the beat of horse hooves as horse-drawn carriages rushed by. The sky was a clear, light blue. Despite the beautiful spring day, I felt unhappy.

There is something insulting about the sun when it hurts one's eyes. It blinded us; we both were squinting as we climbed into Divilkovskaya's car. Inside, Adya embraced us. The ride was brief—the Lubyanka is close to the National Hotel. The chauffeur brought our bags in. Divilkovskaya gave her name to the doorman and asked for a pass for Natasha and me, which we would need to get in and out of the hotel. Important members of the Bolshevik Party and their families lived in the National Hotel—they needed protection.

We walked up to the third or fourth floor, and Divilkovskaya led us to a room that had been prepared for us. It was a typical Russian hotel room, with dark red velvet curtains, armchairs, and a small love-seat. There was a round table in the center of the room; the rest of the space was taken up by a double bed. Divilkovskaya said that the three of us would stay here, and that we would be given meal coupons in the dining room, which was on the first floor of the hotel. She said that she would soon come by to see how we were getting along.

It all seemed an unbelievable dream: steam heating that worked and a sink with running water! At last we would be able to wash ourselves from head to toe, something we had not done for months. And we would have meals prepared for us, like important members of the Bolshevik government!

As we were unpacking, Adya gave us her impressions of Divilkovskaya. She had taken good care of her and had at first put her to sleep on a sofa in her own quarters. But when Adya tried to bring up the subject of prison so that Divilkovskaya would make arrangements about delivering us a food package, she had become unresponsive. Adya told us how she had been taken to see "Swan Lake" at the Bolshoi Theater. Demian Bedny, the well-known Bolshevik poet, had sat in the same box as the Divilkovskys. Fat and jovial, he had joked with Adya during the intermission. And somewhere, in another box nearby, Lenin himself was sitting.

Divilovskaya told us that one night Lenin's wife and his sister had come to dinner. They wanted to see "Chernov's daughter," who was sleeping. But Divilovskaya told them that Adya was not a "trained bear" nor a "circus attraction" and that she should be left alone. Adya regretted this; Divilkovskaya, out of principle, had prevented her from making the acquaintance of Krupskaya and Ulyanova.

Divilkovskaya came back that evening and gave us some ration cards. We thanked her for everything she had done for Adya and ourselves. She sat down and chatted openly with us.

"Word of your arrest has gotten to Lenin," she said. "Hearing that Chernov's daughters were being held in prison, he was outraged and ordered that 'this shocking scandal' be stopped at once. Or else," she added. "Chernov could use this against us abroad, where it would quickly become anti-Bolshevik propaganda."

She did not realize that Vladimir Ilych's anxiety on our behalf had at first looked to us like genuine humanitarian concern. It was clear to us that she herself was probably acting on instructions from Lenin and not solely out of the kindness of her heart.

We were later to learn that Victor had written Lenin after we had all been arrested, congratulating him on not being able to arrest him, and taking instead his children and wife. Victor said that, with such tactics, the Bolsheviks would achieve whatever political ends they sought.

We wanted to wash thoroughly. The running water in the room was cold and we went downstairs to the kitchen and asked for hot water to wash our hair. At lunchtime, we went downstairs again. We were freshly scrubbed, we had put on some clean clothes, and our hair was neatly brushed. We walked to the kitchen where we admired the large, shining stoves, the sparkling pots, the extraordinary spotlessness throughout. The cook, who was dressed in a bright white coat and hat, gave us three warm plates in exchange for our coupons. Though the portions were small, they looked very appetizing. We had potato dumplings with mushroom sauce, cranberry pudding, and a piece of bread.

The dining room was situated directly opposite the kitchen. It was furnished with long, heavy oak tables and matching benches. But there were few people lunching there: most inhabitants of the National preferred to eat in the privacy of their rooms. The three of us sat down at the end of one of the long, oak tables and enjoyed the food and the surroundings.

After lunch we went up to our room and rested. What a treat after those nights in prison on the hard, wooden bunks! We had a large bed with a spring mattress, plump pillows, fluffy blankets. Adya settled down to read on the small love seat. We were all three in a state of physical euphoria. That evening we went down again—to supper. Later on, Divilkovskaya came by our room to check up on us. She promised to try and find out whom we could start seeing, and what should be undertaken in order to visit Mother in prison.

That evening an old friend of our family, Vera Boborova, came to see us. She was a Socialist who had served time in Siberia under the Tsar. She had once stayed with us in Alassio. How did she find us? Was she a Left-wing SR? At that time, they were attempting to work together with the Bolsheviks. I do not remember exactly, but this seems likely. We knew Borborova well, but her behavior that evening seemed strange to us. She was looking about nervously. In a barely audible voice, she murmured that we should be absolutely quiet at all times. We were to be sure not to talk openly even in our room. She reminded us that in Divolkovskaya's custody, we were still under Bolshevik supervision.

On the other hand, the three of us felt absolutely free, at least morally. All the pampering, the heated, comfortable room, the hot meals, were given to us without any strings attached. There were no conditions placed on us in any way. That evening, when we were lying in bed, trying to fall asleep, we were kept awake by the general excitement of well-being. Because of the cold in our prison cell, we had slept for weeks on end in our outer clothes. The clean, silky sheets and the softness of the pillows filled us with delight.

The next morning, I woke up with a fever and a rash. Divilkovskaya became alarmed, and brought a doctor to see me at once. The doctor was still young, a portly, self-confident woman who, upon closing the door behind her, asked squeamishly, without coming near me: "Do you have a lot of lice?"

She made me think of a story about Louis XIV who stood high on the bow of a galley powered by chained convicts. He held his nose with disgust as he walked by them. She was an early example of the concentration camp doctor who scolds the prisoners for wallowing in the stink and dirt in which they are confined.

The doctor did not believe me when I told her that we did not have lice. She continued to keep her distance and would not examine my rash. She nonetheless calmed Divilkovskaya, assuring her that I did not have typhus. She told me to stay in bed until my fever passed.

I was not hurting; my fever only fogged my head pleasantly and I was happy to lie in a comfortable, clean bed. Whatever I had—Natasha and Adya did not catch it. I stayed in bed for three or four days. My sisters went to the ballet at the Bolshoi Theater while I was sick.

When I was completely well, Divilkovskaya invited us to her quarters and introduced us to her husband and daughter. I have a clear image of a very thin man with a small beard and pince-nez eyeglasses. The daughter was about twenty-two. She was tall and blond, not very pretty, but pleasant looking. Well-mannered and not at all condescending, she talked to us willingly, despite the difference in our ages. She told us that she had just graduated from a finishing school in Switzerland, specializing in housekeeping. I was quite surprised to hear that housework could be a course of study. One day, she proudly taught us the basic principles of ironing—showing us how to iron correctly on her own ironing board.

There was nothing particularly memorable about our new acquaintance, except for the fact that she was the fiancee of the notorious, blood-thirsty Peters. A large photograph of her fiance in a trench coat and military cap stood on the marble fireplace in her bedroom. It was inscribed to her in large letters in the lower right-hand corner. When she showed us his portrait, I shuddered. We knew him by reputation; he was said to be one of the most cruel, ruthless leaders of the Cheka.

It is interesting to note that neither Peters nor Divilkovsky are listed in the *Great Soviet Encyclopedia.* This indicates that, *officially,* these men did not exist, although the former was Dzerzhinsky's right-hand man, and the latter an editor of *Izvestia.* This is not that surprising, given the fact that the *Encyclopedia,* while listing "Trotskyism," leaves out Trotsky altogether. In Lenin's *Complete Works* (fourth edition), both Peters and Divilkovsky are mentioned, although there are no explanations as to their positions, nor a word about their close association with Lenin. I have not been able to ascertain how the political careers of these men ended, and where they died. What happened to their wives?

As soon as I recuperated, I began to go out with Natasha and Adya. I had a feeling of estrangement as I looked around the open sky, the trees, the streets. Spring was just beginning. Muscovites walked around with their winter coats wide open. The dreadful, endless winter of 1920 was ending at last.

Divilkovskaya continued to stop by occasionally to see us in our room. She said that we would be able to visit Mother as soon as the appropriate formalities were completed. When, for the twentieth time, she referred to the Cheka as the "Excess-ka," I could not hold back and asked her why she spoke so playfully about this frightening organization. Divilkovskaya explained that the Cheka was fighting the enemies of the Revolution and that it was unavoidable that some mistakes occasionally occurred. It was from her that I heard for the first time the classic expression "when you chop down a forest, chips will fly." Natasha and I argued with her, saying that the Cheka's methods, which included blackmail, lying, provocation, and terror, were unjustifiable. The Cheka was inhuman, its actions were in complete opposition with the Revolution's purposes and goals.

We told Divilkovskaya about our trip the previous summer through the Volga region, and recounted the story of that man in Khvalynsk, who was taken by the Cheka down to a dark cellar where skeletons and skulls with glowing eye-sockets hung from the ceiling. Overcome by fear, the man had revealed where, in the garden, he had hidden the family's possessions. He was not released, but at least his family was left alone for a time.

Divilkovskaya passed our story on to Vera Boborova, who became upset at our lack of tact, and complained in turn to Ekaterina Peshkova, who must have had a hand in our release from prison, although we had not seen her yet. Meanwhile, Natasha and I were pleased that, for once, we had been able to convey the truth to the mother of Peter's fiancée.

Soon the friend of our family, Ekaterina Peshkova, came to see us in the Hotel National. In her usual impassive tone, she told us that Boborova had been frightened by our candor with Divilkovskaya. Peshkova did not give us her opinion in the matter, nor did she offer us any advice on how we should behave in the future. She comported herself in her habitual stern manner, making us feel unsure of what she really thought of us. I got the impression from her coldness that she did not approve of us. Only later did we find out how much she loved us. Secretly, she had been proud of us, but she had been unwilling—or unable—to communicate this at the time.

Peshkova brought us two pieces of soap, one for ourselves and one for Mother. She also gave us a large, round cheese with a light-colored rind, which tasted like Dutch cheese. She and Mikhail Vinaver had already become the directors of the Political Division of the Red Cross. The Red Cross was tolerated by the Bolsheviks solely because of the personal prestige of Peshkova in Dzerzhinsky's eyes. Peshkova reported that Mother had been recently transferred "upstairs," to the Special Division of the Cheka within the Lubyanka. As far as helping us with arrangements concerning our visit with her, she suggested that we get in touch directly with Latsis or Romanovsky. It turned out that they, too, were living in the Hotel National.

-48-

The next day, Divilkovskaya gave us Latsis' telephone number, and we made an appointment to see him. At the appropriate time Natasha and I went up to his luxurious suite. He greeted us as old friends, politely, almost jovially, asking us to make ourselves at home. As usual, he was sprawling in an armchair. Next to him, a very young woman with short, curly hair sat behind an enormous desk. In front of her she had a set of water colors and a copy of *La Vie Parisienne.* God only knows how this magazine had found its way to Moscow that winter. She was making copies of pictures out of the magazine into an album and highlighting them with touches of watercolor.

"Please meet my wife," Latsis said. "How can I be of help?"

We asked him to let us visit Mother at the Lubyanka and he immediately drew up a letter on Cheka stationery, giving us "specific permission to meet in person with prisoner Kolbassina" on the next day. This meant that we could see Mother face to face, and not through a small, barred window.

"Tell me, how is your younger sister?" he asked. "She is such an interesting little girl! She will go a long way. I was thinking that she should be sent to our childrens' camp, which is set up especially for the children of

[240]

Cheka employees. Chernov's daughter in a Cheka school—
it would be very amusing, wouldn't it?" He laughed.

"And how is Comrade Denisevich?" I asked, trying
to divert his train of thought.

"Yes, I must admit that we had to apply a lot of pressure in order to get her to do what we wanted." I then recalled vividly the sad expression on Iya's face, her pathetic
appearance in her new coat with the monkey fur, as she
had stood in our cell.

The next day, the three of us walked over to the Lubyanka. We found ourselves standing at the desk, where
two months before we had stood in the company of Khovrin
and of poor Vera Ivanovna. The Commandant read our
pass and ordered a Red Army man to escort us to the
second floor. The soldier led us up the stairs and along corridors to a well-lit wide passageway with windows on one
side overlooking the Lubyanka courtyard; on the other
side stood a row of newly constructed, cage-like, miniscule
cells made out of freshly cut light wood. These "boxes"
were closed with large locks painted in a shiny black color.

A woman guard came to meet us, and upon reading
our pass, opened one of these doors with a giant key.
Mother came out of it, wearing her purple winter coat. She
looked pale, but she smiled joyously when she saw us. The
soldier and the female overseer stepped aside, but they
could easily overhear our conversation. However, when
people who are close to each other talk in such situations,
they can understand each other by using allusions and frag-
ments of phrases beyond any eavesdroppers' comprehen-
sion.

Mother managed to convey to us that an informer
had been placed in her cell. She was an old baroness who
did not leave her alone day or night, asking her for Victor's
address incessantly. Like Iya, she was "to be freed shortly."
She offered to give Victor a message "just as soon as she
got out." Later, Mother recounted that this women had
gotten mixed up with a group of aristocrats tied to a monarchist conspiracy against the Bolsheviks. She had been

taken down to the Cheka cellar to be shot. There, standing on the blood-drenched basement floor, rifle guns pointed at her, she had agreed to become a "prison hen," that is, a prison informer.

Mother was tortured by this woman. Whenever she began to fall off into deep sleep—and she always had been able to sleep anywhere, even in the absence of exercise—the baroness would put her exhausted, tormented face right against Mother's. She would stare at her, breathing heavily until Mother woke up. Mother would jump up as the baroness asked her with an awful laugh: "How can you sleep like a baby in these circumstances? I cannot fall asleep at all, and look at you, off like a child!"

She would then, once again, ask Mother to take her into her confidence and give her Victor's address. To convince Mother of her sincerity, the poor woman assured Mother that she had always looked upon the Social Revolutionaries with great sympathy. She added naively that she had even been to some of their "parties"—she meant Party meetings. She asked Mother where she should go to attend one of these "parties" when she was freed.

In the tight cell, with the electric light bulb glaring continuously, there was nowhere to hide from the maniacal stare of the baroness who followed Mother around the cell like a hawk. Whenever Mother lay down she saw the baroness's tall, thin figure and heard her pacing endlessly back and forth in the narrow confines of the cell.

Mother was delighted with our gifts of scented soap, cheese, clean linen and a new towel. We told her about the miraculous existence we were leading. She asked us to bring her some fresh vegetables—some carrots or cabbage or an onion—on our next visit, which had been scheduled for the following week by Latsis. Mother's gums were hurting, the first sign of scurvy.

Soon the female guard came up to us and told us that our time was up. We parted, promising Mother to bring her some fresh food the next time. On our way back to the National, we noticed two young soldiers behind us, who seemed to be following us. They disappeared before we reached the hotel. We no longer paid much attention to the fact that we were being followed.

The weather continued to be pleasant. The sun shone brightly, melting the snow, but at night huge puddles still froze again. Slowly, we began regaining our strength. Each day we were able to walk longer distances. At the nearby Okhotny road market, we bought Mother some cabbage and sauerkraut. Luckily it was not too expensive—our money was running out. I have a memory in connection with this expedition; it seems unimportant, yet to this day it fills me with pain. During our outing, we passed a stationery store; it displayed a small toy bunny rabbit which stood on its hind legs. It was cut out of plywood and painted white.

"Look, what a sweet bunny," Adya exclaimed.

Natasha and I looked at one another, but we did not stop. Each of us knew that we had very little money left. We had to save it to buy fresh vegetables to give Mother against scurvy. Adya, who never made a fuss or asked us for toys, was only ten years old. Why didn't we, the older ones, sense how much she wanted this bunny, although she would never have asked for it? Our few kopeks would probably have been enough to buy it. What of it, if we would have had to swallow our pride and ask Divilkovskaya for money on Mother's behalf? Or else go directly to Peshkova? Our refusal to please Adya remains in my mind as one of the instances of what Alexei Remizov calls "the irreparable."

Divilkovskaya never asked us anything about Mother, nor did she volunteer to help her. She could have offered to send her a clean blouse or a book, but she did not. Apparently, having taken on Chernov's daughters, she did not want to show in any way that she was helping other SRs as well.

During our long walks through Moscow, we noticed that two men were following us at all times. Often, one was in uniform, the other in civilian clothes. We understood that they had been assigned to tail us wherever we went. Once in a while, to check up on them, we would split up and go in different directions and then get together again. The men, too, would part, one following Natasha, the other following me. Soon they guessed that we were testing them. They laughed whenever we looked back at them. The Chekists continued to hope that we would lead them to Victor's hiding place. For this reason, we did not visit any of our friends, and continued to live cut off from the world.

A little less than a week after we had visited Mother, we phoned Latsis again, asking him for a pass for another visit at the Lubyanka. Again, Latsis wrote out an authorization for us, but he did this only after we called on him in his suite and he had entertained us with his drawing room humor, asking us all sorts of questions. Next day, the three of us went off to visit Mother. Once again, she came out of a "box" into the well-lit corridor which was already familiar to us. The female overseer watched us as we handed her a jar of cabbage and some dark red cranberries. Mother explained that the baroness had at last been removed from her cell, since she had been unable to get any useful information out of her. Mother was relieved to be alone once more.

And so it went—every week we were allowed a visit with Mother. Whenever Latsis was off somewhere, we went to Romanovsky, whom we would telephone beforehand. He was very polite to us, and unlike Latsis he never entered into personal conversations with us.

Once we decided to make a trip back to our room near the Yauza Gates. We wanted to collect the books and clothing we had left behind at the Sinitsins. Since the Cheka knew that this had been our home and since there was no one at that address that we could incriminate, it seemed safe for us to go back. I do not remember how we got hold of a sled. Probably, Divilkovskaya borrowed one for our use; there were several families with children living in the Hotel National at that time. We chose a week day when Sinitsin would be away at work. The three of us set out across town, and as usual our constant companions followed us, keeping their distance behind us. It was again a cold day and the puddles were frozen over. There was little snow left in the streets of Moscow, but the sidewalks were still lined with small, sooty snowbanks, just enough to con convey our sled.

We found Sinitsin's wife at home alone. Although she was a little embarrassed, she let us into our former room without recriminations. She was anxious to show us how much her daughter had grown since we had last seen her, and talked to us in a friendly manner. Leading us into her own quarters, after we had collected our possessions, she said:

"Back in January someone came to see us. She must have been some kind of spy or *provocateur,* trying to get Victor Chernov's address out of me—I was home alone. She was very insistent, she also wanted the names of all your SR friends. She said she had to warn Chernov immediately because one of his daughters had denounced him during an interrogation. I became disgusted and asked her: 'Who are you? How do you know about the interrogation?' She answered something that was completely unrelated. But clearly she had been sent here by the Chekists."

By the way she described the visitor—a blonde wearing a long coat with a drooping fur fringe, we understood that it had been Iya who had called at the Sinitsins.

With some cord we tied our possessions to the sled and, saying goodbye forever to Sinitsin's wife, we went back to the National, all the way across Moscow. Our load seemed heavy as we walked back, trying not to slip on the icy sidewalks. It was maddening to think of the two husky soldiers walking behind us, empty handed. We stopped and jokingly motioned them to come up and give us a hand with the sled. They laughed, hiding their faces from us. then they continued to play hide and seek with us, peeking out from behind street corners, laughing and poking each other as we walked ahead of them back to the hotel.

49

We were slowly coming back to life. We no longer had to hide. Even to be under direct, open supervision by the Cheka was a relief to us—we felt freer than we had in a long time. One day, wandering about Moscow, we walked by the Popov Gymnasium where we had studied for a few months in late 1917. Natasha and I had the same idea—what if we tried to enlist in its last grade? Never mind if we had in the meantime graduated from the Satrolov gymnasium—there was much that we could still learn at Popov.

It felt as if a thousand years had elapsed since we had attended the Popov gymnasium, although only two and a half years had gone by. What a joy it would be to find ourselves among our school friends, who would be graduating this year! Adya could enter the second grade at the Popov and again be among children of her own age.

Natasha and I decided to try to meet with our former schoolmates and then to go to Divilkovskaya with a request to authorize our reintegration into the Popov. The next day we came up to the school shortly before school ended. It was a clear, sunny day in the early spring. We were overjoyed to suddenly find ourselves among smiling, cheering young people. We had not been forgotten; we were surrounded by our friends who had grown and changed, but were still as open, as affectionate with us: "The Chernov girls! The Chernushkis! Where have you been? Where were you hiding? When are you coming back to school?"

We tried to explain to our friends that this was what we wanted to do, but that in order to do it, we would have to have the Bolshevik authorities' permission. Only then could we go to the school administration with a request to register. We told our friends of our unusual position. We had just been released from prison, but we were under close Cheka watch. We were hostages in the hands of the Bolsheviks, who were still hoping to capture Victor Chernov.

Our good friend, pretty Elena Spendyarova, with her usual expansiveness, ran up to a slender, red-headed boy who was one of the crowd: "Trotsky, Trotsky," she shouted. "Do you hear this? What dreadful things you Bolsheviks are doing! The Chernovs are held as hostages by the Cheka!" Indignant, she was tugging at the sleeve of Trotsky's son.

We were irresistibly drawn to these healthy young people, to their stimulating life. We promised our friends to re-enter the Popov gymnasium as soon as we could.

But as we were walking back to the National Hotel we looked back and saw our constant shadows, the young men who were following us. This sobered us. Nonetheless, without delay we went to Divilkovskaya with our request.

Our guardian did not appreciate our initiative—in fact, she was horrified by our willfulness and our daring. However, before saying no to our idea, she did consult "those in charge." The answer was an emphatic denial. We had been quite naive to believe even for a second that we would be allowed to associate with young people of our own age in one of Moscow's best-known schools. We were dangerous social outcasts.

Shortly afterwards, Divilkovskaya, who could not have relished her responsibility in regard to us, had a talk with Peshkova. She asked her to take charge of us. Peshkova must have felt that life at her house would be more suitable, more normal, for us than our existence at the Hotel National. Thus our carefree, comfortable days there were ended, along with the strange unlimited freedom which we enjoyed in the early spring of 1920.

PART XII

Life with Peshkova

50

A few days later we moved into Peshkova's apartment in the center of Moscow, in a house which now bears a plaque commemorating the fact that Gorky used to stay there. The household comprised, in addition to Peshkova, her mother, who was known to all as Babushka, and her son, Maxim, nicknamed Max, who was about nineteen.

Max was then attending the newly-founded Soviet Military Academy, but sports were his main interest, and particularly the motorcycle which his father had given him as a present not long before. At that time, he seemed altogether devoid of intellectual interests, and this saddened his mother and was a wound to her pride. Max received us cordially; we joked with him in Italian, French and German, as we used to do in Alassio, where Max had often stayed with his mother before the Revolution. However, we seldom saw him. He was out most of the day and his evenings were spent among his friends in the theater world of Moscow.

At first, Babushka received us rather badly. Peshkova explained to us that her mother was the daughter of a general who had grown up in a wealthy environment. When she was still young, her family had suddenly lost all their money. She then developed a fear of poverty which verged on the pathological. Little by little, she had become a miser.

An unofficial member of the household was Mikhail Nikolaev, a friend of Peshkova's who was something like her morganatic husband. Nikolaev, who had a separate apartment in the same building, worked all day long in a publishing house handling foreign books; in the evenings he visited at Peshkova's. However, he seemed to fade away whenever Gorky was in residence there.

Peshkkova lived extremely frugally, as did most

Muscovites at that time. Her entire life was spent in the service of the Russian Political Red Cross, which was then indirectly affiliated with the International Red Cross. In collaboration with Mikhail Vinaver she devoted herself to helping political prisoners held by Bolsheviks, and not only Socialists, as Alexander Solzhenitsyn erroneously maintains in his *Gulag*. Within limitations set by the authorities they visited prisons and distributed to the inmates whatever small necessities the Red Cross had to give. It was a huge, selfless and brave undertaking—there were many prisons in Moscow then and they were overflowing—the Lubyanka, Butyrskaya, the Novinskaya women's prison, the one near Taganskaya for men... The city had no public transportation, and Peshkova and Vinaver would set forth on foot every day with the supplies they had to distribute to the prisoners loaded on a sled which they themselves pulled along. The Red Cross headquarters were located near Kuznetsky bridge in the center of town. Every day the two of them walked great distances; at night Peshkova returned home exhausted. The apartment was icy: in her household there were only enough logs for the dining room stove at night and for a tiny *burzhuyka* in the kitchen.

In her home we were assigned a small back room. Twin iron beds were made up for us, while Adya had to sleep on two trunks pushed together. For us Peshkova had taken some sheets out of a closet in an unheated room. As we went to bed at night, it turned out that these were damp. All night long they would not dry up in our cold room and Natasha and I could not fall asleep. As for Adya, she woke up crying loudly—her arms and legs had started to ache dreadfully. Alarmed, Peshkova moved her onto a small sofa in her own room. From then on Adya slept there.

Peshkova's apartment had a markedly "Art Nouveau" decor. In the large dining-living room, picture windows formed an oval glassed-in winter garden where tall green plants grew in pots. An aquarium with goldfish stood in their midst. There was a desk to one side of the picture windows, on which framed photographs of Gorky and of young Maxim were displayed. Max could be seen as a child, an adolescent and a grown boy. On the other side of the windows stood a black grand piano. By the door a massive dining table and a sideboard formed the dining area. Here meals were served and guests entertained.

Naturally, in view of Peshkova's hard work, Natasha and I immediately assumed most of the household responsibilities while we lived with her. Babushka was in the habit of doing some of it, but she preferred to spend long hours in her own, rather dark room. This room was filled to the ceiling with an indescribable mixture of worthless trash, of souvenirs and of valuables. Once I was to extract a book of poems from under a heap of strange objects. It was Khodasevich's collection of poems, *The Way of the Seed*, with an inscription to Gorky: "To my dear, highly respected master, Alexei Maximovich." Babushka collected everything: glass jars, torn wrapping paper, tin cans, old clothes and string. However, it was not easy to get her to find us a dust rag. She insisted that we use the broom only lightly, without pressing it hard against the floor, so as not to wear it out.

Young Maxim was full of wit and he came up with wonderful parodies of the slogans which the Bolsheviks used for publication during that era, and which were posted in huge letters all over town: "The Kingdom of the Proletariat shall never end"; "Citizens who, like animals of prey, waste water will be sternly punished"; "Children are the flowers of our life"; "All united in a single front against lice." He even hung a placard in the dining room: "All united in a single front against glass and iron in Babushka's room."

Peshkova was harsh on her mother. Tired, irritable, she was often rude to her. Max, too, was disagreeable with Babushka. Perhaps for this reason Babushka, who was always rather dour, came to appreciate our good manners and the fact that we had taken charge of most of the household tasks. We became friends.

Our most complicated responsibility was to have dinner ready by the time of Peshkova's return home, between five and six. We cooked on the small *burzhuyka* in the kitchen, which, alas, was not a genuine Bromley like the one we had used at the Sinitsins. We had to split the few wet logs available to us into minute woodchips and even those sometimes refused to burn. Way ahead of her return we would put a tall enameled saucepan filled with cold water on the fire and start peeling whichever vegetables we had that day: carrots, beets, cabbage or potatoes. When the water finally came to a boil, we added some millet to the water. Often after the vegetables and millet were plunged into it the water would not boil again: we were in trouble.

I remember one such occasion when the water refused to boil, no matter what I did. It was nearing five and I was in a panic. What would Peshkova say? Then I tasted the soup, and, as if by a miracle, it was cooked. The vegetables were ready and the millet appetizingly soft. What a joy! When Peshkova arrived moments later, I could serve dinner at once.

What made our life difficult was the fact that Peshkova seemed not to notice our good will, our efforts and hard work. She came home and remained silent, never uttering a single word of praise or encouragement.

With Natasha and me she was invariably stern. Fortunately, she did smile at Adya on occasion and would say a few friendly words to her.

In Peshkova's bedroom over her bed hung the portrait of a very pretty little girl, who looked remarkably like Max. Babushka explained to us that this was Katya, Gorky's and Peshkova's first child, who had died of meningitis at five. I thought then that, had this little girl lived, much would have been different in Peshkova's life. Her love for young Max might be less exclusive and perhaps her disposition would be mellower.

We were not the only ones intimidated by Peshkova. All the women who worked with her on Red Cross projects feared her, and so did some of the political prisoners for whom she cared. As a rule she was more gracious with men than women. In fact, with men she could often be charming. According to Mother, without exception, all female inmates preferred to deal with Mikhail Vinaver, who was warm-hearted and direct in his dealings with people.

Once, when Max had returned home earlier than was his habit, he saw us all drinking tea in the dining room: "Mother," he said, "what a pleasure and a rest it is for me, after my Moscow friends, to look at Olga and Natasha!" Peshkova smiled with approval. It was one of the rare occasions when she showed her good feelings for us.

We continued to visit Mother in prison every week. Each time, we had to telephone Latsis or Romanovsky in advance and remind them of their promise to give us a pass to see Mother during the coming week. To phone was no easy matter. In Moscow at that time the telephone was frequently out of order. At Peshkova's sometimes it took hours of standing in the hallway where the telephone was located before one was connected with one's party. Once in a while, Peshkova, with some Red Cross problem in mind, asked one of us to put her in touch with an investigator at the Cheka, but this often proved impossible; the telephone would not work.

Mother was again alone in her cell. Her gums were hurting but the vitamins which we were able to bring her saved her teeth. The notion of "vitamin" was not current then; what we did was to provide her with raw vegetables. We were still followed wherever we went. An aquaintance of Peshkova had told her that she had seen "the young Chernov girls in the street in the company of two young men, two young suitors no doubt." We abstained from getting in touch with any of our former friends.

About two weeks after we had settled in Peshkova's apartment, one evening Ida paid us a visit. All of us were assembled for dinner in the living room, and Peshkova suggested that we receive our guest in the privacy of her bedroom. Ida seemed very tense. She asked us no questions whatever, nor did she inquire about Mother. At once she started to reproach us bitterly: how was it that we had given in to Bolshevik solicitations? Accepted their inducements? Agreed to living in the Hotel National? We had been seen one evening in the Bolshoi Theater. Were we not ashamed? We were discrediting ourselves and Victor and helping the Bolsheviks with their propaganda campaign against the SRs.

But to present us with these recriminations was not the only aim of Ida's visit. She told us that she and Victor had decided to try to slip from Moscow into Estonia illegally. They needed money. For this reason she had come for Mother's jewelry which we had to give to her at once.

Indeed, Mother had a few very modest jewels which had come to her from her own mother—a sapphire brooch, mounted in silver, two strands of tiny pearls, and a golden ring with two diamonds. While we lived near Yauza Gates Natasha and I had sewn these inside some of Adya's stuffed animals—Adya had a small bear, a squirrel and a home-made beaver. These had stayed with us throughout our travels and our arrest. They were now kept in our suitcase in Peshkova's apartment.

We told Ida firmly that her jewels were Mother's property, and that there was no question of our giving them to her. We were keeping them in a safe place while Mother was in prison. Ida's voice became thick and very low as it always did whenever she was angry. "What nonsense, this is no time to hang on to family jewels," she said. "In Victor's name, I demand that you give me these immediately! Let me have at least the diamond ring. I have reasons to think that it belongs to Victor, not to your Mother!"

Remaining as calm as we could, Natasha and I refused to comply. Ida stayed for a long time. After a while, she started to shout and waved her arms and tried to intimidate us. This failed to impress us and she finally left, no longer trying to hide her hostility. We went back to the dining room.

Peshkova, who had overheard Ida's shouting, said in an emotional manner most unusual for her: "When I consider some of the people around you, I marvel. Despite pedagogues like Ida Samoylovna you have become good people." Then suddenly she added: "If only your Mother were to agree to it, I would love to keep you here forever. To have you as my daughters. To adopt all three of you." But no sooner had she uttered this proposal, which touched us deeply, than she became again her restrained self, realizing perhaps that neither Mother nor we would ever consider such an adoption.

One evening not long afterwards, Max returned home full of excitement. He requested a private talk with his mother and the two of them went into Peshkova's bedroom and shut the door behind them. Later our hostess told us that Max had run into Victor in the street. He had had no trouble recognizing him despite Victor's shaven beard and his disguise. "Mother, I am a Communist," he had said, "and my party duty would have been to stop Chernov and to have him arrested. But somehow I could not bring myself to do this."

"Max, in addition to duty, there is also honor," Peshkova had told her son. As she reported this exchange to us, Peshkova was visibly proud of her son's decision not to comply with "the new Communist morality."

-51-

While we were staying with Peshkova, Maxim Gorky came from Petrograd and stopped at her apartment. Though divorced, the two had remained good friends. In Gorky's presence, Peshkova was transformed. She lost her stiffness, she smiled and looked younger, her face became soft and her movements free. It was a remarkable metamorphosis.

Now that I see Gorky's photographs taken during that period, he looks quite young to me, but to us then he seemed elderly. He was open and friendly; everything was easy with Gorky. From under his bushy eyebrows, he looked at one cheerfully and directly, with kindly eyes. He always asked many questions and listened to the answers thoughtfully. We were not intimidated by him; he was attentive to people, he looked at them observantly and humorously, with the eyes of an artist. When the customary joking about the resemblance between Natasha and me would start at the dinner table, Gorky declared firmly that he could perceive no similarity whatever between us. All he could see were two individuals. When members of the family tried to fool him by presenting one of us to him in place of the other he was not tricked for a moment. And he fully realized how much we were helping Peshkova with household matters. "These girls work much too much, Katya," he would say.

With his arrival, gaiety took over Peshkova's home. All day long, young musicians, poets and writers called on Gorky. I remember Pilnyak and Leonov, who were to become well-known soon afterwards. A young and talented pianist, Dobrowein, often came to the house and played for Gorky for hours on end. On such occasions the table was set with a beautiful damask tablecloth. As for which tea set to use—Peshkova owned two, a pink one and a blue one—this remained a mystery which only she would settle at the very last minute. Peshkova's mother or one of us would set the table with one set, but the lady of the house could suddenly change her mind, and replace pink cups with blue ones or the reverse. Under her stern exterior, Peshkova was quite feminine and unpredictable.

Gorky was not fond of social formalities, and Natasha recalls how, one day as everyone was sitting down to tea, he had said, pointing to the tablecloth: "Natasha, please remove these rags. Let us drink tea for real, on the oilcloth."

Once, during dinner, Gorky was fishing bits of red beet out of his borshcht, arranging them in a row on the edge of his plate: he apparently hated beets. As he was doing this he told how he once had squashed bedbugs all around the edge of a sheet of paper—just like this, in a row. He was in prison for revolutionary activities in Nizhny Novgorod. On the paper he then wrote a letter to the governor of that city, pointing out that he had been condemned to solitary confinement, not to share his cell with unpleasant companions such as bedbugs.

When Gorky visited, however briefly, all sorts of rare foodstuffs made their appearance in Peshkova's kitchen—white flour, sugar and lard, sent to the writer by the Bolshevik leadership. Sighing, Peshkova would say: "One can get used to anything.... At first, how ashamed I was to accept these things from the Kremlin."

On one occasion, sometime later, when we no longer lived at Peshkova's, but only spent the night with her when we visited Mother in prison, Gorky told us about a remarkable event which had caused a sensation in Moscow. There had been a reception given in honor of a visiting delegation of British workers, representatives of a printer's union. It was combined with a political meeting: it had been held in the great Conservatory Hall in Moscow, now Tchaikovsky Hall. Apparently, Victor made up his mind to make a public appearance during this meeting. Needless to say, the Cheka was particularly vigilant during the Englishmen's visit, seeking to protect them from undesirable encounters or conversations. But Victor, a man hunted all over Moscow, was counting precisely on the surprise which the daring of his action would cause.

With the help of SR printers, who were the majority in that profession, Victor gained entry into the meetings. For this, he, who had long been beardless, now shaved his head as well. Unrecognized, with the help of SR sympathizers posted at the entrance hall, he joined the Russian delegation of printers assembled near the rostrum. When there was a lull between speeches, he requested to speak as a member of the Russian group. Without any obstacle he ascended the rostrum and spoke. Briefly, but eloquently— Victor was a brilliant orator—he compared the fate of the Russian Socialists before the Revolution to that of the early Christians. The Bolsheviks resembled the Church in later years, when it had become autocratic and forgotten the fate of the downtrodden and exploited them, suppressing them in order to maintain its own authority. The Bolsheviks, forgetting the needs of peasants and workers alike, were now instituting a bloody dictatorship, destroying all the liberties and all the hopes of the working class and the peasants in order to maintain themselves in power.

Even before he was finished, enthusiastic applause and shouting greeted his speech. The audience was demanding the name of the orator, and Victor called out: "I am Victor Chernov!"

He was immediately surrounded by excited Englishmen, seeking to congratulate him and to engage him in discussion. But the Russian printers stopped them, shouting, "This is not England for you!" Promptly, they took charge of Victor and escorted him to the hall's exit. They helped him disappear into the night. The Chekists attending the meeting were stunned. By the time they had rushed to the exit of the Conservatory and sought to have the streets leading to it searched, it was too late. Victor had left the area, fading away into Moscow's dark side streets.

As we were all assembled at the tea table, Gorky told us this story with excitement, laughing loudly at the Cheka's discomfiture. This was early in his post-Revolutionary career, years before he embraced the Bolsheviks' credo. Disapproving of Lenin's policies, he himself was soon to go into self-imposed exile in Western Europe.

Time went by, and our existence continued to be as tentative, as unsettled, as ever. Sooner or later our peculiar situation had to have an outcome, yet none was in sight. Politically, things were becoming worse for all those whom the Bolsheviks regarded as potential opponents.

At Peshkova's we had little privacy. The room assigned to us was icy and crowded, entirely taken up by our beds, a wardrobe, an ironing board.... It opened into an inside courtyard; it was dark, even in the daytime. At night, it was lit only by a small bulb under its high ceiling which was inadequate as a reading light. We had to spend most of our life among strangers. Only seldom did we manage to sit down with a book in the dining room or Peshkova's bedroom. We had no life and no work of our own.

In those years, in addition to her Red Cross post, Peshkova was a member of the Russian League for the Salvation of Children. An idea of the liberal writer, Korolenko, the League had been created by the Kadet—K-D—political party, the moderate Constitutional Democrats. For the multitude of children left abandoned in Russia as the result of World War I and of the Civil War, the League had opened a number of children's homes located in what had been, before the Revolution, private country residences, notably in Serebryany Bor—Silver Wood—about twenty kilometers out of Moscow. The educational policies of these institutions were under the supervision of a certain Repyeva, a well-known Moscow pedagogue.

Peshkova had a talk about us with Repyeva, and it turned out that the children's homes of the League were in great need of educators. Peshkova suggested that we take jobs in Serebryany Bor as trainees, while Adya would live in one of the homes there as a pupil. We accepted. We were both anxious to go to work. It was becoming evident that to pursue our studies was out of the question for us—the authorities would never allow us to do this. Working with underprivileged children under the auspices of an organization dedicated to a humanitarian goal appealed to us. Here was an opportunity to do something useful, to be at last on our own.

I remember our interview with Repyeva, a small, rather dry woman with cold gray eyes. During our talk, which was in the nature of an examination, she asked us all sorts of probing questions. Her coolness somehow dampened our enthusiasm for pedagogy. However, after the interview, she decided that we were mature enough to work in Serebryany Bor, in two separate homes. Adya was to attend a third one, for ten to fourteen year olds, as a pupil. Thus, an entirely new existence among strangers started for us. From now on, we were to live exclusively among Russian pedagogues and young children, many of whom proved extremely appealing.

What determined the choice of the children who were admitted to one of the League's homes? As I remember now, the degree of their neediness, combined with a recommendation from one or another among the members of the League, were decisive. Our pupils usually came from working-class homes, sometimes from those of the intelligentsia, which was then destitute. Regardless of their origins, children came for stays of about six weeks to two months, all equally starved, badly dressed, often covered with lice.

I remember the day when, in April, we left Moscow for Serebryany Bor in an open, horse-drawn sled. We were being taken there by Repyeva herself, along with several bags of foodstuffs for the children's homes. In addition, three new wards were traveling with us, but all that could be seen of them were three little heads in warm hats and mufflers emerging from a pile of blankets at the bottom of the sled. Repyeva sat in the front by the driver and we in the back. The sled glided along snowy, sunny Moscow streets. We left town and rode past the suburbs of Krasnaya Presnya. The road was completely iced, the fields a sparkling white, the trees still very black, but there was already a breath of spring in the air.

PART XIII

The Homes in Serebryany Bor

52

Serebryany Bor, a small summer resort, lies in the middle of a wonderful pine forest on a steep bank overgrown with reeds, on the Moscow River. A long descent to a sandy beach starts deep in the woods, leading to the water's edge. There, scattered throughout the pine woods in a most picturesque fashion, were the dachas which housed the children's homes of the League.

We arrived at the snowbound settlements by sled. Our first stop was a wooden dacha known as Home no. II. Here Natasha was dropped off with Alicia Weber. She was to serve as a kindergarten teacher under the direct guidance of this woman of German origin, who was at the head of the Serebryany Bor homes. Before reaching Home no. I where I was to live and work, we left Adya in Home no. III.

The sacks of provisions which we had brought with us —The League for the Salvation of Children was able to get food supplies from the Ukraine for its homes—were divided evenly in three parts and left accordingly at each home.

We proceeded along the roads of the small settlement and eventually came to an elegant, light-gray dacha with a veranda enclosed by partitions of stained glass. This was Home no. I. Three women, the entire pedagogical staff of the home, greeted us upon arrival.

Awakened by the adults, from the depths of the sled two sleepy boys emerged. They were about five or six years old. Confused, yet lively, they looked around with great curiosity. They were to be placed in Home no. I, for children five to seven years old. Following the boys, a tiny girl appeared from under another blanket. This was Raya, whose profile was that of a small owl.

We walked up to the veranda where we were surrounded by a group of bouncy children. At first they all looked alike to me, with their shortly cropped hair and their school uniforms of khaki cloth. The adults, too, wore khaki. Everyone was full of friendly greetings.

One of the three adults—she was the housekeeper, Ekaterina—came up to me: "First, we must help the new children settle in," she said, "and then we shall have dinner. Later, after the children have gone to bed, we'll have tea and get acquainted. You are still very young, and that is wonderful. I hope you will enjoy your life in Home no. I. All of us here are on a first-name basis, for the sake of a family atmosphere. I am Aunt Katya. Please meet our directress—she is the pedagogue in charge here, Aunt Nadya. And this is her helper, Aunt Lyda."

Aunt Lyda was a plump brunette, whose full figure was emphasized by the wide-belted khaki smock she wore. She held a pair of scissors and a comb. "We will give the newcomers a haircut and a hot bath," she said, and asked me to help her. I followed her into a large, comfortable bathroom. There a stove next to a hot-water tank was burning brightly, fueled by small wood chips. Hot water flowed in abundance from a faucet.

Aunt Lyda spread a newspaper on a table in the bathroom. Next to it she sat little Raya on a high chair. Making her bend her head over the newspaper, quickly and skillfully, she cut the little girl's hair. She squashed the lice that fell with the hair onto the newspaper. Then she drew a hot bath for the child, and gave her a thorough washing. She put clean regulation clothes on her, and tied her head with a white kerchief. The sharp profile of the child looked even more owl-like now—soon the other children were to nickname her "little owl." Following the same procedure, a haircut and bath were given to the little boys.

Soon a bell rang, summoning us to dinner. The dining room, located on the ground floor of the dacha, was a spacious room with unpainted log walls. The adults settled the children at long tables of white pine, and sat down among them, keeping order and eating at the same time. The dinner was served by two cheerful young girls who worked in the kitchen. With a janitor and a cook they constituted what was known as the "technical personnel" of the home.

Aunt Nadya, the head of the home, first served a cabbage dish, which the children ate hungrily. This was followed by ample servings of hot, thickly cooked millet kasha. As the children got up from the table, decorously, they thanked Aunt Nadya for their dinner. After the meal they were allowed to play in the dining room. Little Raya, who had eaten her kasha to the last grain, rushed into the kitchen and asked the cook with joyful anticipation: "There will be some dinner tomorrow also, won't there?" Thus, during a whole week, after each meal, the little girl, who had no doubt suffered from starvation, would rush into the kitchen to inquire happily about the next meal.

When the children had been put to bed, the adults gathered for a cup of tea in the dining room. Real tea was poured into enamel mugs. Ekaterina brought out my share of brown sugar, giving me a monthly allowance of a pound. I was overwhelmed by such opulence.

"Are you not a relative of the Tolstoy-follower Chertkov?" Aunt Nadya asked with sympathy. She was an elderly woman with a pince-nez on a black cord, whose gray hair hung straight. She was a typical Russian woman teacher of those years—a woman of good sense and compassion under a slightly forbidding pedantic exterior. The Bolsheviks were beginning to persecute the followers of Tolstoy because of Tolstoy's principles of non-violence. Having probably heard something about our mother being in prison, she had mistaken Chernov for Chertkov.

"Every night you will be expected to attend the evening lectures given by Alicia Weber in Home no. II," Aunt Nadya told me. "She is training the kindergarten teachers according to the Montessori methods." With a small grimace she added, "Here, however, in Home no. I, everything is done simply, in the Russian manner, without foreign theories."

Aunt Katya said with an apologetic smile that at first

I would have to sleep in one room with four children. She hoped that later it would be possible to give me my own room.

In the bedroom assigned to me there was a pleasant smell of warm unpainted wood. By the light of a small night-light one could make out the outline of the children's beds. My own bed was brand new, narrow and hard, like a ship's bunk. Through the double window one could see dimly the trees in the dark garden. It was warm and cozy, another world altogether from everything we had encountered until then in Russia, as if the Lubyanka Prison and the high-strung atmosphere in Peshkova's home had never existed.

In the morning I was allocated a khaki smock, and I became Aunt Olya to the twenty children of Home no. I. Having helped the children get into quilted jackets and hats made of the same khaki cloth, Aunt Lyda and I took them for a walk in the quiet, snowy countryside. Aunt Lyda walked by my side, explaining to me my new responsibilities in a friendly, even voice. The children ran ahead of us in a joyful group. My companion was about thirty-five, with a swarthy complexion and a kindly expression on her plump face. She was telling me that she was devoting herself completely to what she considered to be the most important endeavor in life—the upbringing of children.

It was a sunny, frosty day. The clear-cut shadows cast on the snow by the small fir trees looked like pictures out of a children's book. Leaving the dacha we had crossed the entire settlement. There, at the edge of the woods on fresh snowy meadows, one could see bird and animal tracks. Upon our return, before lunch, there was time for a drawing session for the children. Throughout the day everything was done according to a strict but sensible schedule. Within a very few days the quiet, purposeful rhythm of Home no. I absorbed me completely.

Working in Home no. II, Natasha, too, had become fully immersed into a world which was new to both of us, where everything was done for the children entrusted to us, and no time was left to dwell on our own problems. However, we were deeply concerned about Adya in this new environment. How would she take to this institutional life, so different from anything she had experienced until then? Knowing her sensitivity and shyness, Natasha and I wondered how she was getting along with other children. As soon as possible we made a date to visit her in Home no. III. Aunt Lyda agreed to fill in for me one afternoon. I went off to meet with my sisters.

As Adya came to greet us in the reception room of the wooden dacha, she was smiling, and we knew at once that she was happy in her new situation. In fact, she was to flourish in Serebryany Bor; she made many new friends there and soon became one of the star pupils in her class. All her life she was to remember Home no. III with nostalgia and fondness. To be among children of her own age in peaceful circumstances was an enormous relief for her after our adventures.

The employees of Serebryany Bor were given one day off a week. Natasha and I would each take a two-day leave twice a month. Thus, one of us was able to visit Mother in prison every week. On occasion Adya would come along with one of us. Officially, we were still in Peshkova's custody, and she served as an intermediary between us and the Cheka. She took upon herself the complicated formalities necessary to obtain us prison passes.

Whenever we came to Moscow, we stayed with Peshkova. Each time she greeted us as if we had not been away at all. On her part there was never any expression of pleasure at seeing us, not even any greetings. In her house we were at home. Whenever there, we faced at once a whole world of household responsibilities. But we knew that Peshkova cared for us deeply. Each week, as one of us came to town, what we wanted most in the world—a permit to visit Mother—was waiting and ready for us.

Mother spent another month in the Special Section of the Cheka at the Lubyanka. She had the good fortune to occupy a cell next to those where two well-known public figures were detained. They were E.D. Kuskova and her husband, Prokopovich. Kuskova had been one of the founders of the League for the Salvation of Children. She and her husband were allowed to read books in their cells. In turn they shared them with Mother. In particular the three of them reread all of Lamartine's *Histoire des Girondins,* whose story echoed their own in such an ominous way.

Soon afterwards Mother was transferred into the Butyrskaya Prison. There, sometime after her arrival, the Socialist prisoners had, by means of repeated hunger strikes, obtained exceptionally liberal prison conditions. The administration was prevailed upon to segregate political prisoners from the criminal elements. The political prisoners' cells were locked only at night. During the day they could walk freely along the corridors, visit with their comrades, and exchange books. Representatives were elected by the political prisoners; these were allowed to negotiate with the prison officials on behalf of their comrades.

The walk from Serebryany Bor to Moscow was a long one. We would arrive at Peshkova's only toward tea-time, and hear the Moscow news from our hostess. Right after tea, as soon as we had washed the dishes, we would go to bed in order to be up the next day at dawn. The prison visits in Butyrskaya usually took place in the early morning. They were held in the reception hall of the prison, a large empty room filled with benches and chairs. Two soldiers and a prison guard paced the middle of the room, observing us closely. As a rule, they did not interfere with our conversation.

The visitors were allowed to sit next to the prisoners. They could touch them and embrace them. When the half-hour allocated for the meeting was over, the guards abruptly put an end to the visit. The packages brought by relatives had to be given first to the guards for careful checking.

Once by mistake we were summoned to another kind

of visit—the non-personal kind. On that day the large reception room of the prison was divided by two parallel barbed wire partitions, with a narrow corridor provided between them. Two guards slowly paced the length of this corridor while people visited with each other across the double net of barbed wire. Everyone spoke loudly, people puncuated their words with wide gestures and shouts. Fortunately we visited Mother in these non-personal conditions only on one occasion; I still remember how sad we felt on our way home from this particular encounter.

In Butyrskaya Prison, Mother was quite happy. Under the new prison conditions obtained by the Socialists, many interesting encounters and discussions among the prisoners took place. On certain days, they even lectured to each other on various scholarly subjects. We were overjoyed at Mother's improved conditions and at her good spirits.

After our prison visit we usually returned to Peshkova's and spent the night there. She asked us about Mother in great detail. She also wanted to hear about our experiences and work at Serebyany Bor. Although she remained restrained, we could sense that she was proud of us, and of the way we managed in our new situation.

In Serebryany Bor, the snow was slow in melting, and night continued to occur throughout the spring months. At long last the warm weather arrived with a big explosion; overnight the countryside turned green and full of life.

Five more dachas were opened by the League for the Salvation of Children in order to serve as summer homes for some of the underprivileged children of the Moscow region. The number of young women attending Alicia Weber's classes grew. In the woods, one would meet groups of unknown children led by the new pedagogues. In the evening the staff gathered for professional discussions and seminars. And one day Natasha was transfered into Home no. I, and we were given a room to ourselves.

53

In the beginning of the summer of 1920, the rumor spread through Serebryany Bor that some of the dachas there would be occupied for the season by the families of Boksheviks in high positions. The dacha next to us was taken over by the Steklov Soviet of the People's Commissars—while I was in Butyrskaya Prison in 1918 an article by Steklov, once our neighbor on rue Gazan in Paris, had appeared in *Pravda*, which my cellmates and I had read. Steklov demanded that all of Moscow be put through a sieve in order to find the perpetrators of the terrorist act on Leonontiev Street.

A lovely young terrier called Pika was one of the livelier inhabitants of Home no. I. Pika was beloved by all the children. All day long they played with her, and at night she guarded our compound. No sooner had the Steklovs moved into their dacha than it became known that Commissar Steklov's wife was highly displeased by the proximity of her dacha to a children's home. In the daytime she was disturbed by the children's voices; at night Pika's barking kept her awake. Through the Steklovs' maid, Aunt Nadya was informed that the dog had to go. Indignation seized everyone in Home no. I. It was decided that the best policy to follow was not to acknowledge Steklova's demand that poor Pika be removed.

A couple of days went by; one night we were all wakened by the sound of heavy boots in the garden. Three Red Army soldiers, armed with rifles, were scurrying around the garden in the moonlight, trying to catch Pika. Pika barked wildly; she took refuge in the depths of the underground ice-house installed at the end of our garden. The moon, which was full that night, glistened menacingly on the soldiers' bayonets, as they vainly tried to coax the dog out of her hiding place, using threats and friendly entreaties in turn.

All the children were awakened. They rushed out into the garden, followed by the entire staff of Home no. I. Upon seeing us, the soldiers, who were all three very young men, stopped in their tracks, embarrassed.

"What are you doing here?" we asked.

"We are under orders from Commissar Steklov to kill your dog," one of them answered.

"You have no right to do this! You have awakened the children! Please go away. You should be ashamed of yourselves!"

To our relief and surprise the three soldiers left in silence. But by then the children had heard that they had wanted to kill Pika. They were so excited and upset that it proved difficult to calm them down that night.

The next morning Aunt Nadya asked Lyda, Natasha and me to go over to the Steklovs to discuss the threats against Pika's life. The three of us, as a delegation, walked up to the gate of the affluent-looking dacha next door to us. On the veranda, as on a stage, the Steklovs were sitting on wicker chairs taking tea. He was a heavy set man with a full red beard; his wife was an overweight middle-aged woman with a contemptuous, bored expression on her face. We introduced ourselves. Natasha spoke first. She said that we had come on the matter of the dog. Upon hearing the word "dog," Steklova jumped up. Interrupting Natasha, she shouted that our dog was causing her extreme distress, that it woke her at night and that she would not endure this hardship for another moment.

"It is customary for dogs in Serebryany Bor to guard houses at night," I said. "The dacha further down the road is also guarded by a dog," said Natasha.

"Don't try to fool me," shouted Steklova in a strident voice. "That other dog has a hoarse bark which does not get on my nerves, while your Pika has a dreadful high-pitched bark. It is the high-pitched barking that keeps me awake. Your dog has to go!"

"What right have you to send armed soldiers into our

garden? Who has allowed you to do this?" I asked.

At this Steklov became enraged. "I will have the dog killed, and you are free to go complain to whomever you please!" he shouted. Madame Steklov looked pleased.

"Do you know by any chance Turgenev's short story, 'Mou Mou'?" I asked.

"Call the dog what you will," said Steklov coldly, obviously unacquainted with this classic vignette of a rich woman's willful destruction of someone else's beloved pet, "but I don't ever want to hear or see it again." Steklov got up from his chair and walked back into the house. Clearly there was no arguing with this man, full of his own power. We left in silence.

The inhabitants of Home no. I took it upon themselves to save Pika's life. During the day the dog was not allowed in the yard, and at night she was shut up in the innermost depths of the dacha. The children were thrilled, aware of the fact that evil forces were threatening their beloved dog, whom it was up to them to save. They now called Pika "Snow White."

A few days following this adventure, Natasha set forth to visit Mother in prison. As usual she spent the night at Peshkova's, where Gorky was then visiting. When at teatime she told him Pika's story, Gorky was delighted. He had always disliked Steklov.

"Natasha, please write this story down for me in detail. I want all of it, including the bayonets shining in the moonlight," he said.

Our life in Home no. I seemed monotonous, yet it was always filled with unexpected events, with small trials and triumphs. We now knew well the children entrusted to us. We loved them and got along with them splendidly. Only on Sunday did we have a difficult time. This was the day when the children's parents—those who could—came to visit their offspring. It was always a painful day for staff and children alike. Even those children who seemed perfectly adjusted to collective living suddenly became anxious and restless at the prospect of seeing their parents.

This even affected those children who had not been happy at home. All of them began to yearn for their mothers, and for their own family life. Those who had no parents visiting them were forlorn. On Sunday we too became upset. We were sorry that our wards' parents had no opportunity to observe our happy, purposeful day-to-day existence in Serebryany Bor.

At the end of the summer the entire staff of the numerous Serebryany Bor children's homes gave a day-long party. The weather was exceptionally sunny and warm. Kuskova, Mother's new friend from the Lubyanka Prison, recently released, came to visit, and so did Peshkova and Vinaver, along with other members of the League for the Salvation of Children. Everyone in our community participated in the festivities, including our smallest wards. Plays and ballets were staged against the impressive backdrop of the old pine trees on the bank of the Moscow River. There were songs, sports competitions and a huge bonfire. After the children were put to bed, a dance was held with music provided by an improvised orchestra. The night was balmy, and the couples looked romantic in the moonlight, dancing against the stately trees. All three of us—Natasha, Adya and I—thoroughly enjoyed ourselves.

In the early fall, the temporary children's homes were disbanded. The dachas were boarded up. As was to be expected, the League was not an organization which could survive autonomously for a long time under the Bolshevik regime. That fall the administrative and pedagogical control of the children's homes passed into the hands of the People's Commissariat for Education.

This change of authority occurred without any visible repercussion at first. The personnel of the children's homes remained in place, and the program of studies was not modified for the time being. In 1920, a large segment of the Russian intelligentsia was still boycotting Soviet authority. When the Bolsheviks had taken over, a number of representatives of the liberal professions, including professors and educators, had resigned from their posts. Among the educated classes unconditional sympathizers of the Bolsheviks were few. For this reason, the authorities were not in any hurry to alter anything in Serebryany Bor.

But it was only a question of time—small changes were already occurring in our daily existence. Aunt Nadya was retiring. Soon our good friend Lyda left for Moscow; but Natasha and I coped easily. The number of children increased. With every week I felt more self-confidence and derived more satisfaction from my work. To have my own room with Natasha was a great happiness. It enabled us both to enjoy a measure of privacy even in the middle of our impersonal surroundings. We often saw Adya, who was thriving in the company of her peers.

PART XIV

Last Days in Russia

54

One day the liberal prison conditions enjoyed by the Socialists in the Butyrskaya ended in a dramatic confrontation between inmates and prison authorities. Without any provocation, one morning the Cheka had all the political prisoners seized by Red Army men. Those who resisted were bound with ropes. All were put aboard a train headed for Yaroslavl, an ancient merchant city on the Volga. There was a large prison in that city.

We learned of this transfer from Peshkova and Vinaver, who tried to be as reassuring as possible. But we could sense that they were concerned for the sake of the political prisoners. Energetically they were trying to bring about their return to Moscow, through whatever connections they had among high-placed Bolsheviks.

We continued to visit Peshkova even while Mother was in Yaroslavl. Within a month, the Red Cross had obtained the return of the political prisoners to the capital, but the men and women prisoners were now separated and prison conditions for both were harsh. Mother was now held in the Old Novinskaya Prison, the very one Natasha Klimova and her friends had fled in 1908. At about that time we learned from Peshkova that Victor and Ida Samoylovna had been able to escape from the Soviet Union, taking refuge in Estonia.

Toward spring I began feeling extremely tired. Suddenly the long walks to Moscow became more than I could manage. Natasha became worried and insisted that I consult the physician in residence at the Serebryany Bor health center. The doctor determined that I had a slight heart ailment, and advised that I stop working at once. Everyone in Home no. I was full of sympathy. Alicia Weber asked me to remain in Serebryany Bor throughout my illness. But Peshkova, alarmed, demanded that both Natasha and I quit work and move back to Moscow. Vinaver, who had a three-room apartment in the city, offered to take us in. We accepted with enthusiasm—we felt free and cheerful in Vinaver's company. It was decided that Adya would remain in Home no. III, which she greatly enjoyed.

Mikhail Vinaver, a man of Polish origin, was a person of great refinement and culture. He had kept his Polish citizenship, and often traveled to Warsaw, where his wife still lived. He was a member of the Menshevik Party, and had close ties with the Polish Socialist Democrats.

Natasha and I were delighted to be living with him. In exchange for his hospitality we acted as his hostesses and housekeepers. The apartment was never without guests and it reminded us of Villa Arianna. Political prisoners, just released from prison, were given hospitality there as a matter of course.

In those years, at the insistence of the Red Cross, political prisoners were still occasionally freed. Vinaver, a co-director of the Red Cross with Peshkova, enjoyed a measure of political immunity. Later on, in 1938, at the height of the Stalinist terror, he was arrested aboard a train headed for Orel and disappeared forever. Peshkova, probably because of her connection with Gorky, survived.

I remember some of these people, just released from prison. They had the faces of those who, long confined in darkness, are suddenly allowed into the sunshine. Many were Socialists, SRs and Mensheviks. Others were simply known as CRs, Counter-Revolutionaries. I remember one of them, an energetic, attractive young Monarchist, a young woman who proudly called herself a *Vendéenne*.

At Vinaver's we occasionally had Adya for a visit. She would walk to Moscow from Serebryany Bor with a girlfriend and bring us huge bouquets of wild flowers, bachelor's buttons and daisies gathered along the road. Sunburned and full of gaiety, Adya and her friend would spend the night with us. The next morning Adya and one of us would have a prison visit with Mother. The thought that we were living at Vinaver's pleased Mother. It made it easier for her to bear the isolation and hardships of the Novinskaya Prison.

Vinaver did everything he could to make our days in Moscow pleasant. He took us to the theater and introduced us to interesting Muscovites. He had many friends in Tayrov's theater, the Kamerny. In particular he was close to the painter Exter, a brilliant woman artist who worked as a stage designer in this avant-garde theater.

It was during that period that Aunt Sonya joined us, sharing our room in Mikhail Vinaver's apartment. In the evening, when we did not go out, in her incomparably sonorous voice, she read us aloud the Greek classics in translation, or the poems of Pushkin and Verlaine. Vinaver gave us a heavy green curtain, out of which we made a warm, good-looking dress for her. The once elegant Sonya was in rags, she had no shoes—it had become impossible to buy anything whatsoever in Moscow. Fortunately, I found a ball of fine cord in the apartment. I was able to weave a pair of sandals for our friend. With the help of Aunt Sonya the two of us cleaned Vinaver's apartment in depth. It was suffering from neglect; we had a long and victorious battle with mice, which had invaded a back room where Red Cross supplies were kept.

In Moscow the political situation of those who were opposing Bolshevism was becoming more precarious with every month. The future for our family looked bleak. Mother in her prison and we at Vinaver's were treated as hostages for Victor, who was now safely out of the Bolsheviks' reach. Despite the efforts of Gorky on our behalf, for us there was no hope of continuing our education.

With the beginning of the NEP, a new policy toward emigration was instituted by the Central Committee of the Bolshevik Party: "Let those who are not for us leave Russia," was now the official motto. On Lenin's orders a deportation of Russian intellectuals to the West was being mapped out. By 1922 the philosophers Berdyaev, Bulgakov and Frank, the writers Remizov, Zaitsev and Ossorgin, and a score of others were to leave the country.

Peshkova, herself a former SR, was deeply worried about what lay in store for members of that party. And indeed, a wave of mass arrests of SRs was to take place sooner than anyone expected. The Bolsheviks were about to stage a spectacular trial of the SR Party leaders. Despite pressures on the part of Western Socialists, exile in Siberia or Bashkiria and eventual extermination were to be the fate of every member of what had been not long before the largest political party ever to exist in Russia.

Telling us nothing ahead of time, Peshkova decided to make an ultimate effort to have Mother released from prison and to obtain the right for all four of us to emigrate abroad. With this request she went to Dzerzhinsky, who was had long been a personal friend of hers. Dzerzhinsky acceded to her wish. It all happened with unbelievable rapidity. Mother was freed five days before our departure.

Knowing of Mother's adventuresome disposition, Vinaver categorically forbade her to step out of his apartment upon her release. He feared that she might fall into yet another trap set up by the Cheka. For this reason some of our Moscow friends—those who were very brave—came to Vinaver's house to say goodbye to us. Dasha was there, of course. Having been released shortly after her arrest aboard the train headed for Bashkiria, she had resumed her professional activity in the provinces.

Mother was delivered a passport in the name of Chernov, and we, her three daughters, were included in it. The four of us had to have our passport picture taken together. This was not an easy thing to do; in Moscow at that time photographic supplies were unavailable. But we managed; our passport was officially approved. It bore the yet unknown signature of a certain Yagoda.

We had very few belongings left between us, and they fitted easily into the same brown suitcases which we had with us when we arrived in Petrograd in 1917. They were now with the red wax stamps of the Cheka, which they had acquired at the Lubyanka. Aunt Sonya alone—we were dangerous political outcasts—came to see us off at the station. The last words we heard in Moscow were hers, as she said to us through her tears: "Goodbye, my dears; be happy!" Just before departure, the train bound for Estonia was carefully searched by the Cheka and our identities checked once again. Then our train departed, headed for Tallin. I had a feeling of emptiness, of rupture, as if we were leaving something very important behind us in Russia, some unfinished task. We had lived through so much in less than five years: hunger, underground existence, unrelenting pursuit by a hostile political power. It all had been overwhelming, and we felt little excitement at the thought of what lay ahead abroad, little curiosity about the future.

"This cannot be, this is only temporary, we will soon return," the four of us had the same thought; we knew this as we looked at each other. Through the train window we observed the slowly setting sun. We were riding through the Russian forest, golden in the fall.

A tall Estonian conductor checked our tickets. "You are going to Estonia. How nice," he said. He walked past us and returned with a big crusty loaf of broad. He cut it for us, and gave Mother a packet of butter wrapped in white paper. Mother thanked him and took down our travel bag. She found some small apples which we ate for dinner that night, along with the indescribably delicious bread and butter. The kindheartedness of the Estonian conductor cheered us up, but we remained silent. I was remembering Petrograd in 1917, the woods and lakes of Nyanya's village, the breaking of the ice on the Volga. Suddenly, with extraordinary clarity, I recalled the old woman in Moscow, whose bucket I had helped carry on that icy night. We were going—and all I felt was a sense of loss.

The sunset lingered on, then the window darkened, and the rhythmic beat of the train became more distinct. We were no longer traveling on Russian soil.